↑

The One-Star Jew

BY DAVID EVANIER

NORTH POINT PRESS
San Francisco 1983

Several of the stories in this collection have been previously
published in slightly different forms in the following journals:
Chelsea (The Creator of One-Fingered Lily), *Commentary* (The
Man Who Refused to Watch the Academy Awards), *Confronta-
tion* (The Princess), *Croton Review* (The Arrest), *Midstream*
(The Jewish Buddha), *Moment* (My Rabbi, Ray Charles, and
Singing Birds), *National Jewish Monthly* (The Lost Pigeon of
East Broadway), *Paris Review* (Cancer of the Testicles, The
One-Star Jew, Selective Service), *Pequod* (Jolson Sings Again, A
Sense of Responsibility), and *Transatlantic Review* (A Safe
Route on Eighty-third Street).

To my Dini,
Robert M. Ravven,
Daniel Menaker,
and my father, Seymour Evanier

CONTENTS

1 THE CREATOR OF ONE-FINGERED LILY   3
2 CANCER OF THE TESTICLES   15
3 SELECTIVE SERVICE   32
4 THE JEWISH BUDDHA   48
5 MY RABBI, RAY CHARLES, AND SINGING
    BIRDS   62
6 THE MAN WHO REFUSED TO WATCH THE
    ACADEMY AWARDS   70
7 A SAFE ROUTE ON EIGHTY-THIRD STREET   88
8 THE ONE-STAR JEW   91
9 THE LOST PIGEON OF EAST BROADWAY   133
10 THE PRINCESS   164
11 8:30 TO 10:00 P.M.   178
12 THE ARREST   183
13 A SENSE OF RESPONSIBILITY   193
14 JOLSON SINGS AGAIN   203

. . . above the whistle's shriek, the harsh scream of the wheel, the riveter's tattoo, the vast long music endures, and ever shall. What dissonance can quench it? What jangling violence can disturb or conquer it—entombed in our flesh when we were young, remembered like "the apple tree, the singing, and the gold"?

Thomas Wolfe
Look Homeward, Angel

The One-Star Jew

1

THE CREATOR OF
ONE-FINGERED LILY

I

I read recently of the arrest of a forty-year-old man—a bachelor—for having a Librium pill in his pocket without a prescrip-
tion bottle. The police handcuffed him, took him down to the
station, stripped him, booked him, brought him before the
judge. The judge fined him and slapped him in prison for three
months.

Now the man is suing the police and the courts for humili-
ating and embarrassing him. It turned out he was on his way to
see his mother, whom he visited once a week. It was his—or
her—birthday, I don't remember which.

When I read of this, I had not seen my mother in twenty years.

I sympathized with that man. If I were visiting my mother, I
thought, I certainly would take a Librium along—and probably
without the bottle, just as he did.

A question: why did the police notice this fellow on the
street, decide to frisk him? What was so extraordinary about
him? Did he look so menacing? So pathetic? Was it an impulse

of malice or sadism on their part? Was he wiggling his ass, thumbing his nose at them—this forty-year-old bachelor? It hardly seems likely. It must have been his utter dejection, misery, and loneliness. And sure enough—there, ensconced in his pocket, the little green and white pill to lighten his load, to help see him through. Aha! they got him in the nick of time.

II

1956. I am sixteen years old.
I am lying in bed with my mother, thinking about my girl friend, Judith. "Rub noses, like pussycats," my mother says. Catching my thoughts, she asks: "Why do you run around with that slut?"
The bed is perfumed—it is the bed my mother and father shared for a time. I feel chills as my mother rubs noses with me. "You're limited," I tell her. "God, I hate it when you're snotty," she replies.
Across the roof, there is Judith, but it is as if there were barbed wire between us.
Why does my mother make me think of concentration camps? Nothing written, nothing said, makes them as real for me as my mother does. If she can exist, so could the camps.
One day I said to young Doctor Greenblatt, the bachelor attached to his own mother: "My mother hits me—"
"How dare you!" he shouted, "you ungrateful little creep, you serpent, your mother struggles night and day for you!"
I trembled, but I was not really surprised. I felt sorry for the young doctor. My unexpressed sympathy, my silence, galled him—his face got redder and redder. He would burst. The sight of my tense, sad face was unbearable to him. "Get out of here!" he shouted. Now I no longer visit the doctor, but I still visit the unusual patches of garden and greenery in the courtyard of his apartment house, and think of him when I am there.
The others—the neighbors, the social worker my father brought me to—their faces glaze over if I try to tell them about my mother. They let me know it is a terrible thing I am saying,

and forgive me by not listening to me. "Someday," they say as one, "you will regret—"

III

When people ask me about my mother, I say, "My mother? She is not living." One of my finest stories is called "My Mother Is Not Living."

My mother called me at work one day a year ago. We had not seen each other, or spoken, for twenty years. She did not have my address most of that time, for I forbade my father to give it to her.

During the phone call, my mother wished me a happy birthday, asked me how I liked my job, and said she would like to see me. I felt my pounding heart. She spoke in a slow, lulled way, and I could tell she had sedated herself for the phone call. I thanked her for calling, and said I would think about seeing her.

I have used my father as a guinea pig for my stories and poems most of my adult life. He is an excellent subject, always willing to cooperate with me (although the smirking profile I wrote of him when I was on my honeymoon in San Francisco in 1970 was done from memory). I have written portraits of him that showed him demonic, arrogant, sad, crazy, silly, mean, ridiculous. I wrote of one particular facial expression of his I know very well: Ever since I was a child, whenever I have done something that shocked my father, he sits bolt upright, pops his eyes, looks aghast, and sticks his fingers in his mouth. He carries a copy of this description of him in his wallet and whips it out to show to strangers.

Each time I finish a story about him, I say that I have gotten my father out of my system.

While I have also revenged myself on my mother in my work all these years, it has all been done from afar. I have had the satisfaction, however, of knowing that she read some of my stories about her. I was too afraid of her to confront her up close.

IV

1956. *Today when my mother stood by the window, I wanted to push her out. I can't. She is a victim too. And it would mess up my life.*

Her flashing eyes when she hurts me: THAT *is difficult to understand. "God, you're ugly"—comments like that. And to my father: "I hope you drop dead, you son of a bitch." So many enemies—the grocer, neighbors, Negroes, rock and roll ("dirty music"), even the antique dealers she coos with—Carlo and Enrique—smiling her head off and flashing her teeth—as soon as they close the door, she snaps, "Wop assholes." I don't think they are even Italian. Categories of Jews (her people): the good—the rich; the creeps—those who are honest or poor, the German refugees from Hitler who "have no class," or the immigrants with traces of Yiddish and the old country. She does like a few cute little old ladies. She stares at the exiting blonde in the elevator who is wearing a fur coat and says to me: "She's just a Flushing broad who will never make it to Park Avenue."*

In the closet my mother keeps her school books—Dreiser, Sinclair Lewis, Jacob Wassermann, "Europa," Dorothy Thompson, Ibsen, her college yearbook, the school newspaper where she did her writing. I read what the other students wrote to her in the yearbook.

She is waiting for me to be drafted into the army. Why? "It will make a man of you," she says. "You think it's you against the world, kiddo. Everybody's wrong and you're right. They'll knock some sense into you." She pauses and adds, "Hair like an idiot." I ask her: "Do you want me to get killed?" She doesn't reply. She has a certain honesty, no doubt about it.

V

I decided to return my mother's call of eight months ago. I dialed her number. She instantly recognized my voice. I asked her how she was, and she told me she'd had an operation during the summer. I did not ask her what had been wrong: it seemed like the question of a hypocrite.

I said I would like to see her and suggested we meet in Chinatown.

"I didn't know you liked Chinese food," she said. "We have something in common."

After a moment she said, "How will you recognize your old mother?"

"Will you wear a feather?" I said.

She roared. We set the date and the time.

VI

From the moment I picked up the phone, the hatred of my mother seemed to disappear. When I had contemplated meeting her in the past, I was afraid I might strike her, that she might strike me. Those thoughts have left me.

On the day of our meeting, I deliberately chose a tie to wear that was not too spectacular. My reasoning was that if I looked too good, my mother would devise ways to try to destroy me, or take my money (I have none) away from me.

I placed a Librium in my pocket and set out for Chinatown, where she would be waiting on the corner of Mott and Canal Streets in front of the Carvel store. I did not take the Librium.

VII

1954. My mother is in her happiest, most animated mood. She has snagged her hairdresser Ricardo into the house, into the bathroom, especially to do her hair for her at home. The price— a steal. He adores her hair. She says she can't help but be complimented.

She bustles about, racing through the halls. Ricardo is waiting in the bathroom. She brings me in and introduces me. "What a handsome young man!" he says. "Why don't I cut his hair too, Rosie? Won't charge you a sou."

My mother is ecstatic. "Cut it so he don't look like a Com-
mie." She laughs to show she's kidding.

She closes the door while Ricardo does her hair. Streams of
giggles and laughter.

When she comes out, she asks me, "How do I look?"

"Beautiful," I say. She is not satisfied. "What else?" She
looks at me tensely, her smile gone. I don't know what to say,
and look for a clue from her. She turns away.

"Ricardo's ready for you, Bruce," she says in a moment.

Ricardo is standing in the brightly lit bathroom, beaming at
me. He is cutting the air with his scissors.

He talks all the while I settle down. He places a towel over
my shoulders and begins. In a minute I feel a tickle on my
penis. I start. It stops. I feel another tickle. I look up in aston-
ishment and shock. "Cut that out!"

"Hmmm hmmm—you have beautiful hair, young man—"

I feel the tickle again. I jump up and run out. "Bruce!" he
calls.

I hear a shout. My mother follows me and storms into my
room. "What the hell is going on? Are you going to embarrass
me?"

"He touched me—on the—on the—penis."

"Get back in there," she hisses.

"He touched me—"

"You're imagining it, Bruce, that's all. I'm telling you nicely:
GET IN THERE. Don't you ruin my day."

"No."

She goes into the bathroom. She returns after a moment.

"All right. I talked to Ricardo. He's amazed. He doesn't
know what you're talking about, and he promises he won't do
it again."

"What?"

"What do you mean what? Bruce I'm warning you. Get in
there."

I go back inside. Ricardo is beaming, laughing, and chatting
at once. He is also whistling.

I sit down tensely. "There we are!" He again places the towel over me.

Within a minute he puts his hand on my penis.

I jump up, run out of the room. As I leave the house, I shout, "God damn it," and slam the front door with all my might.

I run for a long time, crying aloud.

VIII

On the corner of Mott Street, I saw my mother first. She looked much older. She is sixty-two years old. She had always prized her beauty.

She did not recognize me. "Rosie," I said. I kissed her. When she smiled, she looked as I remembered her. A very pretty woman. She wore a clasp in her hair, a gray dress, a brown cloak. She carried oriental shopping bags. She still walked her quick little steps on her short legs and high heels.

We sat down in the corner of the Yun Luck Rice Shoppe. "So what have you been doing?" she said.

IX

1954. Surely there is somewhere to go, to get away from all this. I look around corners, in new neighborhoods where gardens will lead me to new friends. There is a house with a well in the garden, and I wonder if I should knock at the door.

Lighted windows. Behind them are girls who will kiss me, families to welcome me. There are people who read books, who do not shout and curse, who do not hate everyone.

When it rains, the streets are filled to overflowing with water. Some of the kids make rafts, and I want to sail on the rafts, away from this. I dream that when I am not there, the kids are actually sailing on the rafts. But in the daytime I never see them doing so.

I like those dark, rainy days; with the streets turned into riv-

ers, I feel as if I can see far away. The world has been stopped,
and cleansed. At night in bed, I sail away.

X

She spoke in the small, childlike voice with the Bronx twang I
remembered.

She touched my wedding band: "My married son!" She asked
me the first name of my wife.

She asked what I liked to do in New York. I mentioned the
theater and films.

"What about opera?"

"No, not opera."

"Somehow I thought you would like opera. What about bal-
let?"

"No."

"Uh *huh,*" she said.

On my mother's face are years of hard work and struggle. The
last time I saw her, she was still a secretary, supporting herself
since throwing my father out of the house.

She has been teaching Junior High for eighteen years: Bronx,
Far Rockaway, Manhattan, Crown Heights, getting up at six in
the morning. I was startled to hear her mention receiving "a little welfare" when she had been in the hospital and out of work
for seven months when teachers were being "excessed" out of
the system.

She brought me up to date on the neighbors: "Kaganovich,
the fat man across the hall, just lost half a leg. Gunzenhouser
died of cancer. Farber, the Frankfurter King, lives in Palm Beach.
Lance Stone, he was your age, is fabulously successful in television or movies. Or maybe finance. People ask me about you—"

"You like teaching?" I said.

"No. But I like decorating the classrooms. That's fun. And I
get many compliments for that. I was doing that this past week,
and the principal said, 'What about the bulletin board?' So for
the typing class, I have the kids draw these signs: 'More Tap,
Less Yap' and 'Don't Be A One-Fingered Lily.' I have a kid do a

drawing of Lily at the typewriter with just one finger. They like that, they get a kick out of it."

"You made them up yourself?" I asked.

"Yes."

She said, "I miss my old job."

"As Rothbaum's secretary?"

"Sure. Look, the Schrafft's wagon came twice a day: in the morning and the afternoon. And there was color TV."

"What were you in the hospital for?"

My mother looked away. "I had an operation."

"What kind?"

"Woman's troubles. They began with your birth, Bruce. It goes back a long way."

"I never knew that."

"Bruce, you remember Eva Stern, my best friend? We gabbed on the phone day and night."

"Sure."

"She died. I was her only friend at the end."

"What was wrong with her?"

"Mental. Valium and alcohol. Her daughter Shirley had an auction of her furniture. But first she said to me, 'What do you want? You can use some of these things. I've heard about your apartment. And they mean nothing to me.' So I took the chandelier and the mirror. Eva had fallen against the mirror and broken it during one of her states. I spent $1,000 to fix it. She always asked me about you."

After a moment my mother said, "Effie died too. She was in and out of asylums. She always asked me about you.

"Some people can't keep their heads together," she added.

Eva and Effie were my mother's two best friends from childhood.

XI

"Maybe you'll come over to the house for dinner with your wife—what's her name again?"

"Susan. Sure we will."

"What do you like to eat?"

"Whatever you enjoy making," I said.

"I'm a good cook. You're so skinny, Bruce. Herbie eats like a horse."

"Who?"

"Herbie. He's a boy your age—a little younger, thirty-one I think. Still a bachelor—I'm looking for a girl for him. He was teaching at the same school in the Bronx. When I need to go places by car, sometimes he drives me. So I cook him dinner."

"Doesn't he have a mother and father?" I asked.

"Sure. But he says his mother can't cook roast chicken like me." She giggled. "He knows I'm seeing you today."

XII

"I won't mention that story, 'My Mother Is Not Living,' " my mother said. I saw a peculiar expression on her face, and realized she was trying not to cry. "Or why we haven't gotten together for so long. We won't go into that, I promised myself. Bygones are bygones."

I nodded.

My mother mentioned that another teacher had pointed out my name and address in a writers' yearbook five years ago, and asked her if it was me. In such ways, I realized, she had gleaned tiny bits of information about me over the years. They added up to very little, almost nothing at all. I had sworn my father to secrecy about my movements and whereabouts, and he had followed my instructions with unusual care. Perhaps it was because I had said, "I don't trust myself. If I see her, I don't know what I would do."

She must have come upon the story, "My Mother Is Not Living," in just such an accidental way, stumbled upon it or had it pointed out to her by an unsuspecting friend.

"Have you traveled?" she said.

"Just London. Have you?"

Her face lit. "England, Italy, Spain, Singapore, Hong Kong. This shopping bag is from Hong Kong. I've turned your bed-

room into an oriental room. Wait until you see it. Do you want
to walk around Chinatown?"

"Yes, sure."

"I love a day off like this. I guess I'm still a little girl."

I helped my mother on with her coat and we walked into the
street.

XIII

It was unexpectedly cold out, and my mother noticed that I was
shivering. She was disturbed about the light coat I was wearing.

Her head bobbed as she looked into the store windows, and
at the merchandise of the street vendors. We zoomed through
stores of exotic Chinese ware. She barely paused at all. "They
don't have it," she said as we walked out of a fourth store.

"What?"

"Seasoned pepper."

We walked down the winding side streets. She eagerly took
in the sights and smells. "I like this better than a show," she
said. "It's an adventure."

"So do I," I said.

She looked at me. "You do? Uh *huh*." She nodded.

She walked a few steps and stopped. "What's that smell?"
There was the aroma of coffee from a Chinese pastry shop.
"Oooh!" my mother said. "Doesn't that smell good? Just the
right thing to warm us up." She paused. "Maybe you don't want
coffee."

"That's a good idea," I said.

"You do?"

"Yes."

"You sure?"

"Positive."

"Okay. Let's go."

We stepped down into the coffee shop.

We sat at the counter. The elderly Chinese waiter was not over-
joyed at our small order. "Make the coffee very, very hot," my
mother said. He began to pour the cream and my mother

stopped him, taking the pitcher away from him. "That's okay," she said, "we'll do it ourselves."

"It smells wonderful," my mother said to the waiter, her smile making her face youthful. The waiter smiled back. In a moment he was back with another pitcher. "Maybe you like more?"

"No, thank you."

He quickly handed my mother two napkins.

XIV

"I'm still pretty cold," I said as we stood in front of the shop. "Maybe you'd like to keep shopping, and I'll get going."

She pointed to her two empty shopping bags. "I guess I'm like my mother," she said. "She always had a shopping bag in one hand and you in the other, Bruce." It was true. I had rarely seen my mother during the day as a child. She had deposited me with my grandmother and taken off.

I took my mother into my arms and said, "I'll call you." There was a pause and I saw her looking at me. Then I added: "I mean, not years from now. Soon."

Touching her cheek, I said it again.

2

CANCER OF THE
TESTICLES

I

I had not seen Samuel for years, but his letters annoyed me.
They were so melancholy, so sad. I couldn't figure it out. In 1970
I returned to Manhattan for the summer and called him. "I'm
double the size I was when you knew me; so is Doris. We eat all
the time. Don't you?" We made a date and I broke it—too depressing.

Following that, several letters arrived. The contents varied,
but always the same refrain: "So many things to say; we must
get together soon; you have been a better and truer friend than
I." Puzzling to me, since I did not understand what we had to say
to each other, and why I was such a good friend. First a letter
came about the sudden death of his father from cancer. I remember Mr. Weintraub's grocery store, Samuel's Marxist stories and poems condemning his father for ringing up sales on
the cash register and conveniently forgetting to put in a bar of
soap, a can of soup, when packing the customer's purchases in
bags. The next letter told of the death of his mother from cancer.
Then good news: his novel published. He inscribed it to me:

"To Bruce—There were four people who thought I might be a writer. You were one of them, and your confidence and friendship were very important to me, during dark, difficult days. Sam."

Not true, unfortunately—I never believed in Sam as a writer. I hope the other three did. I read his book which was, in a strange, unreal way, about black power. All the attitudes were proper, and, if set down more convincingly, might have netted Sam a home in Scarsdale, a sale to Hollywood, a livelihood. But true to Sam's writing style as I remember it, everything was tone-deaf: a black's afro was "crunchy"; his lips "like accordion folds." What emerged incessantly, everywhere, was the theme of masturbation. The characters could not keep their hands off themselves, no matter how militant. Everyone: the beautiful blacks, the fuzzy liberals, the reactionary dogs . . . at every free moment was settling down with a wad of toilet paper. It was uncanny in such a short, serious and shadowy book. And while it was not well written, it had an authority; there was no doubt that here was something the author really knew about.

I waited a long time to write Samuel about the novel, and then suggested who might like it. I compiled a list of people I did not respect. Samuel wouldn't know it, and he would respect them himself, and they really might enjoy the book.

During an interim period there was a letter from Samuel's brother, Moshe, from Montreal. Ten pages handwritten on newspaper, crumpled and hard to decipher. Moshe was now twenty-six, eight years younger than Samuel. I thought of him, a kid of seventeen, singing freedom songs badly in Washington Square. He'd heard I was starting a magazine, and in the cool, lovey-dovey hip lingo of those days he said he was enclosing his fine poems, that I might use them or tear them up or merely keep them, but that he hoped they would make me "happy and content."

I remember a day in 1960—we are all at Coney Island in Samuel's car. I am singing softly to myself the World Youth Freedom song. Samuel shushes his wife Doris and Moshe. He puts his hand on Moshe's shoulder and says, "Listen." There is silence.

"Bruce," he says to me, "sing louder. You have a beautiful voice."

That is how truly tone-deaf Samuel was, and is. *No one*, ever, has praised my singing. No one has ever had reason to. That day in the car, Moshe listened, said "Yeah, yeah" to Samuel and joined me with his guitar. I felt my voice rising in strength, believing with them, and sang all the way into Manhattan.

Another time, another day: Samuel mentions a hit song by the McGuire Sisters. The refrain goes: "May you find someone to love, as much as I love you." He says, with a twinkle and a smile, "Bruce, I'll bet you love that song."

Embarrassed and taken by surprise, I admit it. "How did you know?"

He turned to Doris. "You see? I know, Bruce. It's fine . . . it's good that you're like you are. Don't be embarrassed."

I must have been between girls at the time. Samuel had taken to analyzing me, explaining he had never seen me as a person before, but, as he put it, as "a giant."

A long silence after the letter about the book. A letter came from Samuel when I had hepatitis last year. "Oh no," I said to my wife. "What can it be this time? He must have cancer." We laughed.

I put the letter away for days. Not because I thought that. I placed it between pages of books, in cubbyholes, in drawers. I opened it one day: "I have cancer of the testicles," Samuel wrote me.

II

In 1960 I was working as a typist at an encyclopedia firm. I shared a cubicle with a concert pianist named Arthur. Arthur was in his midtwenties and he spent three months of the year as a reservist in the army. Arthur was a type almost extinct today—extremely well-adjusted, friendly open eyes beaming through horn-rimmed spectacles, his fingers flying over the typewriter keys, his coffee breaks fifteen minutes to the second, respectful, on the ball. Did he like the army?

"Sure! We all have to do it, don't we?"

"But you're an artist."

He glanced nervously over the rim of our cubicle.

"You're not a sour apple, are you?" he said.

God, he was happy. He cleaned his fingernails, he had a girl who kept him in line. He was living proof that the artist could be a good citizen, devoid of nasty thoughts and incendiary attitudes.

He had me pegged. "You're the first to go on your coffee break and the last to leave it," he said, tapping his fingers. "I like my work. I like my girl. I like the army. You've been late to work every morning this week."

"What kind of music do you play anyway?" I asked him.

He got edgier and edgier about me. I felt I was his conscience. I felt I was everybody's conscience. He wanted no part of it. The only thing I was sneaky about was the army. They were breathing down my neck. I had so many plans going for avoiding it that I couldn't keep up with myself: A) Radicalism. B) Pacifism. C) Mental Illness. D) Criminality. E) Homosexuality. F) Flight to Cuba. G) Near-sightedness. Each stance required a different behavior pattern, and I couldn't make up my mind. I visited Communist Party headquarters, grinning and waving at the cameras I knew were hidden all over the building. Once inside the building, a comrade spotted me and started to call out "Bruce O—"
"NO NO NO!" I screamed, looking around for microphones, "HA HA HA! HI HOW ARE YOU." On the way out of the building, I placed my hands in front of my face as a shield. By the time I got to the Automat nearby I was breathless and terrified. I went back to my room, dug up a stack of *Daily Worker*s and burnt them in the toilet. It took hours.

I had chosen, at that point in my life, a psychiatrist to go with my life style. Dr. Harold Jackson was black, left-wing, and short. He had a house in Greenwich Village, he was friendly with Langston Hughes and dabbled in poetry himself.

There was no real difference between sitting in Dr. Jackson's waiting room and sitting in his office. This took me about a year to figure out. He would greet me in the waiting room and chat about politics, weather, restaurants, nutrition, exercise. I would charge into his office, sweating with neurotic symptoms, and wait to get down to business.

Chuckles, frowns, bits of philosophy wafted through the air. "I can't breathe!" I said. "My father—my mother—that bastard at the office—" I tried to get it all out; there was only an hour.

Dr. Jackson looked at his fingernails, clucked his tongue, paused, and finally said,

"Let me ask you this, Bruce—"

I strained forward. "Yes?"

"Are you . . . shall we say, tense?"

Gobbling for air, I said between gritted teeth that I was.

"I thought so. Many of my patients are. Tense, anxious, nervous. Do you frequently feel this way—"

"Yes—"

"I must confess . . . I rather thought so . . ."

"I want to go to Cuba."

"Oh?"

"I can't breathe here; the capitalists have seen to that all right. I don't exist—I'm just a writer, that's all. A useless commodity. Those army bastards are just waiting to kill me. Who will know? I'll be dead before I'll have had the chance to be alive—to live, to publish my book. Wiped out, like a spot on the wall. No way. No way. Will you help me?"

"Certainly!"

"You will?" I leaned forward. "I was thinking of a freighter . . . or a plane via Moscow—"

"Now, now, Bruce, travel to Cuba is forbidden!"

"That's why I thought Moscow first . . ."

"I think, Bruce, that life . . . sometimes . . . has its gray moments. I want you to know that I, too, have sometimes, oh, fits of . . . pique . . . now and then when things don't go just as I might have planned. Do you know about the Club Valhalla?"

I stared at him.

"The Club Valhalla, Bruce, is very pleasant. Singles mingle there. They have the most charming dances, and, heavens, all

sorts of fun things. Why don't you give them a jingle and see if
the rates have gone up? They were most reasonable when I went
there."

"But I don't want a bourgeois dating club—"

Dr. Jackson laughed. "Oh my no, they're most serious.
They're quite mature politically, I can assure you."

"But about Cuba—"

Dr. Jackson looked sad. "Yes. This country's attitudes toward
that valiant land are so silly. You can't even get a good Havana
cigar."

He ushered me out, smiling, cheerful. He was black, he was
radical. I saw him on the streets of the Village with blonde girls
who towered over him. He looked up at them, grinning, and patted them on the ass.

III

I met Samuel on a coffee break at the encyclopedia. He had an
owlish look, very pleasant. He was an assistant editor, twenty-
eight years old. I was simmering; he was placid. I slipped him a
copy of the *Daily Worker*. After work, he was waiting for me
outside. "Come home, meet my wife, Doris." I traveled on the
subway with him to Brooklyn.

They were opposites. "Doris, meet a radical, a poet, a fine
thinker, and a dear friend, Bruce."

She was tiny and flat-chested. "Take it easy, Samuel. How do
ya do?"

"This is wonderful coffee, Doris. Doris is a fine cook. Wait,
you'll see, Bruce. And a wonderful little wife. Sitting here like
this, I can tell, Bruce, we'll be good friends. I didn't know there
were any radicals left. Doris's mother, Hilda, organized the
steel workers. She's still there in Bedford, Massachusetts, in her
little house. I laughed at her ideas. But when you talk about
them, I begin to understand—"

"It's instant coffee, Sam," Doris said. "Take it easy."

"But tell me this, Bruce. What about the Soviet Union? Isn't
it a drab, poverty-stricken place?"

Samuel sat at my feet with his coffee, looking up at me.

"The Union of Soviet Socialist Republics—" I began.

"Doris, turn the lamp the other way. There. Look at his profile. Did anyone ever tell you that you have a Greek profile, Bruce? Go ahead, I was interrupting."

"—is the first land of Socialism. Surrounded on all sides by enemies, mistakes were made. But I'm sick of all this crap! Corrupt? Treehouses! Honeymooners live in treehouses! That's how corrupt it is. And Stalin was a reader of Tolstoy!—"

I was inspired by the dimmed lighting, Samuel at my feet, their quiet, rapt attention.

We talked through the night. "This has been very fine. I can't tell you, Bruce, how you're opening our eyes. I have an idea. Sleep here tonight. Tomorrow we don't go to the capitalist cockroaches' office. We continue talking. You'll educate us. We'll learn. This is fine. Isn't it, Doris? This is really fine."

She stared at Samuel. "Are you crazy?"

He laughed and grinned. "No, no, I'm serious. I feel Bruce knows. I have that feeling. I don't think I'm wrong."

"He can sleep here, of course, but tomorrow you work."

He patted her on the head. "Little Doris. Isn't she sweet, angry like that? It's good to express anger, Doris. And to express love too. It's very good. It's time we began to let go."

I slept on a couch that night. There was no sexual action from the bed. Only later would I discover that after three years of marriage, Doris and Samuel had accomplished an historical feat equal to Lenin's five-year plan:

Doris was a virgin.

Samuel, also.

IV

December in Far Rockaway. It was very cold, the wind whipping against our wooden cottage, the sea spray on the windows. The boardwalk was deserted, the steeplechase and the merry-go-rounds closed. Once, long ago, the Jewish workers considered summer weekends in Far Rockaway a big deal; then came the borscht belt; then the Concord and the Riviera and Las Vegas. Our bungalow was where the workers used to come in summer. Clustered among hundreds of other wooden shacks, all of them vacant, we now lived, Samuel, Doris and I, in the two rooms, for thirty dollars a month. We had an electric heater, blankets, our Marxist texts and pictures of Lenin.

People in the neighborhood found us. Even though it was 1960, once a week a horse-drawn wagon stopped at our door: the milkman. Cards were left from representatives of Father Coughlin, Frederick's of Hollywood, the *Police Gazette*, a committee to drive the British out of Palestine.

Samuel had quit his job and we lived on unemployment insurance. He was very, very happy.

At night we huddled around the fireplace, freezing. "Talk, Bruce," Samuel would say.

"What about?"

"Anything is fine. Really, Bruce, you have a way of saying things. Doris agrees with me. Or sing for us. Or read us your poetry or stories. Any of these things would be fine. Tell us about when you were a little boy and your father took you to the Palace to see all the old-time performers like Belle Baker—"

"But I already have—"

"I would like to hear it again. Or about being a writer. What it means to you to be a writer. I would like you to go into that again. The way you would sneak up the stairway to the roof with your first girl friend. Doris likes the way you talk about that. Or your intuitions about Stalin's innate kindness and decency. Or the venal behavior of the Trotskyites."

I talked on into the night, and sometimes I thought that Doris was pressing her thin body against mine in the candlelight. I was between girl friends. I pressed back.

v

During the first months, at night I listened for stirrings from their bed across the room. There weren't any. Doris vomited a lot, and sometimes he told her happy stories about their present situation: adult fairy tales. "Baloney," was Doris's response.

Samuel had a thing about shoes. I watched him hasten to put Doris's shoes on for her. "Samuel, what the hell are you doing?"

Samuel looked up at her from the floor. "Helping my little Doris."

"Oh for Christ's sake."

"You look so cute when you get angry."

She kicked him. He did not move away.

VI

Samuel had this certain look, or gleam in his eyes sometimes, that came and went. You knew something was cooking when it was there. On the subway, he would stare at a girl's shoes and that gleam was there. At first I thought I was imagining it, except that I had to keep tapping his shoulder to tell him we had reached our stop. I was only dimly aware of what he was doing. We never talked about it.

VII

About this look of Samuel's: "That look," Doris would say. Samuel would laugh then, devilishly, or giggle. He had that look one day when he said, "Bruce, I feel it is time for us to take a more active part in the struggle." A picture comes to mind of that period, a picture of Samuel in my scrapbook in a Lincoln Brigade demonstration. The picture turned up in the *Daily Worker*. A line of demonstrators was grimly walking up and down, glaring at the photographer. Except one, who was grinning and waving and flashing a V sign.

On a momentous day, Samuel and I visited the home of the chairman of the Far Rockaway branch of the Communist Party, Dr. Hyman Bernhardt. Bernhardt, a broad-shouldered, solid man with curly red hair, greeted us at the door with dancing, suspicious eyes. He ushered us in. He stared at my briefcase.

"What a lovely briefcase," he said, and took it from me. We had known him for several months.

His hands roamed over it. "May I look inside? It's so handsome."

"Yes."

His hands roamed through the briefcase as he went on talking to us. "Very nice indeed," he said, and handed the briefcase back to me.

He introduced us to his wife and daughter, and took us into his private study. "Two cracked ribs," he said, nodding.

"What?" I said.

"My daughter, Naomi. Two cracked ribs. She never told me. A doctor friend informed us. In the Washington demonstration."

"Wonderful," Samuel said.

Dr. Bernhardt looked sharply at him. "Yes . . . that too. But that is quite right, Sam. Wonderful in what it reveals to us of the determination of the youth."

On the wall there was a picture of Stalin, and underneath it a quotation from Brecht: "They say that we are evil. But we are the end of evil."

"You're a writer, Bruce. My wife and I saw a play by Tennessee Williams the other night. What magic that fella has . . . what magic. It was . . . excellent. And the marvelous revolutionary anger of Kowalski. In my youth, I traveled the South, organizing the party. He knows the South. My eighth book, incidentally, on black slavery will be issued by the Red Hammer Press in March. It demonstrates, I think, indubitably, the incredible, scientific superiority of the blacks of that day in their terrible bondage. I don't know if you are acquainted with my work . . ."

He paused.

We both said we certainly were.

". . . but I have endeavored to pierce the lies and . . . dare I say . . . the deliberate, disgusting, and scurrilous myth perpetrated by the white Southern oligarchy that the blacks accepted their situation. The scholarly research that I devoted to this book was not easy. One can do many things with so-called facts. Therefore, in this book, my thesis: that one black slave out of three not only revolted against their slave masters, but called them 'the man' . . . and toward each other . . .''

He lowered his voice. "Toward each other, these fine, brave men, in celebration of their blackness and in their extraordinary revolutionary awareness, these men . . . addressed each other . . . as . . . comrade."

He paused, walked across the room and looked out the window. "Comrade . . . that word of fraternity and brotherhood, one hundred years ago . . . that is my discovery, and I trust that despite the blackness and cowardice of these days of fear, the book will be passed from house to house, that it will be known and help to ignite the fires that will sweep this country . . .

"Yes. They are with us . . . but they are still afraid. Tennessee Williams . . ."

"Really?" I said.

Bernhardt let it hang in the air. "Faulkner, Hemingway, Frost . . . they are waiting. I can feel it. Here, in the quiet streets of Far Rockaway, the masses also wait. I go to my office at headquarters daily. I climb the stairs, push open the door. Not a soul comes in. But I remember when those rooms were filled with people. A special room for babies and children. Cookies. Cakes. Games. Those people are *waiting*. They are angry. But now they will be joined by their black brethren and topple those detestable vermin in the capital."

"But . . . isn't there also some kind of disillusionment because of the . . . oh . . . moodiness of Stalin?" I said, quickly adding, "Not that I believe the capitalist press."

Dr. Bernhardt paced back and forth. "The man say dis, the man say dat. Well, de glory lies with de fool, not de mule. If I lie, let me die. Listen heah: don't let nobody turn you 'round, heah? Samuel, Bruce? 'Cause on dat great gettin' up mornin', see, dat great big bright gettin' up mornin', when de trumpets blare, you arc gonna be able to bare yo chest, I say bare yo chest, and *dee*-clare, and *dee*-clare, you *be*-lieved, you *be*-lieved. And you'll get what's comin' to you. Oh yes, you will. 'Cause dem folks are talkin' about concentration camps run by Stalin. By a *Com-*

munist! DO YOU BELIEVE THAT? Man? That the Jews burned the
Reichstag? WHATEVER they say, WHATEVER, you—will—*bee-
lieve* that a Communist does NOT HURT PEOPLE. He don't. HE
DON'T! He LOVES people. And that is why, my dear comrades,
that picture is on my wall, and will remain in its place. This is
one fella who is not going to be moved. This is one fella who
does not say one thing on Sunday and sell out to the *New York
Post* on Monday! This is one fella who has written EIGHT books
of which he does not repudiate ONE solitary word. 'Cause I stand
here now and you see my shadow there on the wall. And when
you leave this house you can know my shadow will still be on
the wall, and NEXT week, and the week after that. And my library shelves will remain intact:*Marx-Lenin-Stalin.* Oh yes.
There will not be a mysterious disappearance one night, and
you say, 'Where Stalin?' and I say, 'Who he? Never hearda that
mother!' No sir, no . . . my baby daughter's cracked ribs . . ." He
chuckled . . . "She believed something that I conveyed to her."
    He was silent for a moment. "The isolation has not been easy.
I say to my wife: 'Where are the people?' When someone comes
up to my office, I assume he is a spy. And he is. He is too eager
to say yes. He fawns. He is a good eater. I watch him. Steak for
lunch. What does he have for dinner? It's a little disgusting to
watch him munching away."
    There were tears in his eyes. "Who will carry on?" He looked
away. Samuel promptly said, "Look, we give you our word."
    I tried to shake my head.
    We departed with gifts of books by Dimitrov, Hikmet, Fu-
naroff, Ernst Toller, and Stalin. As we walked through the streets,
Samuel talked about the strength and affirmation he was finding in Marxism. I had thought Bernhardt's daughter was very
pretty, and felt sorry about her ribs. I wondered if it was worth
it. But if I could get a date with her, I wouldn't say so.

VIII

Samuel had a legendary friend, Emory, from college days. Emory
had worked nights as a hotel clerk at a shady hotel in Boston; he
was working on a novel; he was a flamboyant figure, "open to

life," as Samuel put it, although with "sexual confusions." When I tried to pin Samuel down on Emory's qualities, I found out that Emory had the most uncanny ability to capture, through mimicry and satire, the essence of the Jewish mother, and particularly *his* Jewish mother.

One wintry morning, there was a knock at our bungalow door. "Yoo-hoo, Mr. Weintraub!" a high voice called. Samuel jumped and rubbed his hands, flung open the door.

A fat, bespectacled, blinking Emory stood at the door, scarf flung flamboyantly around his neck. He said, in no particular order:

"Children are starving in India . . ."

"I'm only your mother, may your nose clot . . ."

"What are you an Einstein, with all that hair? . . ."

"Eat your heart out, you little schnorrer . . ."

"Go to Ginsberg the robber, see if I care . . ."

Samuel sank to the floor in laughter. Emory sat down at the table, not pausing to take off his coat, his face red, his chest heaving: "Essen, my little kinder . . . a bissel schmaltz, if you please . . . stay away from the *shvartze*, they stink . . . do I know *goyim*? You can smell liquor from a mile away . . .

"So it's your birthday. What are you gonna give me . . . ?"

I noticed that Emory wasn't laughing at all. His voice got more strident; he was breathless. Samuel pounded Doris on the back, and Doris said "Ouch!" He looked at me, laughing and pointing at Emory, and noticed that I wasn't laughing. I was a little jealous of all the attention Emory was getting, and didn't really think he was that funny. I hoped, though, that Samuel wouldn't take out the red taillight that he had recently purchased. In the evenings, when I talked to Samuel and Doris before the fireside, Samuel would turn off all the lights and shine the red light gently on me.

Emory was standing up now, pounding the table and screaming:

"Eat, eat, you little pisser, with a face that the neighborhood shakes their heads at . . . don't pull your putz, you'll get a craziness in the head . . ."

"Ha ha ha," laughed Samuel.

IX

It was the absence of sex that made you aware of sex with Samuel. It was the total absence of sex. He talked about his brother Moshe's crush on a girl: "You should see Moshe, Doris. He has this very deep feeling about Judith, the daughter of the furrier. He said that he would like to do certain things with her, nuzzle her . . . things like that. I saw him pat her on the head Thursday morning. I really think . . . he feels affectionately toward her. I have a hunch he's already kissed her . . . did you do things like that when you were his age, Bruce?"

"What things . . . nuzzle girls?"

"You know . . . display affection?"

"Fuck them?"

Samuel blushed. "You know. Drift toward each other . . . share things . . . foibles, tales, stories . . . like in a fairyland, a dreamlike sensation . . ."

"He said *fuck* them, Samuel," Doris said.

Samuel changed the subject, but later on in the evening he came into my room and said he wanted to shake my hand in thanks for my "incredible honesty and spontaneity."

"You are teaching us things, Bruce, and we are learning."

"What am I teaching you?"

He shook his head. "—you extend yourself so that we may imbibe, and that we do. It is not wasted on us, believe me, Bruce. We are profiting from your experience, and your suffering—"

"I—"

"You are wiser than your years, Bruce. Because of you, I'm changing. I'm becoming revolutionary in every way. I feel my manhood pulsing and surging with every revolutionary step I take." He paused. "I honestly feel, Bruce, that one day soon, I shall come to a climactic stand for the revolution."

X

It was during those winter days of unemployment insurance and welfare checks, of picket lines and walks along the deserted boardwalk, that I made a suggestion that Samuel felt changed his life. I suggested that he see a psychiatrist.

It is hard to explain why this suggestion meant so much to Samuel. After all, I had seen dozens of them besides Dr. Jackson: all sizes, shapes, races and creeds. I knew their styles and their tastes and how to talk to them. In fact, I was running out of available ones. I would look new ones up in the Yellow Pages and imagine what they were like from the sound of their names. My father paid the bills. I found it hard to remember who said what: I remember that for some reason one of them had a bad back and was lying down on the couch while I was sitting on a chair. He said that what he really liked to do was sculpt and that his greatest pleasure came from banging away in the basement. The clearest idea I got of why he was a psychiatrist was that it allowed him to social climb. Since those days he has written a book on the joys of marijuana and is a desired guest at all parties.

I mention all this to indicate that my suggestion to Samuel was not the result of some deep sense of compassion for him, but merely what every person in therapy says to every person out of therapy: why are you *not* in therapy?

It was, however, a great moment in Samuel's life. The gates opened. It was the beginning, too, of a friendship, and even of a business partnership: for Samuel eventually invested in a drainage corporation with Shmuel Goss, his psychiatrist. This corporation eventually went bankrupt, but that came later, long after Samuel had been treated successfully and had gone into the business world.

Shmuel Goss, like many psychiatrists, had a following: his patients. They thought he was extraordinary. Samuel added him to his gallery of greats, beside myself, Emory, the great satirist, and Hilda, "the Communist Rebel Lady" (this was a paraphrase of a description of Elizabeth Gurley Flynn as the "Rebel Girl" of the I.W.W. and bestowed on Hilda, who in fact was Doris's mother. Hilda owned her own house in Bedford, Massachusetts, had once been expelled by the Communist Party, and made wonderful potato kugel).

Goss had a big body, a booming voice, the usual attributes.

But it was new to Samuel. Goss was casual; he let patients meet each other and even overhear bits of each other's conversation and gossip. He let it all hang out.

This was during the time that I moved out of the cottage. I had found a girl. Samuel told me, though, that Goss believed that "Everything was healthy in sex." Shortly afterwards, Samuel somehow conveyed to me, amidst Victorian blushes and stammering, that his marriage was consummated.

It was during this time, too, that one night I stayed over with Samuel and Doris at the cottage. By some chance I had gone to the bathroom and when I came out, their bedroom door was open and a red light was shining over the bed. I saw Doris in knee-high black boots. Samuel was lying nude on the floor, and she was stomping on him.

XI

During the next ten years of my own anguished life, as I have said, Samuel has kept in touch with me, reminding me of what a good friend I had been to him.

I recently received another letter from Samuel.

Dear Bruce,
It sounds like it has been a difficult year for both of us, although we have both had our share of satisfying experiences as well.

All my medical examinations have proved completely negative and I really have gotten to the point where I don't consider myself in jeopardy. I appreciated your concern.

I have in recent days been thinking of our friendship and I am strongly reminded of how much you helped me at a very critical time in my life.

Take care.
Sam.

I'll conclude with a card received from Samuel some time back, on the birth of his child. It was a quote from Dylan Thomas:

And then to awake, and the farm, like a wanderer white
With the dew, come back, the cock on his shoulder; it was all

> Shining, it was Adam and maiden,
>> The sky gathered again
>> And the sun grew round that very day . . .

I do not want to give the impression that my friend Samuel was always tone-deaf.

3

SELECTIVE SERVICE

Even when I ran into Grinaldi, my psychiatrist, seated on a bench with a pigeon on his head in Washington Square Park, or eating dinner in Bickford's among the old men who lived in single rooms, he had an air of calm and certainty that reassured me. I saw him as a rebel. His phone number was unlisted and he was afraid of the authorities. He had no license to practice, but none was technically required. His psychiatric magazines were filched for him by friends and patients from libraries and medical waiting rooms. His life was a thin thread, but he carried it off.

I was almost eighteen. The draft board was breathing down my neck.

"When I came to this country from Sicily," he told me during a session, "I ate out of garbage cans to keep alive. When the Communists and the Jews tell me that man is basically good, I have to laugh—"

"The Jews," I said. "Did you say the Jews?" My heart was pounding. Grinaldi's face flushed and then he laughed. "Yes, the Jews."

"I'm Jewish—I mean I'm not in a religious sense, I'm a pacifist and a socialist—but . . . I'm Jewish."

"Yes, I know, Bruce."

"You're not anti-Semitic?"

Grinaldi laughed and shook his head. "Jesus," he said.

"What does that mean?"

"Take it easy, Bruce. A great many Communists are Jews. Everybody knows that. I'm stating facts. Ethel and Julius Rosenberg—"

"*Are you in favor of capital punishment?*" I stood up.

"God damn it," he shouted, "will you get off your high horse, please? Just sit down and listen for a minute. You, Bruce, *do not hear, do not see. You*, Bruce Orav, argue and negate. You have the answers to everyone else's problems but not your own. In short, Professor, A for intellect, zero for belief."

"True, but you're changing the subject—"

"I am not changing the subject. You said you were a pacifist—"

"Yes, I am—"

"Sure, and I'm a horse's ass. What are you going to do about the army?"

"I'm not going!" I screamed. "Not in a thousand years!"

He popped two ice cubes into his scotch and downed it. He stared at me with a smile. "You don't want to be a soldier?"

"NO!"

He smiled. "I think you'd make an excellent soldier. In fact, you'd make a terrific commanding officer." He spoke slowly, and he leered at me.

"What—what the hell are you talking about? I'm non-violent—"

"You're what?"

"Non-violent! I believe in peace!"

He drew out each word. "Oh no you're not. You're boiling. You take all that anger with you on the battlefield, Bruce, and you'll be a credit to Uncle Sam."

"You son of a bitch," I said.

"Hey," he laughed. "Hey, listen to that! Do you hear yourself?"

"So what?"

"Your voice! The resonance and tonal quality! Usually you sound like a weak sister! Why can't you always make it forceful like that?"

My head was spinning. "I can't follow you, I can't follow you—"

"Bruce," he said, "do you believe your mother is basically good?"

"That bitch! I could slit her throat!"

"Oh?"

"My mother is one percent of the world."

"I rest my case," he said.

"Anyway, I don't want to get killed . . ."

"Oh . . . well, why didn't you say so?"

"Because it's more complex than that."

"Sure it is. Have a drinkee, Bruce. Won't hurt ya. You got a lot to learn, Bruce. You want it all nice. You and FDR and the fags and Adlai."

Selective Service. All the school counselors, the advisors, the neighbors, the shrinks, would say soothingly, "After you finish your stint in the service—"

"What do you mean, after—" I wanted to scream— "I won't be alive after!"

I carried my Selective Service letter in my jacket pocket. A long white envelope, it contained my 1-A classification. I did not know how to get rid of it. I was afraid that my Communist connections would become known to the draft board and that they would induct me immediately out of revenge. I couldn't leave the letter in my room. One of my enemies might enter when I was out, find the letter, and inform the board of my communism. I was afraid, too, that the letter might fall out of my pocket at a demonstration and be picked up by the F.B.I. who policed the picket lines.

I lit a match to the letter in the kitchen sink.

I placed the ashes in my pocket and walked around with them.

I went out one midnight and, when no one was looking, emptied the ashes from my pocket into the grate in the street. I looked around angrily at the suspicious types who might be watching.

But then I wondered if the draft board tapped my room. I talked aloud to myself all the time.

I began to whisper in the room. Damn it, it was hard not to talk aloud. I moved my lips silently and the words struggled to get out.

I paced around my room. I clicked my teeth shut on a word. I slammed my fist against the wall. The annual civil defense drill was coming up Thursday. The sirens would sound, the streets would be cleared. Every year the *Catholic Worker* crowd—Dorothy Day, Ammon Hennacy—got their names in the paper as they were carried off from Battery Park protesting. Thursday was the day. If I took part, the draft board would be convinced of my sincerity as a pacifist. I would be on TV and in the *New York Times*. But I would have a jail record. What if I trembled in front of the cameras? What if they placed me in a cell and took away my glasses? I wouldn't be able to read. What if the TV reporters asked me for a statement and I was unable to speak? Confrontations always made my heart pound and reduced my words to gibberish. I might forget I was a pacifist and scream "Fuck capitalism" or "Free Sacco and Vanzetti" in my confusion. What if a guard hit me? If I was a pacifist, I couldn't hit back. Or what if he really hurt me? They could do anything they wanted to you in jail and call it an accident. One day at a Communist rally, I had meant to tell the comrades that I was going to the bathroom. Instead I said I was going "backstage." They had stared at me. I was so befuddled I broke out in a sweat.

I sat down on my cot and tried to read *Esquire* and tossed it aside. Time to read the *National Guardian*, article by article, to deepen my Marxism. Oh shit, why was it so boring, so deadly, why was each paragraph torture? How could people with a vision of paradise sound like a machine cranking along a parched road? Anna Louise Strong writing about being released after years in a Communist Chinese prison—how pleased, how proud

she was that the Socialist system proved its virtue by releasing
her! Anna Louise, all smiles, in her maidenly dress, New England glasses, grateful for imprisonment and for release. Was
she guilty—yes and no. Yes when they jailed her, no now that
she was out. Whatever they said was fine. Let's see, who's been
expelled from the American C.P.? Oh, Nat Binder, the visionary
working class leader as of last Thursday, now a vermin, an agent
of imperialism, a capitalist stooge. I had always thought he was
a creep. Oh, Kumar Goshal, fuck you, oh, Cedric Belfrage, why
are you people so hard to like? You're supposed to be saints, God
damn it, and you're not even passable.

I thought of my father's face when he would hear of the arrest.
Now he would know I was serious, that I wasn't kidding, that I
wasn't afraid of my shadow like him. But I would need a pair of
jeans and a workshirt to get arrested in, wearing a suit would
look ridiculous. Oh Christ, where would I get the money to buy
the jeans? I had spent my weekly allowance already. I would
have to call my father and plead with him, and he would be suspicious. He always wanted me to wear a suit and a tie so that I
could find a good job.

I was called to the phone in the hallway. "DON'T DO IT,
BRUCE—"

"What?" It was Grinaldi.

"You heard me."

"I don't know what you're talking about—"

"Don't do it, Bruce—"

"What are you talking about?"

"Thursday."

"Thursday?"

"Thursday."

"But how do you know about Thursday?" I had to admire the
bastard, although I felt weak. I had never said a word to him.

I held on to the wall. "I don't know what—"

"Shut up," Grinaldi said, and clicked off.

I had a part-time job at a Communist bookstore in Queens.
Thursday was a working day, and when I got to the store I felt
relieved. It was far from Battery Park. I knew I was safe.

The owner of the store, Harry Stemm, had bulging eyes, and urged me to join the party, burn something, bomb something.

When I came in the door, Harry put down the books he was marking. "Tsk, tsk, tsk," he shook his head. "So you're not going through with it? I was hoping not to see you today."

"I'm sorry, Harry." I searched for the words that would satisfy him. "I wasn't sure politically it was the right tactic."

"Hmmm," Harry said, "perhaps you're right." He was happy to see I had made my decision on political grounds.

The phone rang. Harry picked up the phone and looked puzzled. "Guy wants to talk to you. Sounds like a ruffian."

"DON'T DO IT, BRUCE—"

"I'm in Queens, for Christ's sake, at my job—"

"Okay, Bruce. Don't let that Commie sell you a bill of goods."

"I won't." I said good-bye.

Harry stared at me suspiciously. "Who was that?" he said.

"My therapist."

"Progressive?"

"Very."

At that moment, a girl I had never seen before came into the store. She was dark and pretty, her name was Angela, and she was looking for *Look Homeward, Angel*.

Suddenly she said, "God, I feel guilty about today. I wanted to take part in the civil defense protest, and my parents wouldn't let me."

Harry looked up. "Oh ho! Listen to that! Young lady, Bruce here had the very same idea!"

"You're kidding!" she said.

We all burst out laughing. Harry was beside himself, doing a little dance around us.

"I would really have liked to," I said, "but it's too late now. Here we are all the way out in Queens—"

"What's wrong with Queens?" said Harry.

"It's an hour from Battery Park," I said.

"So who says you have to do it in Battery Park? You'll be the first to take a stand in Queens!"

And we'll be carted off to jail, I thought, with no press, no TV, no nothing.

Angela looked at me. Her eyes were warm.

"This is really amazing," she said, and she and Harry burst out laughing again.

The air raid sirens began whining.

"I don't believe this," she said. She stared at me.

Harry gave me a push, a twinkle in his eye. "So?" he said.

"I'm going out there!" Angela said suddenly, and marched out into the deserted street.

I stood still for a moment.

I rushed out after her.

Angela and I walked along the sidewalk. Policemen passed us, told us the drill was starting, and kept walking. A few people shouted at us to get off the sidewalk, but no one stopped us. Finally we walked out into the street to attract more attention.

When a policeman finally stopped us, we had to explain what we were doing. I wasn't too clear. "Being as this is a day of drilling," I began, "that is, in preparation for—"

Angela interrupted me. "We're protesting the civil defense drill."

"Oh," the policeman said. "Well, you kids will have to go inside—"

"We refuse," Angela said. I shook my head in total agreement.

"You want me . . . to arrest you?"

We said yes. "Really?" he said. "Well, okay."

He said to me, "You seem awfully nervous. Are you all right?"

"Perfectly!" I replied.

At the jail, I was separated from Angela, and I crumpled to the floor. I was not protesting, I was just unable to move. They picked me up and carried me to my cell. They asked me if there was anyone I wanted to call. I gave them Grinaldi's phone number.

I was afraid my chest was going to explode. I was unable to get up, and they brought my food to me.

When my father came, he paid my bail, and, with the aid of a policeman, carried me to his car.

I felt better the next morning, and rushed out to buy the *New*

York Times. There was a large picture of Dorothy Day and Ammon Hennacy on the front page. At the end of the story, there was the news that two young protesters had been arrested in Queens. No names were given.

Trial was set for the following week.

I called Grinaldi on the phone.

"Yeah?" he said.

"It's me, Bruce."

"I know it's you, Bruce. How did they get my phone number?" he said furiously.

"I wanted you to know—"

"You gave them my phone number—how dare you?"

"But, you're my therapist!"

"Listen, Bruce, I'm not anything to you. Don't get me involved in this bullshit. I told them I didn't know you!"

I almost broke out crying. "I'm sorry, Marius, you're the one friend . . ."

There was a long pause. Grinaldi sighed heavily. "Oh Jesus, Jesus Christ. What did you have to go and fuck up for, Bruce? I warned you, didn't I?"

"I did the right thing! To protest against nuclear warfare and Hiroshima and the killing of millions of innocent people is the right thing and you goddamn well know it!"

He sighed. "Keep regressing, Bruce, and you'll be permanently fixated at the oral-anal stage of the puberty circle."

"And the girl felt the same way!" I said, gasping for air.

"Say that again."

"I said the girl felt the same way!"

"What girl?"

"Angela Goldberg!"

"Which masochist are you talking about? I don't remember an Angela—"

"I only met her that day!"

"What?"

"I met her at the bookstore!"

He whistled. "Ohhh . . ."

"We did it together—"

"I get it." A warm note crept into his voice. "Well, Bruce, you
didn't mention a girl—" His voice became merry, he laughed.
"Now I get it. Bruce, why didn't you tell me?"

"Tell you what?" I said, confused at the switch but relieved
at his friendliness.

"Cunt."

"Wunt?"

Laughter surged across the wires at me.

"You can't stay away from it, can you, young man?"

"That has absolutely nothing to do with it!" I said angrily. "I
didn't touch her!"

He sighed. "Well, hurry up! And come see me when you're
out of jail. You've made me happy, Bruce. G'bye, Papa." He hung
up.

My lawyer was late for the hearing. I stood with my father before the judge, and Angela stood with her parents and her lawyer. Her parents looked balefully at me; they wanted Angela to
say that I made her do it against her will. She had refused.

My heartbeats were so loud I was sure I would not be able to
hear what the judge said. I heard nothing. I might get a month
in jail. How did I get myself into such a mess? Pacifism, communism (which one was it, anyway, I tried to remember)—they
were far away. A member of Pacifist International had come by
to cheer us up, and I heard him as if he were speaking from
across the street to me. He was tall and blond, with a blatant
Irish name. You're a cold bastard, I thought, an anti-Semite at
heart, with the biggest Adam's apple in God's green world. You
don't give a shit about me; if you did, you would get me out of
this; I might go to jail. Angela wouldn't talk to me. If only she
would, it would be all right. She acted as if it had all been an ab-
erration. Her parents surrounded her, shaking their fists at me.
But she wouldn't even betray me. That, somehow, made it
worse. She wasn't a fink, but she didn't love me. My father held
my hand, and I shook it off, afraid Angela would see.

We stood around, waiting for my lawyer. "Is your lawyer
here?" my father said.

"I don't know. I think I would recognize him, but I'm not
sure."

"Oh, my God," my father moaned. He buried his face in his hands, as someone called "Here I am, Judge!" A short, squat, black man with the face of an aging squirrel, thick lips and heavy horn-rimmed glasses came smiling down the aisle carrying a pile of law books. It was my lawyer, Eugene Collins. *"Where did you get a Negro?"* my father whispered out loud, his face ashen. "You're trying to destroy me, aren't you?" he said, shaking his head, and making shrugging motions with his shoulders to the judge as if asking his forgiveness that his son was so disturbed that he would resort to this.

Eugene Collins grinned at me and at the judge. He apologized to the judge for his lateness.

The judge said it was an open-and-shut case, but that he would consider suspending sentence if I would promise never to do it again.

"Oh my, no," Collins said, smiling. "Your Honor, this young man would not in good conscience promise that. He considers what he did an act of good faith and moral conscience, an act of defiance of the vicious capitalist war machine that is trampling the freedom-loving peoples of all nations—"

My father gurgled.

"All right, all right, never mind," the judge said. "I'll pronounce sentence then—"

"If you don't mind, sir, I am sure that Bruce would like to make a statement at this time, as a pacifist, as an enemy of this heinous war—"

No, no, no, no, please, I wouldn't know what to say, I'm a leaf, a pebble, a feather, a pulsing heartbeat, that's all I am, I don't know why I'm here, I just want to go home—

"Never mind all that," the judge said. "I don't want to hear what he's got to say."

I remembered to look angry, muffled, and offended. The relief was so great that I could think more clearly. I looked around and stood up straighter.

"Inasmuch as this is a felony," the judge began, "I must—"

"Uh uh uh!" Collins said, pointing a finger in the air. "Excuse me, Your Honor, this is not a felony. If I may, may I cite, excuse me, let me find it—" Collins had taken his books in his arms and was thumbing through the pages of one of them, sticking his finger in his mouth to moisten it so that he could turn the pages more quickly. The judge looked annoyed, but waited.

"May I cite—" Collins cited page and reference. The judge grunted and asked to see it. Collins stood on his toes, smiling, and handed up the book.

The judge read. "You're right. Misdemeanor."

I had no idea what they were talking about, although I sensed that something was happening.

The judge pronounced sentence. "Twenty-five dollars or ten days in jail."

My father rushed up to Collins to thank him and asked him what his fee was.

Collins patted him on the back. "No charge; it's an honor. Your son is a hero, Mr. Orav." Collins told me to call him sometime, shook hands with my father and me, and scooted off.

I looked for Angela. She nodded coldly, and walked off with her parents.

I went to see Collins at his office to talk about evading the draft. I had heard many stories about him: that he shipped guns to Cuba, that he had been in jail himself during World War II as a Trotskyite because he refused to fight in a capitalist war.

"I'm afraid my connections to the Communist Party will get me in trouble when I claim I'm a pacifist," I told him.

"What you gotta do, Bruce, is get into one of the far-out numbers. The C.P., that's run by the F.B.I., so the draft board ain't scared of that shit, no way. In the old days I'd tell you to join the Trots, but they're class collaborators now too. No, you gotta join somethin' crazy, if you know what I mean. Selective Service gotta be *scared* of you. Like Progressive Labor. The draft don't mess with those guys." Radical papers and books were scattered all over Collins's desk. He held up a copy of the Progressive Labor newspaper. A slogan in big black letters said: "CASTRATE CAPITALISM." Collins laughed, his white teeth shining.

"Wait a minute, something even better." He riffled through

the pile and held up a four-page sheet called *Proletarian World*. There was a poem beneath the masthead:

Black and White,
Get Your Machetes Together, Brothers!
Unite and Fight for a Proletarian World.

"It's a family, just a husband, wife, and daughter, Bruce. You call up, see, spell out your name slowly and clearly so the F.B.I. gets it right on the tap, make sure PW puts you on their mailing list. That's very important, in case the F.B.I. misses your call or fucks up somehow. Have a money order made out for a dollar with your signature on it, and mail it to them. The F.B.I. and the C.I.A. will open the letter.

"The PW—Vince Piker is his name—he won't bother you much. He's harmless. Meanwhile you can keep your C.P. connections, nobody will know the difference."

Collins stood at the door, umbrella in his hand. "Gotta run, Bruce."

I decided to deliver my dollar money order in person at the offices of *Proletarian World*, the day after I made the telephone call in which I carefully spelled out my name.

The Piker family lived in a run-down apartment on Ninth Avenue and Twentieth Street. When I rang the bell, Vince Piker called down, "Is that Bruce Orav down there?"

"How did you know?"

He came bounding down the steps and put his arms around me. A red-faced, friendly man, he seemed saturated with alcohol.

"*How did I know?*" he said. "We've been talking about you all day! Come on up and meet the other comrades."

His wife and daughter were seated in the living room. The daughter was cute. "The way you called up, unafraid, ready to step forward in the name of the revolution, so positive sounding. And now that I see you, what a hot little Red you are! This is my wife, Sophie Cannelone, and my daughter, Iris Callaghan. She heads the youth and women's cavalry division."

The phone rang. When he returned, Vince said, "Guess who

that was? Eugene Collins, and he was calling about you! I told him you were here, and he was delighted. Told me about your civil defense trial—excellent class action. You *are* a hot little Red, aren't you?"

I handed Vince the money order, and he was moved. He showed it to his wife and daughter. "Well, comrade, I don't like to have to take money from you. I know what the struggle is like out there, trying to earn a day's bread in the factory while the bosses rob you blind."

I left as soon as I could. They all stood in the doorway looking at me fondly, Vince staggering a little. I continued to send them dollar money orders with my name in large letters and they mailed me their newspaper and party literature. But to my surprise, they did not call me or bother me in the slightest after my visit that day.

I thought about the draft board constantly. When I neared the army recruiting booth on Times Square, I crossed the street so that they could not see me through the window. They would spot me, see the hate snarling out of my eyes, and propel me through the door and ship me to Korea. They would ask to see my 1-A draft card. At night I would walk up to the booths; they fascinated me. I wanted to throw a rock through the window. But even at night, they were dangerous; what if a silent camera was taking pictures of me, or what if a piece of paper with my name on it fell out of my pocket? I spit into the street at the thought. They would find the piece of paper, they would trace me, knock on my door, see my hate, and kill me. I wasn't sure what frightened me more: combat, or having to live in army barracks, taking showers in the nude, wet towels snapped at my ass by crackers, hiding all traces of myself. I was even self-conscious if I walked into an Irish bar, and would hide my book under a *Daily News* or in a paper bag, the way Grinaldi had taught me. Of course they would kill me in the barracks—a dark Jew Communist with tortured eyes—I'd go first, a pistol shot in the night or the day—an accident, jovially agreed to by all races and creeds.

The draft board summoned me to a hearing on my petition for draft exemption as a conscientious objector. I read the letter over and over again; I looked up the signature on the letter in the phone book—LaRue—and wondered if I should disguise my voice and wake him up at 3 A.M. every night.

The hearing wasn't at Whitehall Street, but in the forties in Hell's Kitchen. I stopped off at the porno shops on the way. Death made me horny. I looked at the women in leather with whips and my prick hit the wall. I carried Gandhi's book on non-violence, my statement of conscientious objection: "I Choose Life," and a saintly expression on my face. But there was time to kill, and there were porno shops on every block in the area. I was confused; I looked away from the ghost faces of the shop proprietors who stood up on raised platforms staring at me.

Suddenly I rushed out of a shop. There was a bunch of Communist material I had forgotten about in my wallet and my pockets—evidence I hadn't had time to burn in the toilet. I had stayed up all night burning *Daily Workers* and *National Guardians* and correspondence and books in the sink, the flames jumping toward me, then mashing the ashes and thrusting them into the toilet. There was no end to it. I ran out of matches by dawn and was still carrying three volumes of Stalin's collected writings, a recording of Paul Robeson at Peekskill, a picture book of Red Army maneuvers published in Moscow. How could I have forgotten? The stuff was in my arms. There was only an hour left before the hearing. Looking casual, I stepped off curbs and dropped the stuff into the grates of sewers. The Stalin books were too thick. I retrieved them, the garbage and sewer water falling from them. In a shop hallway, I tried to tear them apart—the red leather binding wouldn't budge. I cursed and just left them in the hallway and ran off.

I disposed of all the material. Ten minutes to the hearing. I hurried through the streets. I was confused. I tried to get it all together, to remember who I was as I entered the stone building of the Selective Service. Maybe I could be a Rabbi bop bop bop? Or a priest? Or a Hare Krishna Krishna? Or a superb tailor? Gandhi's book was prominently displayed in my hand.

Six gray heads looked up from a conference table as I entered. Red faces, red eyes, gray suits. I smiled, beatifically. I folded my hands.

"What would you do if a madman with a knife attacked your mother?" they asked.

"Nothing whatever," I replied easily with a smile.

The man who was asking the questions ruffled some papers.

"How often do you go to the Community Church?"

"What?" A hook there maybe, definitely; they knew, they knew, the Rosenberg rallies were held there.

They repeated the question.

"Never," I said. How would they know I had been to the rallies—but they must know, but I wasn't sure if in fact they were held there.

"Are you sure?"

"Yes."

"Have you read Arthur Koestler's *Darkness At Noon*?"

"Yes I have. It's a fine book." A pacific answer.

"Yet you claim you don't believe in resistance to totalitarianism?"

I paused. The bastard had a point, and not the kind I had expected.

"If you'll read my statement—"

"We've read it."

"I don't believe that a violent answer to violence will ever bring peace, no. We have to learn to love all our fellow men, and answer hate with love."

"And you never go to the Community Church?"

"Not that I recall."

"Not that you recall. Do you believe in God?"

"In a sense, yes."

They looked up. "What is your religion?"

"I was born Jewish."

"What are you now?"

"I'm a member of the Wider Quaker Fellowship."

"Do you believe in God?"

This was the crucial question, I knew. The law stipulated that no one was exempt who replied no.

"In a sense."

"Do you believe in a Divine Being?"

I hesitated. The sweat was falling from me. "No."

They looked at each other. "You realize your claim isn't recognized then?"

"Send me to jail then. I won't lie, and I won't fight. Never. I'm a pacifist with all my heart. I believe in God as a force, an ethical, spiritual force for good. But I don't see a face up there."

A fellow with a sharp face on the left talked for the first time. "You mention in your statement the influence of a man named Silverzweig."

I felt my fist tighten. "Yes."

"Who was he?"

"He was my teacher."

"What kind of teacher?"

"English teacher."

"Did you ever take long walks with him?"

"No, I—why do you ask?"

I looked up, saw the sneer and realized.

"You never took walks with him?"

"I never took walks with him. No." I felt my face blush with shame for them. I felt cold. Their faces receded. I was ashamed of having given them my statement.

I was a liar maybe. Maybe I was a goddamned liar, since I hated them so much. But no lie of mine, I thought, was as ugly as their coal and iron selves.

They dismissed me.

4

THE JEWISH BUDDHA

My psychiatrist is crazy. I sit silently, nodding my head, while Dr. Wechsler talks about my teaching "The American Jewish Novel." I could start, he suggests, with synagogues—why not call my local rabbi? I say mildly it would be difficult—the "Jewish" part of my novel is mainly references to food and neighborhoods. He nods, smiling, goes on—*he* knows what he is talking about. He is a handsome man—curly hair, a large, ingratiating face dark and perspiring—a square, broad body—and he is a *kind* man. For I am sitting in his office for a private consultation at no fee.

Outside, nervously planted on the couch, is my father. We are guests of the Wechslers for Passover. Passover! Soon we will go to services at Harvard. Surely this is a joke, a private whim; or is Wechsler cracking up? I have dreams of him announcing one day that he is giving up psychiatry, that he is becoming a rabbi and emigrating to Israel. Good-bye and good luck. But are these delusions? He has been to Israel two years ago, last year, he's going again this year. He is there more than he is here in Boston.

My thoughts are interrupted—I hear Wechsler speaking. "And then we were planning to move to Israel, but there are doubts, the hardships . . ." This is no dream. My eyes roam around the room: Judaica everywhere. When you're crazy, the whole world is Jewish. Then I listen again to what he is saying: ". . . when you wrote me that you were at the writers' colony, of course I was delighted and wanted to see you before you returned to Vancouver. So you're going back to the frontier—" Oh my God, now he's unwinding a map of Vancouver, his curious eyes scanning beautiful British Columbia. What is he so happy about? The frontier—it's a city of rain and gray, you could go crazy there—put away that map, you optimistic . . . his lips are moving: "You're not happy there?"

"*No*. The rain doesn't end. Ever. And I have no money. I stand in the rain waiting for buses that creep up to the university—" I go on.

He nods. He understands, but keeps peeking at the map. What can you do with this man?

"Now that you are no longer in therapy with me, Bruce, of course I was hoping that our friendship would continue—" I listen closely, nodding at every word. It is what I have been waiting to hear for so long. For the silences between us while in therapy could have meant anything—but long before now he had stopped charging me—and when I called him after moving away from Boston, he was always there, ready to see me . . .

Although I am cracking and crumbling from loneliness and despair, I am listening now to every word. At the colony, I wrote well—crumbling, I wrote well about crumbling people.

He stands up, his huge frame as always curiously graceful, smiles, shakes hands: friends. Friendship in the twentieth century. And waves me into the living room.

In the living room teacups, honey cake, the Talmud, my father on the edge of his seat, Wechsler's wife . . . and now entering the room, his daughter. "I have heard so much about you!" she says. "You know," he says to her, "of Bruce's writing fellowship—"

"Have a lot of rain here, Doctor?" my father says, smiling,

cupping his ear and nodding in response to the answer that will come from Wechsler. But Wechsler doesn't reply, goes on with the conversation with me and his daughter.

We plan to meet that evening for dinner and Passover services . . .

Back at the motel (across the street from Wechsler's home) my father: "He didn't even speak to me! Not once!"

"It isn't true," I say.

"All he did was talk to you. His wife was nice—she at least talked to me—but would he even answer my questions? That isn't nice."

I take two Libriums secretly in the bathroom. "Shut up!" I scream. "Can't you see I'm cracking?" Without thinking, I bang my open hand against the wall.

My father quiets down and looks at me. "You go tonight. He doesn't want me—"

I pull myself together, for with my father there is little choice.

"He does—" I comfort him.

"No—no—don't mind me." My father looks ahead, crimson. "Anyway, I hate services. Ever since my father made me sit through them when I was a boy. You go, Bruce. And calm down, kid." He pats me on the shoulder. "Please."

At Wechsler's house, we prepare to leave for the ceremony at Harvard Hillel. Oh my God—Wechsler is fiddling with his prayer shawls. Trying to drape them neatly around his shoulders, getting them mixed up. I can't believe it's happening—I look away—I look back, he's still fiddling.

His daughter doesn't want to go. Neither does the Israeli friend who has dropped by: "I'm a hedonist," says the friend.

"No more than I am," Wechsler replies, laughing. I perk up my ears. I have never heard him speak in this way. What does he mean he's a hedonist—he eats a lot of plums?

But then we are in the car: Wechsler, his wife, and me. In the synagogue, he still fiddles with the shawls. The services are good—simple, and sincere. I tell him on the way out they are the best I have ever been to.

"Yes. I've stopped going to the regular synagogues because

they're so mechanical," he says in the car as we drive through Cambridge.

I am silent as we drive back home. We arrange to meet again the next day. After honey cake and tea, I say good night and walk across the street to the motel.

The summer has not just been the writers' colony . . . graduate school in Vancouver ended for the season in May. May, June, and July in Manhattan. August and September, the colony. Sleeping on my father's sofa in the heat. Trudging Manhattan in my one gray woolen suit, sweat pouring down my face, looking for work. I am thirty years old. My father keeps handing me nickels, quarters, when we meet at the Automat at six o'clock for dinner. First, a job at the NAACP as a typist: hiding when a writer I know comes into the office. For we have published in the same places. If he were working for the NAACP, he would know (I think) it was temporary. But when I work for the NAACP as a typist, I AM a typist. My father introduces me to his friends as the typist, although, he says, I will soon be going to writers' "camp."

I rise higher in June: assistant box-office cashier at a theater. The full-time cashier, Bill Bird, is an out-of-work director in his fifties who keeps combing his hair in the reflection in the box office window. His own theater has burned down. He keeps talking about his "stepson." He is not kidding; he has adopted a juicy adolescent. "I don't have the certainty of judgment I used to have," he tells me. He shows me scripts he likes. He is right; he has no judgment at all. I tell him my opinion; he never forgives me. He is, as people go, malevolent.

The high point of his summer comes when a famous aging playwright takes an ad in the *Times* to complain about the critical reception of a play he keeps rewriting; he sounds suicidal in the ad. Bird takes a pencil and paper, sits down in a corner, and carefully composes a letter to the playwright. The critics are nuts, he says; the play is beautiful; he, as a director, should know. Then he comes to the point: he is at the playwright's disposal for directing his plays. He shows me the letter: it is obvious and hungry, but I don't say so. I hate him for writing it, for adopting the boy he keeps calling over the phone and who, he eagerly announces to everyone, is cracking up.

Suddenly there is a crisis: a phone call. "Well, that's just too bad. I've had her in my house and she has peed all over the tiles." When he hangs up, he tells me that his mother is in a nursing home and the social worker wants him to take her back to his apartment. "The woman is helpless; I will not wash up her mess."

The stepson runs aways from his apartment; the mother, somehow, has been moved in. He is combing his hair furiously. The city is hot; I am cracking; he is cracking; the playwright, in his air-conditioned suite, composes suicidal notes and pays to have them published in the *Times*.

One day, when someone inquires who I am, Bird says of me, "He is nothing."

If I do not keep the job, I will have to accept my father's quarters.

I am, as always, seeing a psychiatrist, at fifty dollars a week, paid for by my father. He is one of a line I have seen since leaving college in Boston and Wechsler six years before. In writing about him now, I cannot recall his name, although I can remember the names of janitors, teachers, and rabbis who have crossed my path twenty years ago. I recall his grimace.

Every day my father calls me at the theater.

I visit him in his office. He is part of what is called the "bullpen," those insurance salesmen who do not produce enough business and do not have private offices. These men have known each other for twenty years. When one of them goes on a plane trip, the others hand him quarters and ask him to take out insurance policies on the flight. They handle each other's suits in appraisal. When I come into the bullpen, they look me over. I know they have been informed of the psychiatrist and nothing else. My father likes to give the impression that he is carrying a heavy load.

I published a poem about my father in a well-known left-wing magazine six years ago. It was perfect for that magazine:

ideological invective. It began: "My father sells insurance for death to people who have never lived . . ." My father carries that poem around in his wallet, and whips it out to show to everyone he meets.

The men in the bullpen gather around me, their eyes sharp. Those in their eighties are the cadaverous ones; they don't have long to go, and they long for slices of flesh. One of them addresses me, but not by name. "How old are you by now, anyway?"

"Thirty."

"That's a nice suit you got on—summery."

I feel the sweat pouring down me. His eyes are triumphant.

"You look good," he continues. "Where you living— the Village?"

My father sweeps over and says, "Don't be nasty, Nat."

"Me nasty?"

They stand around me, waiting to take turns. My father leads me out.

When I leave him, I go to the library. On the subway, a man leans closer and closer to me and coughs in my face. "What are all those books for?" he says. "Who are you? You're not gonna tell me you really read those books? WHO ARE YOU?"

"Beat it, Pop," I say carefully.

"Pop? POP? I'm a lawyer of the city of New York, and you call me Pop? Who are you anyway? You show-off."

The train comes to my stop, and I hurry off.

"Pop? POP? Give me your name, you phony. You nobody. With a pile of books you'll never read. Who do you think you are?" He shouts at me, jabbing at my shoulder as we walk along the subway path beside the tracks. I stop. Another train is coming, and I want to push him off into the tracks. I start to run. "You better run. You better run. Ha ha! That's right, RUN. RUN."

I tumble up the steps into the heat of Cooper Square.

I have moved into a sublet apartment on Saint Mark's Place. The stout old Russian woman next door smiles at me and locks her husband out. I hear his cries at all hours. I walk up and down

Saint Mark's among the freaks and heads, and I panic in the crowds and the heat.

A few blocks away is the girl, and the apartment we lived in together for five years. Six flights up, the three rooms, the barred windows. It was a beginning. Thinking about it on Saint Mark's Place, I weep, and write about the girl. I sit in the charcoaled broiling Tompkins Square Park where there is no refuge from the sun, and try to get with the relaxed freaks around me—no use, I am too old, or too shy, or too critical, and my scrutinizing eye makes them angry. The rock band blasts away—people are swaying in the heat. I find the music uninteresting and too loud.

I go back to the Saint Mark's apartment, furious and lonely, and write more about the girl.

An old girl friend discovers me. She is married to a skinny Latin businessman, and lives on Park Avenue with their baby. She finds me at the theater, and is amazed at my situation. "You're still in SCHOOL?" she says. "In VANCOUVER?" She goes on like that, and I know better, but I agree to see them because they are the first people to have invited me.

The Latin mixes cocktails for us on the breezy balcony. She says, "So you're going to CAMP in August?"

I bristle. "Writers' colony."

"Writers' camp?"

When we're alone, she says, "It must take a lot of courage to do what you are doing."

When I am alone with her husband, he says, "At thirty, some of us take a nine-to-five job. Others are artists, and take a chance."

On the balcony, we discuss Fellini, et al. She whispers that her husband plans on more babies, but that this one is the last.

She has a brilliant idea. She is bored. Why not have a party of all MY friends at THEIR country house? She would so like to meet interesting, creative people.

Near the end of the month, we set the date. I round up a few friends, or near friends. It doesn't mean much to me, but as the day gets nearer, it means more.

The morning of the day comes, and no message from them. I

call, and there is no answer. I reach them at five. They have forgotten.

I inform my friends.

She calls me the next day. Her husband, she says, is furious at
her. It was she who was supposed to remember. She begs me to
come out for the weekend.

I hang up, and July ends.

The next evening at Wechsler's, he has another notion. His
daughter, Tammy (how can a growing girl live up to a sweet
name like that—Tammy Hitler, paging Tammy Hitler), has
written a piece of creative writing about Israel. Impressionistic,
sort of. Wechsler calls Tammy: "Go get your creative writing,
Tammy." She brings back fifty-two pages. I know what it will
be like: oranges grow and flowers bloom in the once barren des-
ert. Wechsler looks at his only daughter lovingly. Her favorite
novel, he says, is Howard Fast's *My Glorious Brothers*. Tammy
sits down beside me. She is ten years younger than I am, very
sweet, and fresh. Wechsler never takes his eyes off her. Wechsler
stands up, crosses the room, and joins us on the couch.

"Will you take Tammy's manuscript with you to Vancouver
and let her know what you think of it?" he says.

I think of Vancouver, and all I can remember is rain, and my
one-room apartment with a bridge table, one chair whose wood-
en legs keep falling off and I keep screwing back, a lamp, a television set, a bookcase, a bed, and dust. Yes, I say, I will take his
daughter's manuscript back with me. Wechsler leaves us.

I am talking with Tammy, but hear rumbling noises and look
up.

"We were in Seattle in *June*, 1965," his wife is saying.

"July," says Wechsler.

"June. I remember distinctly."

"Well, we can verify it with my correspondence—"

"*June. June.*"

"Oh, mommy and daddy are getting into one of those again,"
Tammy says to me.

I look up, fascinated. Wechsler seems unperturbed. "The Jewish Buddha," a patient in group once called him. Wechsler had smiled.

I suddenly think that I have never discussed sex with Wechsler. There are certain subjects you cannot bring up with certain kinds of people, even if they are psychiatrists. Oh, I mentioned it to him on occasion, but the atmosphere became charged, or so I thought. But then, why did he never bring up the subject himself. I remember standing in the bookstall at Harvard Square, looking at a copy of *High Heels* magazine. There was a story, "Lucky Merv," about Mervin Spott, whose dream wife kept in her closet high heels that were all the colors of the rainbow. How ridiculous, I thought, but why was my pulse pounding? I never told Wechsler.

The rest of the evening is spent on Jewish subjects: arguments about the Torah, Philip Roth as a Jewish anti-Semite. Wechsler has another suggestion for me: that I teach the Jewish novel in Israel. He gives me a pencil and paper. I am writing down names and addresses of professors in Israel, and stacking pages of notes on top of Tammy's creative writing. I scribble industriously, look serious, and sip Manischewitz wine which makes me high with the Librium I had taken before coming.

I ask about members of the group I was in six years before. I hear my voice uneven with feeling, and I am surprised. I look at Wechsler, and I see that he is not. There is the same gentle smile that a long time ago I thought was mocking me.

The group had lasted only six months for me, as Wechsler was going to Israel for a year. The patients were in a panic; some were booking flights to be near him. I had only been seeing him for a year, and I could not understand why they were so upset.

An old woman in the group had stood up and said, "*Fear! Fear!* When I think back now, I know that my entire life was motivated by fear. Why? Why? Why?" Tears rolled down her cheeks. "And I am *not* free of it to this day! Not to this very day!" Her arms moved up and down fiercely.

I had listened to her words, and thought it could have been said better.

The old woman had not gone to Israel, but several members of the group had.

Within two months, I had arrived in Jerusalem.

At the kibbutz where I worked, Wechsler had come to see me with his wife and a tubby, younger Tammy. "You came a long way to see me, Bruce," he had said.

From the time of the decision to go to Israel, on the flight, in the months before that day, I had never thought of that.

In the living room, Wechsler is saying good night to me and inviting me to a private session the following morning. I say good-bye to his wife, and to Tammy. I gather up Tammy's opus and the useless pages of notes about teaching in Israel. Wechsler closes the massive door behind me.

My father is waiting up for me at the motel. He is lying on his back on the bed, watching television. He tells me to shut it off.

"I saw Henry Gold tonight, Bruce. What a character. When we were kids, I was so poor I didn't even have marbles. Henry did. I would go over to his house and we would play. But before he would let me leave, he would count the marbles."

A few months ago, my father mailed me a baby picture of myself, bundled up in a carriage on an apartment rooftop. "I have cherished this for twenty-nine years," he wrote me.

Now my father comes, as always, to his central thesis. "I'm so lucky, Bruce. You think I'm miserable. But I'm not. You are. I have my apartment. In the afternoon I go to the stockbroker's. In the evening I eat in the cafeteria. What more can I ask? I have good, loyal friends. You don't have any friends, do you?"

"God damn it," I shout at him. "I don't want to hear this shit. Do you know I could recite word for word what you're going to say, I've heard it so many times? Don't keep telling me about how your lonely, miserable life is so great. It makes me so sad I want to cry."

My father is straining forward in the bed, his eyes bulging.

"How can you say that to your own father? *You're* the miserable one—"

"No! No!" I pound the wall with my fist. "Don't give me that. I won't have it, no more, you bastard—you're the most frightened man I've ever known, and you're my own father."

When I stop, I look over and see that my father is weeping. "You cruel thing—"

He turns over on his side. He is wearing only his underwear. I walk over and touch his arm. He flinches and moves away. He is red in the face.

"Dad," I say softly, "can't you see that I am drowning?"

For the first time, I really tell him about the girl.

I read him a story I wrote about him as a young man courting my mother, marrying her, and about my boyhood. In the story, I imagine my grandfather, a man who wanted to be in vaudeville, ingratiating himself with my father by dancing on a table top.

My father listens to the story and says, "I was never as shy as you're making me out to be."

Then I read him the part about when he would sing me his favorite songs: "I Want a Girl (Just Like the Girl That Married Dear Old Dad)," "Buckle Down Winsockie," and the song he once sang to my mother on a rare Sunday morning when the three of us were laughing in bed together: "The Best Things in Life Are Free."

My father does not sing this night.

But we are friends again.

He jumps up in bed. "Bruce, remember Ben Alexander? I told him I was seeing you and he gave me a message for you. He said he doesn't do it no more!"

"He said that? Again?" My father and I kicked our legs.

Ben Alexander, a fellow agent, was a man with a moustache, a dirty white shirt and tie. When I was seven or eight, we ran into him. He was stuffing an insurance circular into a baby carriage.

"Oh my God!" my father had said that day. "Do you see what he's doing, Bruce?"

I absorbed my father's attitude, and I barely spoke to Alexander. He never forgot it. For years after, he ashamedly gave my father a message for me: "PLEASE TELL BRUCE I DON'T DO IT NO MORE! NO MORE!"

My father always relayed the message to me.

Every time we ran into Ben Alexander on the street, he approached my father, shirt sticking out of his pants, and backed away when he saw me. Moving backwards, he said to my father

in front of me: "Tell him I don't do it no more!" Not looking at
me, he turned and hurried away.

Then my father tells me about the agent who slept on the
floor in the office and bought a piano for his alcoholic girl friend
who beat him.

And about Melvin: "Bruce, tell me what you think about
this. I went up to Grossinger's and I was dating this lovely girl.
I never liked her very much. Sheila. She had a trick knee. Then
I saw on the dance floor Melvin, who I hadn't seen in five years.
His wife just had her left breast removed. Frankly I never much
liked Melvin, Bruce. But I felt sorry for him. 'Sheila,' I said, 'do
me a favor. Dance with Melvin. His wife just had her left breast
removed.' So Sheila danced with him. Suddenly I look up and
they're dancing very close, and Melvin is kissing Sheila's fingers. And she's letting him! I couldn't believe it. This goes on
for half an hour. Then she has the nerve to come back to my table. I refused to talk with her. 'What's the matter?' she says. 'I
felt sorry for Melvin,' I said, 'because his wife had her left breast
removed. But I didn't expect you to let him kiss your fingers like
that.'

"So I never went out with her again. Can you imagine such a
thing?"

I ask my father, "But how did you know that Melvin's wife
had her left breast removed?"

"THAT'S NOT THE POINT!" my father bristles.

Before we go to bed at 3 A.M., my father tells me never to hate.
"I don't hate anybody," he says, "not even Melvin," and turns
over.

A few minutes later, he says, "Wechsler is a nice man, isn't
he, Bruce? Do you remember when his father died, and we read
in the paper that he had been an insurance salesman?"

"I remember," I say, and I suddenly do.

In the morning my father presses two expensive ties on me to
give to Wechsler as a gift. I refuse. My father is furious. I leave
him at the motel to visit Wechsler for the last time. I am deliberately early, and approach his house by a wide radius, circling

around it. I pass through the spacious tree-lined streets, and walk down to the park where children play. Wechsler's strength is so great that it extends to the streets around him: they have a serenity for me that I can never find in my own life. The houses are not the brownstones of the Boston I love; they are the solid, well-fed edifices of Brookline. Yet I feel that if Wechsler lives here, it must be all right.

And I keep trying to remember that I am here this morning not as a patient, but as a friend. I approach the house, and take a side glance at the screen door near the garage, the patients' entrance, and stride up to the wide wooden door in front.

He waves me in, and we go into his office. He leans back in the swivel chair, looks at me, and smiles. He starts in on Israel, and I want to scream. He is asking me a question: would I like to listen to a news broadcast from Israel on the short wave radio? He checks the time on his watch and says it is 6 P.M. in Israel.

We listen together to fifteen minutes of news. Produce prices in Haifa are holding steady. He nods, satisfied. I too nod.

He flicks off the radio. He watches me. All the time I have known him I have kept some secrets from him so as not to disappoint him. And yet I know that he has caught them all. I sift through all the subjects I want to pour out to him, eliminating the things I feel will trouble him. "Thomas Mann—" I begin. His eyes light up. What I forget is that this is a subject that makes me happy as well. And that he knows this.

I cannot hold back any longer. "Do you remember Sarah?" I ask him.

"Who?"

"Sarah. In group. I can't forget the words she said to us one day. She said: 'Fear! Fear! When I think back now, I know that my entire life was motivated by fear. Why? Why? Why?' " I clench my fists as I speak.

"Yes, I remember. It must have had a strong impact on you."

"Not at the time. At least I didn't think so. I didn't understand it then, but now I know what it means. *When do we get rid of it?*"

He was silent for several moments, looking at me.

"Well, it varies. In your case, it has been receding for some time."

"You think this is a temporary setback because of the girl?"

"Yes I do," he says.

"So do I." I take a deep breath.

I pause. There is one expression of thanks I can give him that I know will mean something, and I can give it: "You know, going to Israel changed my life. As I have become more of a writer, it has become interwoven with being more of a Jew. And I do not understand why."

I say it passionately; yet it is so much what he wants to hear that I will never know if it is the truth or not.

He rises and we walk to the door. We shake hands.

"Visit us whenever you come back," he says. "Next time why not stay here?"

I grin, and using a Jewish inflection I have always been too embarrassed to use, reply: "Why not?"

At the airport, my father is as taut and strong as a pretzel. He jolts back and forth with my bags, not letting me lift them because he is afraid I will get a hernia.

"Caroline —" he begins. My girl's name has been enough to break me down all summer.

I say to him: "I saw Coric in Tompkins Square Park in July. She was doing what she wanted: smoking pot and cuddling a queer. She suddenly saw me and said, 'You can't change a girl by pouring a glass of water over her head.' "

I embrace my father, and stop to wave at the exit door to Vancouver.

5

My Rabbi, Ray Charles, and Singing Birds

I thought of my rabbi recently when my wife underwent a dangerous operation at Mount Sinai Hospital. (I call him my rabbi although I have not seen him for four years, since I left Vancouver, Canada . . . for no one has taken his place.)

During the day, in her hospital room, I had watched the doctor probing the hole in her neck. I closed my eyes, but opened them again, because it was her skin.

When I went back to our apartment alone at night, I couldn't sleep, and I put a Ray Charles record on. When he sang "For Mama," I lay in our bed and saw the doctor all over again probing Susan's neck. Again, in the dark, I shielded my eyes and opened them.

I thought of my rabbi then, for he let us play a Ray Charles record at the beginning and the end of our wedding.

My wife is well now, and I think again of Rabbi Levine. We played the Ray Charles record one day at his home and asked his permission to use it at the wedding. It was during one of the conversion sessions he was conducting with Susan, whose parents were nonobservant Protestants. We had brought the record along and played it for him and his wife, Chickie.

After the song, "All I Ever Need Is You," ended, Chickie said to us, "Are your friends pretty informal?" and without waiting for an answer, left the room. We sat a moment, looking at Rabbi Levine and his majestic beard. Suddenly he smiled. "I like it! It has a meaningful message."

One Sabbath, Susan and I were seated with twelve others in the church where his tiny congregation was forced to meet. (They had no building.) Rabbi Levine was giving his sermon. Birds outside began to sing very loudly. He stopped talking. "What can I say that is as beautiful as that?"

The following Friday, Rabbi Levine was incensed about an ad that had appeared in the local paper. Queen Elizabeth was visiting Vancouver, and a local citizen had taken a full-page ad entitled: "Queen, You Have Nothing To Be Ashamed Of!" He had traced the Queen's lineage back over the centuries and had come to the certain conclusion that she was descended from King David.

Rabbi Levine held up the newspaper in his hand and proclaimed, "This is a terrible insult to the Queen!"

We heard muttering in the congregation, and a lady beside us said aloud: "You call *this* a sermon?"

He had trouble with bar mitzvahs as well. The church would be filled for a change on such occasions with the family and friends of the bar mitzvah boy—some of whom might conceivably join the fledgling congregation if the rabbi were appealing.

One Friday night, the bar mitzvah boy had completed his speech, and it was time for the rabbi to speak. People around us looked up proudly at the boy and expectantly at the rabbi.

The rabbi placed a hand on the boy's shoulder. "Sidney, I could ask you to try again. To do the whole thing over again. But I won't. I know it wouldn't do any good. Sidney, I sincerely hope that someday you will remember this day and wish you'd done better."

People around us stood up, some walked out, one man shook his fist at the rabbi.

When my wife and I planned our marriage, we had to find a rabbi who would convert her. That left us only one choice, and that is how we came to know Rabbi Levine, the one Reform rabbi in Vancouver.

He said he would perform the marriage, but on the condition that Susan faithfully attend conversion sessions with him for several months during which he would immerse her in the history and meaning of Judaism.

I sometimes went with Susan to these sessions, which were held at Rabbi Levine's home—a one-floor house next to a row of like houses. We sat with him in his closet study, the dog barking, the children running about, and Chickie battering the dishes in the kitchen. His study had no door.

"Where did I leave off last time?" he would begin his conversion session.

"Greenland."

He smiled. "Oh yes. My army days. Chickie was in Brooklyn and I was in Greenland. I was young, I couldn't stand it. Stop me if I'm repeating myself . . ."

"Kugel or tzimmes with the roast chicken?" came a shout from the kitchen. Chickie, a fulsome lady, rested her elbow against the wall.

"Kugel."

"Kugel it will be." She went back to the kitchen.

"I was young, I was intense. So the guys worked it out. On alternating weekends, when planes flew to the States with missions, I was on those planes. I spent the night in Brooklyn, the next day I went back to Greenland . . . I wish I could go back to Texas."

"Texas?" I said.

"My last congregation. What a difference. My own building. Committed, motivated members. Here there is an emptiness. They only wait for the jokes."

Which is perhaps why, on the following night, Rabbi Levine's sermon was on the theme that Jonathan Livingston Seagull was Jewish.

We joined Rabbi Levine's congregation. I had never belonged to a synagogue before, and often felt like a stranger in one. In Hebrew school, I was taught to read without learning the meaning of the words. Services, too, often seemed mechanical and by rote.

But in Levine's congregation, watching him stumble, grope, argue, and express his arbitrariness in truly amazing ways (One night he said three times: "Maybe I'm tired of being Jewish. Why do you insist that I be Jewish?"), I felt at home.

Rabbi Levine called me once and said he wanted a favor of me. There was a girl who had come to him and shown him her poetry. She was alone, a little troubled. He thought that as a writer and editor, I might offer her encouragement. Her name was Sheila Green.

On a Friday night after the service, Susan and I were having coffee and cake when Rabbi Levine walked over to us. Beside him was an obese, limpid girl in a swollen black dress. She had a vacant, sullen, withdrawn look. The look of someone who wasn't used to talking with people anymore.

"This is Sheila," he said, and walked off.

"I've been watching you both," she said. "You're so pretty," she said to Susan. "You are so lucky." She stared at Susan. "You are so lucky. You don't know how lucky you are. No trap doors will slam down on you. I have no one. Perhaps you'll let me come to your home and spend time with you. I won't set fire to it. It would be a good deed. You have everything. I wish you the best but you already have the best. You're very, very lucky. I won't set fire to you. I'll leave your pretty face alone. Don't trouble with me if you don't want to. I'm used to it. You have everything going for you. Can I call you up on the phone?"

"Yes, sure," I said.

Her stare swung to me.

"But your phone is unlisted. You're getting rid of me very easily. You're sitting on top of the world. There is kindness in your eyes."

"Here is our number." I wrote it down.

"You edit a magazine?"

"Yes."

"Will you publish my poems?"

"I don't know. I would have to see them."

"Will you publish my poems?"

"I would have to see them, naturally."

"You can't see them."

"Why not?"

"My poems are written for rabbis. I only show them to rabbis."

I tried to laugh. "But how can I judge them if I can't see them?"

"I don't want you to judge them. I showed them to Rabbi Levine. I trust him. He likes them. You can ask him."

"Well. But look, call us." We backed away.

"You're getting rid of me. I'm used to it. Ask Rabbi Levine about my poems. I smell bad."

We walked to another corner of the room and talked with other people. But wherever we moved, we saw Sheila, standing alone, staring at us. Shaken, we left the building.

Weeks passed, Sheila did not call us, and we did not call her.

One day, I was seated alone at a restaurant.

She stood over me. "I heard what you called me that day."

"What?"

"I heard what you called me that day," she hissed.

"What day—what are you talking about?"

"*Jew.*"

"What?"

"Jew. You called me a Jew—"

"I didn't."

"You called me a dirty Jew."

"I never—I would never—"

"You called me a dirty Jew."

I signaled for the check and started to move away.

"YOU CALLED ME A DIRTY JEW."

I left five dollars on the table and left her standing there, shouting at me.

I called Rabbi Levine and told him what happened.

"I'm sorry. I thought she was getting better," he said. "I will have to call her psychiatrist. Actually it was the psychiatrist who told me she was improving. She'll have to be sent back. I'm sorry."

Sheila did not bother us again.

At our wedding, we had also asked Rabbi Levine to read a favorite poem of ours, "Kaddish," by Charles Reznikoff. The poem begins:

Upon Israel and upon the rabbis
and upon the disciples and upon all the disciples of their
        disciples
and upon all who study the Torah in this place and in every
        place,
to them and to you
peace;

The poem goes on to ask for safety for all the persecuted Jews of the world. It was written in 1936.

upon Israel and upon all who meet with unfriendly glances,
        sticks and stones and names—
on posters, in newspapers, or in books to last,
chalked on asphalt or in acid on glass,
shouted from a thousand thousand windows by radio;
who are pushed out of class-rooms and rushing trains,
whom the hundred hands of a mob strike . . .

Rabbi Levine agreed to read the poem aloud, but made a suggestion: that we remove the last two lines. We asked why, and he said he thought they were too depressing, too disturbing.

We said we wanted the poem to be read intact.

He finally agreed.

It was human darkness that he had trouble understanding.

On Passover, he went through a crisis with the congregation.

On our way into the services, there were two armed guards stationed at the door.

We stared at their pistols as we showed them that we were entitled to enter the synagogue.

Later in the week we sat with him on the couch. He shook his head. "The board of the congregation, they're businessmen, you know. They decided the only way to make sure we would collect fees from people coming to services (the ones who only come on the holidays) would be this way. It's the big opportunity of the year to make money. I pleaded with them that it was a terrible thing, but when I came to the services myself, there they were. They had real guns!"

He lowered his head into his hands.

Shortly after that we were at his house again for Susan's next conversion lesson. His face suddenly lit. "You know what I really want to do? I've thought about this for a long time. I'd like to open up a storefront synagogue. Put on a pair of jeans, go to where the people are, and take them off the street."

My wife and I decided to leave Vancouver and return to New York.

When we called Rabbi Levine to tell him, I began, "We've decided—"

"—to get out of Vancouver," he finished the sentence for us.

We went to see him for a last time.

"Perhaps you too should be thinking of moving on," I said.

"Of course that has been in my mind. Not moving on, but making a change."

"What kind of change?"

"Well . . ." he paused for a moment. "I've been thinking about leaving the rabbinate."

"And doing what?"

He paused again. "For some time now I've thought of opening a bagel shop. Actually it was Chickie's suggestion. She would work out front. Bagels are a big business in the States. They have onion bagels, cheese, pumpernickel, garlic, blueberry, sesame, and so on. It would certainly be a first for Vancouver."

We were silent. He looked rueful, and stroked his beard.

He remained a rabbi.

May the birds continue to sing for him, and may Rabbi Levine continue to stop at their song, look up, and not know what to do.

6

The Man Who
Refused to Watch
the Academy Awards

*I dream that my friend Michael and a crony are in Hollywood,
beside the pool, dressed in red, white, and blue suits, and top
hats. Michael asks me, "How is your father?"*

*"Still the most ridiculous person I've ever met!" I reply. Mi-
chael and his crony bark with laughter at this, pleased. I have
said it to please, but am shocked to hear my own words, which
I do not mean at all—*

I have been waiting three months for a letter that will never arrive. From my friend Michael, who is a director in Los Angeles.
It would be a response to the letter I wrote to him: the first letter
in which I ever lied to him. I had falsely praised his last play (the
second to be produced on Broadway in two years), a black gospel
musical about the murders of the civil rights figures.

In Michael's play, the assassination of Malcolm X, for example, is followed by the reaction of the cast. One actor turns
to another and says, "My God, this is terrible—I feel sick." The
other person says, "We're not gonna let anything keep us

down," and sings a song, "Keep on Truckin'," with handclapping from the audience and, after jumping off the stage, some fancy prancing up and down the aisles. Then the murders of John F. Kennedy, Martin Luther King, Jr., Robert Kennedy, and Chaney, Schwerner, and Goodman.

I waited several weeks to write him after seeing it, a delay he must have noticed, since he'd given me passes to the fourth night. I did not know what to say. I finally wrote him. "It was even better than your wedding!" (Michael had staged his wedding in a theater, with people performing on stage and dancing in the aisles.)

I had lied. It was not at all like his wedding.

He did not reply.

A year and a half ago, I was seated in my cubicle at *Animals* magazine, where I am an editor, flicking the pages of *Variety* and swallowing hard. There, in the list of notables who were traveling to one of the three places *Variety* considers important enough to mention, "New York—L.A.—Europe," there in the "L.A. to New York" list was Michael's name: Michael Greenberg. He had made it. His first Broadway show was opening the following month.

I smiled to myself. I put on a hearty look of congratulations. A "give him credit—he worked for it" look. But I was upset for a number of reasons. Mainly envy. Also hurt—he hadn't told me he was coming to New York. Most importantly, his success was another nail in my coffin. Or so it seemed at that minute. When my secretary poked her nose in the door, I screamed, "*Who cares about animals anyway? What are we wasting our lives on?*"

I took a Librium. I felt miserable. I hated myself for what I felt. He had moved too fast. It was only yesterday he installed the tape machine on his phone that gave you his recorded voice when he was out and a minute to talk your message into the receiver. *That* was impressive—especially if you knew, as I did, that he was living in two closet-size rooms on Fourteenth Street and Eighth Avenue. That was pure *chutzpah*, that machine—a

$250 investment in his future. I should have known then. There was already a certain change—an iciness—talking to a machine, hearing my friend's voice from that spooky remove.

And wasn't it just a few years ago, Michael and Linda thumbing their way to L.A., his teeth rotting? I hadn't had the time to adjust to his wonderful success. The four years in Vancouver, where I studied creative writing, didn't help either.

Of course I had to remember nastily his father. Long before I met Michael, I sat in the sun in my bathing suit at Greenacres in the Catskills. I was fourteen years old. A short man with a big dog was giving a lecture to the guests at poolside: Michael's father. The staff psychiatrist. A nephew of Greenacres Senior. He smoked a pipe. He told a joke to warm us up. He addressed us all as "darling." He'd been doing this a long time. His talk was called "Whores I Have Known." It got quiet. Five minutes later he switched to "Bores I Have Known." Then, "Shores I Have Known" (travel lore). He answered questions for thirty minutes, including two about sunburn.

A short, chubby man: the dog lent him a certain style.

Michael kept him a secret for five years—as well as his entire Greenacres heritage. His father had become famous, but Michael summed up succinctly his own opinion: "He sold out." New School radical, crazy about the oppressed—Michael starved on Fourteenth Street rather than take a dime.

He stayed free, *and sold out on his own*! What am I saying and what am I thinking? I should have hung on in therapy for an eleventh year and achieved rationality. My therapist said I was just about to break through.

A previous therapist interpreted a dream I had about Michael when I first met him in 1965 at the New School. In my dream, I place Michael in a box. I close the lid. I enclose the box in another box, which I enclose in another box, which I enclose in yet another box.

"Is he aggressive?" my therapist asks.

"No. He's short."

"But is he aggressive?"

"Yes."

"Very aggressive?"

I smile. "Yes, I guess he is."

"Are you afraid of him?"

"No. He's my friend."

"But are you afraid of his aggressiveness?"

"No.

"Yes.

"Yes, I am."

Michael has a way of looking at people. If you are suffering, he suspends any movement; he seems to have put everything aside and is focusing only on you. There is pain in his look. Yet it is hard to catch him at it. For when you pause, stammering, his gaze seems to shift to an inch over you, or around you, so that you do not become self-conscious. But you know he is with you. When you are in control, he looks directly at you again.

Sometimes he would catch my panic and it would become his.

He had migraines here for days on end, leaving him unable to function. What happens to migraines in Hollywood?

Michael finally did call me at *Animals* that day. I got over my relief and immediately became anxious about demonstrating to him that my career was progressing. I deepened my voice.

My wife and I met him for dinner. He had seen LaBelle, the rock group, the night before. He said reflectively, "Black and gay—that's the wave of the future."

To anyone else in the world I would have said, "What the hell does that *mean*?" and "Isn't there a certain contradiction there?"

I only smiled and nodded my head vigorously, my muscles tensing, my eyes twitching. I had to cut through the bullshit and establish what *I* was doing that I was proud of. My wife and I took him up the elevator to my studio in the office building off Times Square. We got off at the twenty-sixth floor, and we walked with him up the narrow winding orange staircase to the studio tower where plaster fell from the ceiling in chunks. I opened the door.

Ducking the plaster, he stood by the window. We talked about our work, about our hopes.

He asked me how my father was. I told him that my father, who lived alone, had recently taken to tagging along when the prisoners at the jail near his house were taken out on pleasure trips, and that he ate his meals at the prisoners' cafeteria.

Michael shook his head.

He looked out at Manhattan, the Public Library, Bryant Park, and the river, and said, "Here you will write many stories about the city."

In a minute he was gone.

The next day I called him at the hotel. A female answered. I thought he was playing around. He wasn't. It was Linda, who, instinctively, I never really liked. An icy wind always blew from Linda—in the old days, and now. There had been no change.

I had awakened the baby. "Do you want to speak to her? She's very cross at you for waking her up."

A voice said, "You woke me up!" There was a pause. "You woke me up!" Pause. "You woke me up out of a sound sleep!"

I could not believe it was the baby. I thought Linda was putting me on. Two-and-a-half years had gone by since I had seen her and the baby in Santa Monica.

The baby's voice stayed with me, all that day and the next.

Michael flew back and forth and then it was preview night. Opening night was two days away. We had been invited to the preview. The disturbing meaning of that occupied my time and I swallowed a pint of rum to relax.

I scanned the program and noted that Michael, director of the show, was, among other things, vice president of Imprisoned Creators, Inc. Of course—he'd been especially interested in prisoners for years, working as a volunteer with them in workshops—but still it surprised me now. Michael, who had settled into a Hollywood home, who at this moment was circulating in the lobby with the kissers-and-huggers set. When did he have time for prisoners? I saw his curly hair, the bald spot in the back, his shaggy proletarian jacket with patches of corduroy as he reached to kiss.

I overheard him talking to one of the beautiful people about the swimming pool he was having installed. He had not told me. He caught my surprise—and laughed self-consciously. A bad moment between us.

When the show began, I grasped Michael's comment over dinner that night, for he had worked part of it in.

Black basketball stars, making their theater debut as black prisoners talking extemporaneously and singing about their experiences. It was hard to make out their words. I frequently heard them say, "You had to be there to experience it" and "Damn the Man." The audience cried out "Amen!" The set was a back canvas of a prison wall. The music was a piano player. The audience was weeping from the time the curtain opened. At the end of the act, the actors joined hands with the audience. The audience joined hands. Swaying, they all sang "We Shall Overcome." Tears were streaming down my cheeks. I was confused.

At intermission, they sold souvenir pictures and descriptions of the basketball stars for a dollar. The bar did a booming business. The show would run forever. Michael handed over Linda to talk to us while he circulated. She was guarded and cautious, the way she had always been. She loved L.A. She sounded defensive, as if we'd take it away from her. She was writing for "Kojak" and *Cosmopolitan*. She said it was all crap, but she didn't mean it and didn't expect us to agree. What fed her dislike was my agreement. Still, she had a certain pity and compassion toward me after all these years. I felt like screaming.

Michael walked over to us, left, came back. The strained conversation with Linda went on. We were all standing in the crowded street, lights and smoke. A woman walked out of the theater saying, "You hope someone will say 'hi' to you—"

"Hi!" I heard my own voice.

It got a laugh, but I didn't know what I was doing.

Being a hit, I continued. I said hello to strangers, answered questions directed to people near us. I was babbling away, uncharacteristically convivial.

Michael and Linda weren't around at curtain. We waited outside the theater. I greeted more strangers.

Michael didn't appear.

Michael was quoted in the press that week as declaring that the attitude toward blacks in the theater was still racist. "They all said, 'Don't bring the play to New York. Blacks won't pay to go to the theater.' It was a lie. Blacks *will* pay!"

I first met Michael in the New School cafeteria in 1965. I was neurotic. In the East Village church where, as a Jewish socialist atheist, they let me live in the tower, I laughed aloud at the news of JFK's assassination.

Michael lived in two rooms with a hot plate on Fourteenth Street. He had an energy to him. Notes, address books, magazines poured out of the pockets of his jacket and raincoat. He wanted to be a director.

We climbed up the fire escape of the church together to the tower, where I read him my poems and stories. He encouraged me and brought me candles.

In winter we would stand outside the New School, in the freezing snow and rain, exchanging phone numbers of girls and articles we liked. One day he mentioned a girl he had met. Linda. I knew who she was: the fabulous blonde in my literature class who kept injecting the word "Revolution!" into literary discussions.

It was the time of the Beatles; Abbie Hoffman stripping nude at Fillmore East; Paul Krassner's youth; the Fuck You Bookstore on Avenue A tended by Ed Sanders; Jack Micheline, Ray Bremser, and Allen Ginsberg reading at the 9 Arts Coffee Gallery run by a sailor in a loft above Ninth Avenue and Forty-third Street; Dave Van Ronk and Bob Dylan at the Gaslight on MacDougal. It was a dismal time.

Michael was part of that period—not me. I had nothing to do

with it. I attended classes. At midnight I left the tower and walked in the snow along MacDougal Street past the San Remo, where O'Neill had worked (and Bodenheim and Joe Gould had begged), to the Cafe Figaro, where the young bohemians hung out. I sat down with my notebook, a pen, drank a double espresso. I waited. My pen started flying as I really gave it to my father, my mother, and several mean teachers. The waiter came by periodically. I waved him away.

At 4 A.M. one morning he asked me if I wanted anything else. I looked up wearily, picturing myself doing it. "Can't you see I'm writing?"

At 5 A.M., he said, "Are you sure you don't want anything else?"

"Perfectly!" I said.

"Get out," he said.

"What?"

"Get out."

"I'll order something."

"Get out."

I grabbed my things and, trembling, weaved my way down MacDougal Street. It was deserted, except for a man in a hallway who screamed again and again, "I don't hate—*nobody*. I don't hate—*nobody*." The snow was falling. It crept into my shoes. I felt a weariness and a sense of persecution. I felt good. I walked into Washington Square Park, white with snow coating the leaves of the trees. It was dawn.

I leapt into the air.

I was going to Israel for the summer. Michael and I both chuckled. "Shit, it's the only country my father will send me to."

Michael shook his head in commiseration. "A counterrevolutionary arm of American imperialism."

"Exactly."

At the memorial, Yad Vashem, outside of Jerusalem, there was an eternal flame for each of the concentration camps.

The dancing on the kibbutz accompanied by flutes moved

me. The sight and sound of children—Jewish children—in the
breezy garden in Haifa. Normal things.

When I got back to New York in the fall, the *New York Times*
reported the death of Daniel Burros, a member of the American
Nazi party, and disclosed that Burros was Jewish. Michael suggested that I write a play about it. He suggested the title: *Jew-
Nazi!*

I tried to get into the head of Burros. I couldn't even imagine
him. I gave him my bar mitzvah, my first girlfriend, my sex fan-
tasies. Michael was crazy about everything I wrote. He ripped
the pages from my typewriter as I typed and kept muttering,
"Sensational!"

He suggested a childhood scene in which Burros's authori-
tarian tendencies are first revealed. Burros is shown insisting on
directing a line of children his age at school, ordering them
around. Then Michael wrote a song which he intended to have
the chorus sing. The lyrics went: "Why do I feel so brutal/When
at heart I know I'm a Jew?"

The first rehearsal was held at Michael's new loft. I trembled
all through it. *Jew-Nazi* was more of a comedy than I had intended. The potential backers, embarrassed, drifted away.

Michael was hopeful. "It needs work, but it's already quite
wonderful." My friend Michael. I am sure he meant it.

Michael had rented the large loft for himself and Linda. There
was plenty of work space: an act of celebration after Fourteenth
Street. Space to make love, to work, to have rehearsals: light and
air. Bookshelves everywhere, posters, records, productivity. I
had always lived in one room. Michael's bicycle was in the hallway. He bicycled around the city. A basketball was in the corner. I pointed at it, speechless. I had only played Ping-Pong and
potsy.

"I play on my lunch hours," he explained.

"Huh?" I was trying to absorb it.

"Yeah, you know, these little corners of buildings, vacant
lots, with the Puerto Rican kids."

Normality, fearlessness, health, sunshine, brotherhood in

Manhattan. I was deeply impressed. There were sides to him new to me.

Then Michael and Linda were getting married, and I was getting ready to break up with my girl before she broke up with me, and flee to Vancouver. I had sublet a room on Saint Mark's Place.

One day Michael suddenly said, "Write a poem for our wedding."

"Just like that?"

Michael smiled and shrugged.

On the day before the wedding, I went back to my girl's apartment to pick up my books. She had called me insistently, giving me a deadline. It was a steaming hot July day. I stood on the stoop in front of the apartment house on Stuyvesant Street waiting for Michael. He had promised to help me carry the books. I had drunk a pint of rum. I leaned against the brick wall.

Michael was late. I waited. Then I saw him, grinning, waving, walking his bobbing, busified walk; slung over his shoulder was a green canvas bag.

We shook hands and embraced. "How the hell do you think of these things?" I asked, pointing to the bag.

"How else are you going to carry them, dummy?"

We walked up the five flights of stairs.

My girl was at the door. "This is Pepper." A short man with glazed eyes waved at us and went back to his phone conversation. I stared at him.

"Hey, come on—" Michael called.

I tossed the books into the bag.

On the way down the stairs, I said, "Did you see that guy?"

"Poor passive schmuck," Michael said. We carried the heavy load of books to the room on Saint Mark's Place.

I had been working on a story about the girl.

"How's the story going, Bruce?"

"You haven't got time now, Mike—"

"Sure I do."

We put the books down and I read my story to him.

I looked up occasionally as I read. He was smiling. When I finished he made a circle with his finger and thumb. "You're being very productive, Bruce. It's wonderful."

I walked back down with him to Saint Mark's Place. It was difficult to speak. Crowds pushed against us.

I watched Michael going off down the street, the empty green bag over his shoulder, hurrying to Linda.

I was shivering.

It was early morning of Michael's wedding day. I lay in bed drinking rum and read the personal ads in the *East Village Other*. One girl wanted to meet a fellow whose middle initial was J, and no one else. Another said she had trouble talking with people, nothing serious, but would prefer to correspond with someone for the time being. A third was seeking a "combination of Eldridge Cleaver and Holden Caulfield, but Jewish and sincere."

Five hours to the wedding. I dialed an ad: Club Mogen David. A voice told me they had someone very special for me to meet: Martha Goldberg. Martha was twenty-four, and would soon make *aliyah* to Jerusalem.

In a flat, gravel voice, Martha spoke to me over the phone: "I am tender, affectionate, sincere." I quickly walked to Twenty-third Street and Ninth Avenue. Now I wouldn't be alone at the wedding. I would bring along this affectionate Jewish girl and casually mention to Michael and Linda that we were emigrating to Israel. Michael would be so happy for me.

Martha answered the door. She was heavy but not fat. She wore a blouse, skirt, and sneakers. She did not smile. I heard growls.

Four huge dogs headed for me, gnashing their teeth. "Down!" Martha commanded them. She pointed her fist at the floor. "Down! You will obey me." The dogs moved toward her. She settled herself on the bed, the dogs around her. She stroked them, and they licked at her partially opened blouse. When I opened my mouth, they growled. She leaned back and stretched, thrusting her breasts outward. The dogs licked her. She dangled her thick legs.

She spoke only when I did and after a pause. Yes, she was headed for Israel. There was a growing horse and dog market there. She would raise them.

I told her I had been to Israel.

"Good," she said after a long pause.

"I have a wedding today, where I'm going to read a poem to my best friend and his bride." I explained that Michael was directing his own wedding at a theater.

"I'm not much on weddings," she said.

"Oh. You don't want to come?"

"Not particularly."

"Why."

"It sounds mod and phony to me. Why hold a wedding in a theater?"

"He's a director—"

"I'm not interested in the theater."

I stood up. The dogs stood up and surrounded me. "Down!" she shouted, stamping her sneaker.

I said good-bye and staggered down the stairs.

At the wedding, Michael's father stood on the stage and told the story of Michael as a schoolchild ordering around a line of children at school, as an early sign of his son's directing ability.

It was very quiet then. I moved into the lights, to the center of the stage. I took the paper from my pocket and held it. My voice trembled as I read:

TO MICHAEL AND LINDA.

    One.

"But the real issue is revolution!"
Said Linda to the instructor in the New
    School class

And shortly after I met Michael in the school
    cafeteria
Carrying his armload of books,

The Nation, National Guardian, notes
numbers, appointments.

One day he said, "I've met this girl . . .

How does friendship grow in the city?
How does love?

Two

Some of us submerge those we love.
But Michael and Linda shouted, fought, planned
        revolution, marched on picket lines.
Shaped each other. Michael: director.
Linda: lyricist. Beside Michael, she wrote and
        sang, "I sleep so still."

Three

Our friendship: common struggles . . .
Jobs, New York in winter, therapy, the draft,
reading my work to them.
Common joys: Michael's first plays,
And I at the *Tribune,*
        publishing.
The passage of time.

Four

Michael and Linda in the two closet
        rooms on Fourteenth Street
Corie and I on the fifth floor,
        17 Stuyvesant Street

George Burns said of his late
        wife Gracie Allen:

"Then, in 1928, I got my big break.
And I married her.
And we were together a long, long time."

Then Rabbi Rick Levi spoke. He had recently been fired as
chaplain at Yale for his revolutionary politics. He talked about
his experience for a long time. The audience shouted "Right
on!" but after a while they became restless. They began to talk
among themselves.
    The rabbi finally finished.

When it was over, I walked out into the hot sunlight, and down the Bowery.

The next week I left for Vancouver.

Michael had gotten a job with a theater company in Los Angeles. Michael and Linda settled in Santa Monica.

He wrote me often over the years, encouraging me, his letters frantic, surging, the letters half-typed in his impatience, filled with half-words I learned to decipher.

He had a perfect job, his own theater, a lunchtime program for local workers, a prison program of theater workshops with kids from the reform school.

In 1972, he wrote: "The movie people are brutal and demanding . . . like the garment industry . . . Am planning next season's work and reading, refurbishing my soul and thinking of parenthood—very strange."

We exchanged happy letters. I was married, and publishing.

In December, my wife and I left the rains of Vancouver for the holidays and arrived in Santa Monica, where it was warm, bright, and sunny, to stay with Michael and Linda for a week.

We slept in the baby's room, surrounded by a crib and toys for the coming baby. The house was filled with books and playscripts. Michael's sun-dappled workroom was lined with posters for children's, Vietnamese, mental patients' and prisoners' liberation, as well as theater posters of plays he had directed. He had a complete file of our correspondence and my writing.

There was a book on Michael's desk, *Forming Your Own Corporation*, lying alongside a pamphlet on combating American imperialism in Asia and Latin America.

Linda showed us a closet of lavish suede clothes—jackets and suits—she had bought for Michael, which she saved for him, but which he defiantly refused to wear. He wore the clothes of the people—as did everyone in the theater and movie colony in Los Angeles.

They had a maid, a college student. Linda paid her a dollar an hour, but also threw in lessons in Marxist theory.

Michael and Linda's bicycles leaned against the trees in their back yard. Avocados fell from the trees and dropped into the yard.

Michael and Linda spent the evenings watching television. He hoped to direct TV films, and watched carefully. They told me that when visiting New York they had taken a taxi and when the driver turned to them, it was Rabbi Rick Levi.

I told him I had thought of him when watching Joel Grey receive the Academy Award on television. Grey, with his elfin look and smile, reminded me of him. He had said, holding the Oscar, "Don't let anybody tell you this isn't a terrific feeling," and I had pictured Michael.

Michael laughed. "Oh, I never watch the Academy Awards. I made a vow never to watch that commercial bullshit."

Our room was next to theirs. Michael did Linda's pregnancy exercises along with her every day. We heard them counting. We also heard a lot of laughter, and the sound of continual munching.

The refrigerator was filled with milk, yogurt, coconut juice, health foods. Everything reeked of health. We hid our liquor.

In the baby's room we awoke to their laughter.

One morning, I awoke, heard their laughter, and wept. My wife cradled me in her arms.

"The *L.A. Free Press* is crap," Michael said. Before I had a chance to agree, he went on. "But they've got one really good service. If you send your grass or any dope to them, they'll analyze it for you and let you know what's in it and if it's safe."

"Have you used the service?" I asked, trying to get into the spirit.

Michael nodded. "Yeah, sure. It was very helpful."

"This is the town for you, Bruce," Michael said. "These laid-back, bland blondes don't have the energy. It's a terrific place for a New Yorker with talent and brains. You know, Bruce, I'm surprised you didn't blow your brains out in Vancouver. We've got to get you out of there."

He earnestly, arduously set about finding me a job in the movie colony. He found an apartment for me and my wife to sublet behind theirs. He came by in the morning, leaving pastry at the door and copies of the *Daily Variety, Billboard, Cashbox,* the *New York* and *L.A. Times.* During the day he phoned me with interviews he had set up. In the evening he waited for the news.

The first week I saw three people. The second week, four.

Nothing worked. Michael looked away or directly downward as I talked to him, giving explanations, expressing my hopes.

When he was especially hopeful, he would say: "You won't get it."

I didn't.

It was while Michael and Linda were away for a week that I saw the ad for the job at *Animals* in Manhattan. I left a note for Michael and Linda and flew to New York for the interview.

I am left with a recent dream, and with a memory of certain changes on that trip to Los Angeles.

My wife and I are visiting Michael at his new home in Hollywood. There is no talking. Michael is just too busy. Linda doesn't talk to us at all. Michael is on his way out to dinner. I stop him and ask him about the story I recently published and have mailed him two separate times. He claims he didn't receive it the first time.

"Did you get the copy of my story?"

"Which story?"

"My story."

"Uh. No," Michael says.

"But I sent it a second time."

"That's very possible. The secretary probably got it and didn't know."

"But then how can I get a copy to you?" I ask.

"I don't know."

"But don't you want to read it?"

"Sure."

"But there's no way to get a copy to you safely."

"Well, I can't sleep with it, you know," Michael says in a surly way.

Then, trying to mollify me: "Look, we'll think about it. We'll work something out."

He's on his way out to dinner. He brags: "Three-fifty for shrimp marinara, fifty cents tip." He recites it proudly.

On the way out, Michael and Linda show me and my wife where we will sleep: the garage. It is neat, spacious, and clean, with big bookshelves. I say: "This is nicer than our house!"

Michael cackles, pleased. This breaks the ice. He repeats it to Linda. She likes it too. We all laugh now, more relaxed.

And the memory:

Over lunch in Los Angeles, before I was going for a job interview that Michael had arranged, he suddenly said to me: "Have you got a ten-dollar bill on you? I'll pay you back later."

I hesitated, looking at the impatience in his eyes. I was sure he had taken to doing this often, and that he would never mention the ten dollars again.

On the night before we left, Michael took us to see the newest Franklin National Bank of Santa Monica. He stopped the car and gazed at it in the moonlight. We sat politely.

His last letters were not written in his personal, almost illegible schoolboy's scrawl. They were typed on a letterhead, written in pristine language, and signed: Much love, DREAMLAND PRODUCTIONS. Beneath, the secretary had written in his name and their initials: MG/lbd.

New York is rancid now. I can't do the things I loved: walk across the Brooklyn Bridge at sunset, sit in Washington Square Park. The Hell's Angels have taken over the East Village, the terminal-sex crowd is in command of the far reaches of the West Village.

The Fillmore East is a charcoaled ruin, the wreck of a marquee ghosting Second Avenue. The Automats are empty halls, shared by senior citizens and bums, and at night the lights are dimmed and belly dancers shake for a five-dollar admission.

I scour the city, evoking the past. *Animals* isn't that bad; I have good insurance and medical benefits, and I can write at night if I don't have a drink first.

Michael is in Los Angeles. He is sitting in on boardroom meetings where the smoke is thick, the air full of crazy energy. I see him. His laugh, his charm are well liked. The other executives also have beards, wear denim, and, like Michael, have firm social consciences.

I even hear his laugh now, and it disarms me, as does his voice, and his face.

But I keep seeing the look on his face when he waited for me to give him the ten-dollar bill. The repetition of the memory is as insistent as the look itself was.

In the midst of chatter, memories, stories that day, what mattered was the passing of the bill from my hand to his—the tension before it happened, while he waited, and the resolution of it when he took the bill, pocketed it, and signaled to the waitress.

I remember the scraping of our chairs as we stood up to go.

7

A SAFE ROUTE
ON EIGHTY-THIRD STREET

"Dora Lee . . . Dor-ra Lee . . . that's what she would call to me
. . . and how your wife reminds me of her."

Miss LeGrand, a former actress who was trying to sublet her
Manhattan apartment to us, sat on the sofa beside my wife,
stroking her shoulder, and taking sips from a full glass of what
looked like water.

"Is that your first name, Dora Lee?" I asked.

"No, it isn't," she said, stroking my wife's hair. "No, it isn't,"
she repeated, giggling.

"You have such a beautiful face, and oh God, you do—you
do—look so much like her." She paused, raised her voice an oc-
tave and gave it a Southern lilt and cried again, "Dora Lee . . . oh
Dor-ra Lee . . ." Tears rolled down her cheeks.

Miss LeGrand lived on Eighty-third Street between Amster-
dam and Columbus Avenues. On her block drunkards and
methadone patients huddled on the stoops, Puerto Ricans and
blacks stared ahead in the heat, hustlers in platform shoes

cruised up and down. The sound of sirens and shouts and screams came through the window as we sat talking to Miss LeGrand about the safety of the street.

"This is the safest street. You see, they *live* here. They go to Seventy-sixth Street to rob and kill. They wouldn't do it in their own neighborhood.

"And I know how to walk these streets. If I just did it in a straight line, of course I'd get killed. But you see, I have a route. I cross in the middle of streets, go up certain streets, and down others at certain angles. It is completely secure. I have mapped it out.

"Of course, I drink—you see. I go out to bars—sometimes I have to at 3 A.M. They know that. So I have to be careful."

She looked thin and bare, her skin white. She looked like the apartment.

"I've been ill. If you take this place for the summer, I'll move in with a friend while you're here. I need to get my head together. Cash—I haven't *any*. I didn't pay the phone bill. Now they want a $120 deposit, so I simply have to get out for a while."

"You must want to go back on the stage," I said.

"I can't. I haven't worked since a Lillian Hellman play years ago."

"Why not?"

"The illness—it is in my throat. That's why I talk so low. No one would be able to even *hear* me on the stage."

There were two chairs, a couch, a sink. On the wall there was taped an advertisement in Chinese.

"Do you speak Chinese?"

"No, I don't."

"Why—"

"I think it's fun-nee. Don't you think so?"

"Do you see many plays now?"

"No. I don't care for much of what they're doing. I watch TV.

The Avengers. Remember that? The gore and the blood—God! To tromp the men. I *like* that." She turned to my wife. "Don't you, gorgeous?"

Miss LeGrand fell off the chair as she tried to embrace my wife.

We told Miss LeGrand that we could not take the apartment.

At the door she called, "Coming, Dolores."

We were not sure if she recognized us any more.

She was holding the glass. It was almost empty.

We went down the stairs and out into the night. The faces brooded and stared at us, two children jumped rope, a bottle smashed on the sidewalk and the sirens sang.

8

THE ONE-STAR JEW

Part One   I

Stiff as a ramrod, a straight arrow, six foot three, his face a starched white, Isaac Zavelson stands in the elevator beside some of the other employees of Jews for Israel, waiting for it to move. Entering the building, he has saluted the American flag and the Israeli flag. In his hand he is holding an envelope addressed "Hon. Richard Nixon, San Clemente, Calif." Inside the envelope is a birthday card. Zavelson heads the Ethnics Division of the organization. He is sixty-one. Under him are shorter men than he, more indecisive men, who shuffle when they walk, who do not speak English as well as Yiddish, who like to remain on the sidelines. Zavelson drives them hard—a ten-hour day, and weekends—except Ruthie. Zavelson takes long lunch hours with Ruthie at her apartment; they return to the office beaming, and, forgetting, immediately send down for lunch. Ruthie did not climb the ladder to get her position and salary, or wait ten years as the others did in the department. In order to move her up more quickly, Zavelson became impatient with one of his men, Mendel Berger. Zavelson took away his desk, his Israeli flag, and made Mendel sit on a chair by himself in the corner waiting for assignments. Mendel packed his things and left one day. Ruthie was given his job.

A man enters the elevator and moves into the corner as much as possible: a thin man in his midfifties, with a beard and a moustache, his gray hair forming a ponytail in the back, held together by a rubber band. He wears a sports jacket from May's, has a red handkerchief in his back pants pocket, and carries a dungaree bag over his shoulder, his initials sewn on the bag in suede: L. G. for Luther Glick. He has a paperback in his hand—Zavelson peers sharply at the title: *The Way and the Light* by Krishna Ramanujam. Luther is just returning from a month's vacation.

"How are you, Luther?" Zavelson says.

"Tip top."

"Luther!" barks Zavelson. "So when will you read a Jewish book for a change, a novelty?"

Luther Glick pauses. "I'm not a six-star Jew like you, Isaac."

Zavelson laughs his polite laugh. "I am a full-fledged, proud Jew, Luther. I have nothing to be ashamed of."

"You know, Isaac," Luther begins, "there are other things, other states of consciousness in this world besides—"

But the elevator has opened again and Zavelson has marched out, leaving Luther with his unfinished sentence. Luther shakes his head and joins the line into the office.

Luther is a member of the three-man publicity crew, or as he calls himself, a "minion" of Jews for Israel. He walks slowly this morning, his first day back at work, for Luther is tired. He is not a well man. He has had four heart attacks. And he spent six hours the previous night kneeling on the wooden floor of a church attic in Westchester with six others (all of whom happen to have been born Jewish) who are interested in a new Buddhist sect in the neighborhood. Luther is not a member, but, with the new "cosmic consciousness" he discovered five years ago, he is searching.

II

Jews for Israel (or JFI) is not a place for listeners. Almost every-one there has finished with listening. So Luther is not surprised by Zavelson's behavior. I am not used to it, as I have only been with the publicity staff for six months and am, by twenty years, the youngest member of the organization. Our department oc-cupies a corner of the office—a glass alcove for our head, Ste-phen Greenberg, and two desks on the outside for myself and Luther. Luther sits behind me. He greets me, our obese secre-tary, Bea, whom he calls "Queenie," and our second secretary, Jill. Luther waters his plants, lights his pipe, thumbs through his copy of *Ms.*, and unfolds today's *New York Times*. He settles back.

III

Luther has spent his month's vacation in the New England area. First he traveled to Vermont with his wife for the trial of one of my predecessors in this job, the man who sat at my desk ten years ago: Rom Schwartz. Rom, a poet, teacher, and the son of a world-famous Jewish scholar, was on trial for murdering his wife with a pickax. The two children testified against him. He was found guilty. Luther tells me that he went up to Rom while the trial was still going on, held out his hand and said, " 'Rom—Glick, Luther Glick, from JFI. You may not remember me. I was a colleague. Rom, if you want somebody to just lend an ear, someone to talk to, I'll be glad to come back and see you to-night.' He looked at me and he had a glazed air, as if he was far away, and suddenly he smiled—just for a moment—Rom's old smile—a light of recognition—I think—of who I was, and then that look of despair came back, and he said, 'I'm just so—' and he couldn't say any more—he choked—and walked away with his lawyers." Luther did not stay for the remainder of the trial, but has brought back the newspaper clippings from the Ver-mont newspaper about the trial, which he shows to me, Ste-phen Greenberg, and our two secretaries.

(Rom, who was sentenced to thirty years, has changed his mailing address in the *Poets' Yearbook* from his Vermont home to the jail in which he is staying.)

Stephen Greenberg, a short man also in his midfifties with a round cherubic face, is seated listening to Luther, his short hands folded in his lap, his feet not touching the floor, shaking his head. When he is not at JFI, Stephen is a scholar and historian, the author of more than twenty books. One book he has been working on for years is a biography of Rom's father, who bequeathed him his private papers when he died.

About the second half of the trip—which he had taken alone, without his wife—Luther is less communicative. Luther had been carrying on an intense correspondence with Molly Bethune, the Maine author of a best-seller about living a simple country life, in tune with the lakes, the forest, and the birds. Before the book became widely known, Luther had been delighted with it and had mailed Molly Bethune a cassette in which he talked about himself, his life, his new consciousness, and her book. She had been taken with it and in turn mailed Luther a cassette.

Luther had been very excited by this contact with an author whose book began to move up the best-seller lists and whose picture on the jacket was of an attractive woman in her thirties. He had told us that he had planned to travel in the vicinity of Maine—"Molly's territory," he had said with a possessive, intimate smile—but would not elaborate. He had let it hang. Now we both ask him about Maine.

"I was there," he says and doesn't seem to want to go on. Then he says, "I didn't see Molly."

"Not only didn't he see her," says Stephen to me in his glass cubicle as soon as Luther has gone out to lunch, "he told me he didn't even call her. Luther probably didn't tell you this, Bruce, but—" Stephen begins, crossing his legs. Stephen is a gossip, but the least malicious one I have ever met. He really cares about Luther.

"—This is really quite moving. After Luther and Molly Bethune exchanged a few more cassettes, one day last fall she writes him that she is coming to New York. She gives him the name of the hotel, she gives him her room number, and she tells him the *time* she will be there. Luther was so excited. He talked about it for weeks. He had two of her books but he had a hell of a time tracking down the third—a poetry book. The crisis became finding that third early book— he had a search service looking for it. Finally he had all three books. Then the time came. He was in quite a state. He put on a modern suit and tie. "Well, he didn't see Molly. He took her three books and rode the subway to her publishing house. He walked in the door and stood before the receptionist, who didn't know him from Adam. 'Look,' he said, 'my name is Glick. I have here all three of Molly Bethune's books. She knows who I am. Would you ask her to autograph them for me?' The receptionist shrugged and said she would try. Luther returned in a few days to pick up the books. They were autographed."

IV

I remember one of the first things Luther said to me. It was on the third morning of my first week at the office. He was sniffling. "You know," he said, "sometimes I'm crazy—foolish, just like my wife says. I sleep in the nude. There was a storm last night. I woke up, went down to the kitchen, and then I just walked out into my backyard. I just walked on the grass, the water pouring down on me, looking up at the sky."

V

Since he returned from his vacation, Luther has spent several nights with another sect, a Nichiren Buddhist group. They hold their services in the home of a woman he knows. "Last night they set up the new altar," he tells me. "The leader, a black man, kept making it parallcl. Hc startcd the service and then stopped it again. 'It's too low,' he said. He's six foot four, by the way. So all of his little flunkies started lifting it.

"This leader," Luther continues, "is thin as a pencil, all teeth.

When he smiles, you see teeth. He stopped the services again in the middle, annoyed, and turned to this woman who donates her house for the evening: 'When we chant,' he says, 'the leader should be predominantly heard. If others chant louder than the leader, the leader is not heard and cannot lead.' She smiled and shook her head, thanking the leader for the whipping, and said she would be quieter. The Nichiren Buddhists stress positive benefits. This same woman testified to the positive effects of chanting: in order to get compensation from her medical insurance, she had to produce evidence of medical bills of several years ago. A letter had arrived that day from her doctor with a large contemporary bill, which he had dated, by mistake, several years back. So she submitted the doctor's mistakenly dated bill. She didn't question the honesty of what she was doing...

"The chanting," Luther concludes, "sounds like a railing buzz. It's hard to take at first."

VI

I am replacing Melvin Bronstein, who sat at this desk for ten years. Rom Schwartz was here earlier, and it is Mel who most people at JFI talk about. "A saint," they all say, looking me over as if it would be impossible for me to be as good, as useful as Mel was to them. Mel died three months before I arrived.

There are pictures on the wall of the three of them: Stephen, Luther and Mel. Luther and Stephen's memories are of their long association with Mel, sharing his tribulations. They talk about how Mel could never turn away from anyone, could never say no; of his alcoholism; of how his wife helped to destroy him, his wife with her three-inch high heels that drilled holes into the floor of his car, and who did not come to Mel's funeral because she wanted to see California. They talk about how half his stomach was removed, his kidney, his weak heart. They talk about the huge hotel bills his wife racked up on credit cards while Mel was in the hospital, because she said she could not bear to be at home alone. The finance companies still call the office and are upset to hear they have lost Mel. "Kind, wonderful Mel," the people in the office all say. They shake their heads. "He was too good for this world."

Except Luther. "I never liked him," says Luther. "He should have been a whore. He could never say no. He had no backbone." Luther thinks about that for a moment and adds, "That's true of Stephen as well."

"Mel used to say to me, looking away, not facing me, never facing me, when he sat at your desk, 'You know, Luther, I wasn't always like this. There are certain things that do something to people.' Well, he was trying to tell me—trying to hint that once there was a stronger, angrier Melvin: a dynamo. But I didn't believe that for one minute."

They both talk about the extra little jobs Mel took on at the office. He drew signs.

"Signs?" I say.

"Sure," Luther explains. "Like 'Quiet Please,' 'No Smoking,' 'Admission Two Dollars,' 'This Way Out,' and so forth. Whenever the secretaries needed a sign for one of our dinners or rallies, they would come to Melvin. He printed very well. Watch out, Bruce. They'll be asking you."

"We'll never forget his last party," Stephen says. "We just arrived, me and Luther, and we were standing in his living room. We started sniffing. We smelled smoke. Sure enough, there was smoke coming from the next room. 'Mel, there's a fire!' we said.

"Mel looked at us and beamed, his beatific smile, and said, 'No, no, it's nothing. Nothing is wrong. Everything's fine. My daughter had a little problem earlier but it was resolved.'

"We had to take his word. But the smell got worse and worse, and the smoke was filling the living room. Finally we said, 'Mel, you better do something.' He insisted nothing was wrong, but Luther and I opened the door to the next room.

"What we saw was amazing. The entire room was burnt to a crisp. There was water and debris everywhere. Everything was black and charred. Water buckets stood in a row. The remaining pieces of wood were crackling. The walls were charred. The smoke was heavy. Mel's daughter had set fire to her room an hour before the party."

They both shake their heads. "Where is the daughter now?"
I ask.

"In a mental institution."

I look at Mel's face in the pictures. He has a blank, brown corduroy look. He smiles. I look for traces of him in the desk. There
are none.

I ponder the fate of my predecessors at this desk.

VII

I look behind me. Luther is doing twenty-five pushups on the
floor. He touches his toes twenty-five times. He prepares his
lunch. It is bright on his desk: carrots, celery, tomatoes, chicken,
okra, an orange, and a quart of skim milk. He talks about his
new consciousness.

"Nowhere is it written that I have to be numero uno. That's
the most important thing I've learned, Bruce. I know where it
came from originally. I was a skinny malink of a kid . . . my
brother, though, was a husky busker. And my grandfather was
a butcher. That's how it started.

"When I went back to Toronto after some years, there was no
excitement on my grandfather's part about my arrival . . . nothing. Then my brother came down the street. My grandfather
dashed across the street to him. He brought him into the kitchen.
He plunked black bread on the table, sour cream, sat my brother
down and said 'Eat!' I noticed the difference.

"I used to be so influenced by what other people thought . . .
and that was *so wrong*. Competition is nonsense. Nature did
not decree that it be this way.

"I began reading books about different religions. I realized,
and formulated for myself, that there are just two things, Bruce,
that we need: peace and purpose. Peace and purpose. I found
that I disagreed with not one thing about Islam, one thing about
Buddhism (can't remember which), and many things about Judaism.

"Have you heard of an author who signed his name, 'The Gentleman with a Duster'?"

I said that I hadn't.

"I've been looking for his novel for ten years. I read it as an impressionable youth, but it would have more meaning for me today: *Julius Levine*. It was about a young man who searches out an erudite uncle to teach him about Judaism. But the uncle teaches him about the East—he isn't hung up on Judaism. He knows all the religions have wisdom.

"People around here aren't tuned in to this wavelength. Being a truth seeker isn't an easy thing.

"You know, Bruce, recently I had an experience. Alvin was someone I knew thirty-five years ago. I used to sneer at him. He was an astrology expert, a truth seeker even then. He had become a big business success. On an impulse, I took a journey to see him.

"I traveled far. When I arrived, I went up to his offices. When I saw him in the hall I said, 'Hello Alvin,' and Alvin throws his arms around me, flashing his smile. I was conscious of his admiration.

"I sez to him, I sez, 'I recognize that lovely smile, Alvin—your father had it when he greeted strangers. But you don't know me. Glick. Luther Glick.'

"He closed his eyes, opened them, recognized me, and threw his arms around me.

"He took me into his private office. He sat down behind his desk, and I sat facing him. 'I have a series of questions for you, Alvin.'

" 'Shoot,' he sez. 'Anything you want to know.'

" 'Alvin, when did your daydreams stop . . . ?'

"He paused; then he said, 'I don't remember.'

"Then I asked, 'What do you say when people scorn you for your séances, for your ideas, when they laugh at you? How can you stand it?'

"And Alvin smiled broadly, paused for a long time, and said, 'Nothing. *I know what I know.*' "

Luther smiled at me, repeating the phrase, shaking his head in admiration.

VIII

Luther has many scrapbooks in the office. He saves clippings about events, books, but mainly about people he admires. He has two Norman Mailer scrapbooks: Mailer stabbing his wife, Mailer running for Mayor of New York and answering a reporter's question about what he will do to clear up the snow if he is elected: "I will piss on it."

Luther is reading the *Rolling Stone* interview with Mailer. "Jesus!" he keeps exclaiming. Then he says, "Listen to this. The man's insight is amazing. Charles Manson chose horseshit—not dogshit or human shit—because his girls came from upper-class homes where they had been around horses all their lives. He had them roll in horseshit. It was much less objectionable and more familiar." Luther looks up, giving me that same admiring smile, inviting me to share his admiration with him.

I look up. Stephen is running back and forth with assignments from the director. I have come to realize he does most of the work. As our secretary Bea says, "Luther panics if he has more than one piece of paper on his desk at one time. Also if he is called into the director's office."

Stephen's face is chalk white from running. "Stephen really knocks himself out, doesn't he?" I say to Luther.

Luther raises his head from the *Rolling Stone*. "Yes. That comes from a sense of responsibility."

IX

Luther takes his job seriously—a possible source of contention between us. "Our standards are not one whit lower than the competition—unless there is a weakening at this desk." He snaps at Jill: "I countermanded my comma after Fink." Or at Bea, who is talking to her husband on the phone: "Hang up. We have priorities. When I open my lips, let no dog bark." Stephen reminds me, "The job is his whole life."

X

The most difficult person in the office, lately Luther has gotten worse. I feel him storming behind me at his desk, his back rigid, his breath war clouds, his fingers tapping. We are talking about China, a country he approves of, since he firmly believes in the theory of the survival of the fittest. I really don't give a damn about the politics of China, but I do say, "Well, but of course, China is a totalitarian country." On my way out the door at lunchtime, a voice reaches me across the entire length of the office. "BEFORE YOU GO OUT INTO THE WORLD TO TELL THEM, BRUCE, I AM NOT TOTALITARIAN!" Luther's voice carries above the talk of fifty secretaries, the clatter of their typewriters, and the conversations of over a hundred JFI fund-raisers. My hand is on the doorknob. "BRUCE! DO YOU HEAR ME!"

I walk slowly back to our desks.

"Tell who, Luther?"

"TOTALITARIAN! TOTALITARIAN! YOU SAID I WAS TOTALITAR-IAN!"

"I didn't mean you—"

"IN YOUR QUIET WAY, BRUCE, YOU REALLY TWIST THE KNIFE."

I try to mollify Luther. I reassure him that I will not talk to anyone about our conversation.

XI

That afternoon, Luther says that he has had a long-standing argument with his wife. She has opened an antique store in Westchester and has wanted Luther to work there on weekends. Thinking of his heart condition, I say, "When would you rest?"

"During the week at the office, according to her."

He says that immediately after his third heart attack, he continued to work in the garden he loved. He felt like collapsing.

His wife and four daughters told him not to do the gardening, but they left it for him.

"They didn't know how I felt . . . it was overwhelming . . . the pain . . . sometimes I thought I would collapse in the compost heap . . . that I would die there . . . but I never told my wife. I was afraid to lose her love . . . her support would continue, but it wouldn't be the same . . . and I gradually got better. I suppose I remembered as a boy my father breaking his back in the machine shop with a heart condition. I know how I felt toward him . . . and toward my mother, who was sick too. I hated their illness. It was a drag, going on and on. And I thought my wife would feel that way towards me."

XII

Luther stays late tonight. He talks about his correspondence with Buddies of the Earth, recommending Molly Bethune's book to them; we talk about an article concerning an artist who shoots bullets as his art form (Luther asks my opinion of that), and then he suddenly says, straining forward, "You see, my wife left me last night."

Part Two   I

"Hare Krishna, Hare Krishna, Hare Rama, Rama Rama. Hare Krishna, Hare Hare, Hare Rama, Hare Krishna."

Luther is chanting behind me. In the last weeks since his wife's departure, he has moved more closely toward mysticism and Eastern religion. Luther chants the words from a file card he holds before him. The book on his empty desk is the *I Ching*.

Before going home this evening, Luther is in an animated mood. He gives me and Bea an example of ESP. He shows us his raincoat with a button missing.

"I was walking along at lunch thinking I needed a button . . . then suddenly . . . there on the ground . . ." Luther scoops out a blue button from his pocket and places it against the brown buttons on his raincoat, and says, "Exactly!"

We look at the button. "But it's a different color," we both say.

"It certainly isn't," Luther says, hurt. "It's as close as you could come to finding an exact duplicate—"

"But—" Bea and I say.

"And it's the same size!" Luther says angrily, "You hard-nosed rationalists!" Stalking out, he calls back to us: "You people don't know how much a button costs nowadays . . ."

Luther has been dating the woman who has the Buddhism group at her house. She wants Luther to join her circle. She is looking for recruits.

She calls him at the office and asks him how his Buddhism is coming. "You're the master," he tells her over the phone. "There's so much for me to learn—technique, background, rhythm."

He tells me he has had a conversation with her the night before in which he said, "I want to see you and you to see me as more than a member of this group." She replied to him, "I thought you thought that."

She went on to tell Luther that her sex life during the last year with two black men "has been more completely satisfying than ever before."

"She attributes this to the benefits of chanting," Luther comments, "but I don't know—I think she's trying to tell me something."

He says the song that keeps running through his mind is Ray Charles singing, "I Can't Stop Loving You."

He reminisces with me about his boyhood, his father, his years in Hollywood, and his wife.

Luther takes out a roll of quarters. "Like my father," he says. "I like to have a lot of change in my pocket, for the sound of having money." He jingles the quarters and smiles.

"One time, just one time, my father told me about sex. He was standing by the window and he said 'Come here. Look down there.' I looked down. One flight. We lived one flight above the street. 'You see him?' my father asked me. I saw a kid from the neighborhood: sagging mouth, popping eyes, a lop-sided walk. My father said, 'That's what comes from self-abuse. That's all I want to say.' And my father walked away.

"My father wasn't a violent man. One time I played hookey

from school. I remember coming home and an aunt was waiting for me on the corner. She was a mean one; she told me I was going to get it when my father got home. My mother said the same thing. So it built up, and when my father arrived he saw what was going on. He looked grim. For the first time I saw him reach to his belt, and slowly take it off, fingering it. Then he waved me into the next room. When we were alone, he said, 'I have a story to tell you. There was a rowboat out on the sea in a storm. You don't throw away the oars when you're out there.' Then my father hit the bed with his belt three times so they would hear." Luther laughed gently.

"My father invented words without knowing it. Like in his candy store. He'd say, 'I have to relemplish my stock.' Or, if I came home late, he'd ask, 'Where have you been pulverooting all night?' "

II

"I was always a questioner. Even as a young man I made waves. I always had to know how things worked, and why. And I was always getting myself into trouble—I was full of piss and vinegar. I worked in Hollywood for a while, at Paramount. There were two categories: extras and wavers. All the wavers were allowed to do in a scene was wave. I was a waver. The extras belonged to the union, they got paid more and didn't even fraternize with the wavers. They shunned us.

"As a truth seeker even then, I got into hot water. The director was giving instructions, see, and he's telling us we should react to a home run in the baseball game with enthusiasm: the extras should cheer, the wavers should wave. It didn't make sense to me as I understood the script up to that point. I didn't understand what he was getting at. Then he said were there any questions. No one had ever asked questions—it was just a formality. I raised my hand and said, 'Yes. I have a question. Isn't it true that in this scene if we applaud this play—'

"I heard murmurs and then boos and hisses from the extras.

There were catcalls. I heard them calling out, '*What guff! And he's only a waver!*' "

III

On the lunch hour, Stephen says to me, "When his wife walked out on Luther, I wasn't at all surprised. You may not know this, Bruce, but Luther hasn't slept with his wife in five years. He moved out of their bedroom into his own room after his last heart attack. I asked him if he thought the lack of a sexual relationship had affected their marriage. Luther said he had thought of this and he had asked his wife. He said she said no. I also asked him if his daughters and friends were surprised at his wife's leaving. He said no, no one was surprised except himself."

IV

Luther tells me that since his wife left him, he has a funny feeling of weakness in his chest. "I've tried to remember what it is," he says, "and now I do. When I was a boy, looking for a job, out on my own, leaving my mother, I had this feeling." I ask Luther if the separation isn't a challenge to live a freer life. "No," he replies. "I'm not a WASP . . . I don't want to prove myself . . ."

V

Luther has begun to collect green bottles. He has a shelf of them in his bedroom window. In the morning when he wakes, the bare branches of the trees and the copper of the sun are reflected through them.

VI

Mornings are Luther's best times. He comes in, announcing that his "evacuation and digestion" are both excellent. He shows me the copper bracelet he wears to cure his arthritis. "The body needs certain minerals," he explains.

On his walk from the garage to the office he frequently sees people who interest him. "I don't want to come in to work. I see people I just like, something about their look and their gait . . . I want to spend the day with them . . . a feeling of freedom. But you can't hold on to it . . . by the afternoon you're back in your suit . . .

"I saw a girl . . . very pretty . . . lollygagging down the street . . . I wanted to talk to her. But I had the wrong uniform on. She was wearing jeans. She would have been turned off the minute she saw me . . .

"I hear a guy behind me as I'm walking say, 'I'm getting tired of looking like everybody else.' I turn and I see a guy with a beard, unshaved hair all over his face, torn jeans and sneakers, and he's seated in a hallway talking to three other guys who are dressed exactly the same way." Luther laughs and shakes his head.

VII

He is waiting to see if his wife is serious about the separation. She is living in a single room in the home of friends near her store.

"I've been leaving hard-boiled eggs in the refrigerator. I had one left over, and so in order to know it was the oldest, I drew a cartoon on it. Then, knowing my wife comes by while I'm gone during the day, I drew a little balloon on it with the words, 'Hello Nosey.' A week went by. I checked the eggs every day and nothing happened. Then, last night, there it was. She had written— not on the same egg, but on another—'Very funny.' Which is her way of saying something to me. She doesn't take a joke well. But it was okay—it was her way of talking the same language."

VIII

Being single again, he has to learn how to cook. He puts two saccharin tablets in his soup by mistake.

Jill explains to him: "If you have three apples and four men, you make apple sauce . . ."

"There's a lot more freewheeling in this cooking business than I thought," Luther comments. "I thought it was scientific."

He gets information from all the secretaries about cooking, on the difference between a roaster, broiler, and pullet. He has a two-and-a-half-pound roast beef and wants to know at what heat he should cook it and for how long.

IX

Things are disappearing from Luther's house. His wife is removing them. He finds the bone china cups and saucers that were wedding presents gone. He can't bring himself to object to his wife.

One day the reading lamp over his bed is missing.

He gets up in the morning and goes into the hallway to knot his tie before the mirror. The mirror is gone.

X

His wife notices the effect of the sun on the stained glass lamp in the living room. She is visiting him one evening. She praises the effect. Luther is pleased, as he has placed it there. But then his wife says, "I think I'll take that with me."

Luther's house is burgled. He returns home to find the TV set gone. The hi-fi is neatly stacked on the floor, unplugged, ready to go. He must have interrupted the burglars. Now he is afraid they will come back when he is gone, since there is no one at the house.

XI

Being alone, Luther now rises at 6 A.M. and listens to a radio program every morning in which blind people talk about their lives.

The word gets around that Luther is single again.

Ann Stark, a woman in the office, is about sixty. She has a beaked nose, a homely face, a dowdy figure, and she carries two shopping bags.

She approaches Luther, and stops several feet from his desk. From that distance, she says, "I love you," and walks quickly away.

She does the same thing the next morning.

When she meets Luther at the door, or by the elevator, she whispers, "I love you."

"My speed," Luther comments.

He goes to a singles night at the insistence of a friend. "Not being a gay blade, I was reluctant. But I went. There was a big fat woman at the door and a sign that said 'Admission $3.50.' She asked my name and wrote it down, and, unsmiling, slapped a sticker on my shoulder with my name on it, and pointed the way. I walked into this cold, dank, stone church cellar. There I was. People were standing around. I did see one attractive woman and thought to myself, 'This is wrong of me, chauvinistic. I'm thinking only of her physical appearance, not her mind.' I stood around. No one approached me. They had coffee and doughnuts. I decided I would sit down in a corner and let them come to me. No one did. Although I noticed the attractive one's eyes moved toward me a dozen times, or at least I thought so.

"I've often wondered why attractive people so studiously avoid other attractive people. On a train, if I see a pretty woman, and there's an empty seat beside her, I'll never sit there. And if a pretty woman walks into the train, and I'm sitting alone, she'll never sit down beside me . . . Anyway, I'm sitting alone and a woman wearing a black beret comes through the door. She looks like Nancy Walker, worse, and, just as I thought, she made a beeline right for me. Why do these types always find me? She said she found these singles nights 'valuable, very valuable experiences' "—Luther laughed—"talked away like that with complete ease and assurance. Then they got us together in groups and the leader says, 'I'm not your leader. Don't look upon me as a leader. I'm just here to get things moving. This is not group therapy. This is not psychoanalysis. This is just a rap session . . .' Then he said the topic was: Would I marry myself? And he went around the circle asking. They all said yes. I said no, I wouldn't. After I said no, some of the others also said no. So there we were, paying $3.50 to talk to other people.

"I feel . . . it's like being back where you started . . . when I was a young man. I know why I married my wife: she fed me, clothed me, took care of me . . . she was my blanket against the world."

XII

Luther looks thinner and more haggard. One morning he tells me that his wife has returned from a trip to Michigan. When he saw her, he proposed that they get together again. "She said no, she couldn't . . . that I was overpowering. She said that she was afraid of me."

XIII

The town in which Luther lives has a large Chassidic Jewish community. "When I walk into town I see all these arcane Jewish types . . . with their black hats and suits and long black beards . . . there's not much possibility of finding a friend."

XIV

Luther fingers the things on his desk—a dried meat bone, a Buddha made from crushed concrete—and says, "There was an old man who used to visit our family when I was a kid. His name was Harry Bard. He was a distant relative. He came by for handouts: old clothes, food, whatever my mother gave him. He had an apologetic, smiling, impotent air. I felt sorry for him." Luther pauses. "Now I feel like that old man—Harry Bard."

XV

Peter Black sits talking to me at my desk. He is considered a JFI eccentric—a man in his late sixties with frightened eyes and a scatterbrained way of talking. Luther often gives him a long blank stare and begins reading the newspaper when Peter is talking to him. Peter laughs a lot, and boasts that he has never been sick a day in his life. He was a poet in Russia; he knew Mayakovski and Andreyev and Gorki; he takes out of his pockets crumbling yellowed pages of pamphlets published fifty years ago of Russian poetry and short stories, and literary journals from Chicago and Greenwich Village in the twenties when he came to America. One day he brings in a pamphlet from Meyer Levin's marionette and puppet theater in Chicago in 1935. "As a boy in the Ukraine," he says, "I would lie in the woods, reach up, and eat an apple . . . so many apples on the trees . . . I got diphtheria! The apples were red, with red cheeks! But some had fallen off before they were ready . . . like many writers . . . I'm still a little apple . . . I'm still on the tree."

"The Jews are an enigma!" he says one day, his fingers pointing at me. Pleased with the phrase, he repeats it, "an enigma, yes, what they have accomplished"; his eyes light to the phrase, and he walks away, his shuffling walk, mumbling and smiling to himself. He likes the Publicity Department best of all; he lights on us and says, his eyes twinkling, "I sense a creative force here. Yes, a creative power. Am I right?"

One afternoon we are chatting and somehow I say, "Do you have any brothers and sisters?"

"Yes," Peter answers, "I had a brother—a doctor. He's gone. He was in Buchenwald; they burned him at Auschwitz." I see the tears falling from his eyes; he shakes them away. He chokes on the words. "Excuse me, I am not crying," and he hurries away.

In a few minutes I look for him, but he is not at his desk. My phone rings. It is Peter. "Someone came over to me and asked me why I was crying. They saw me at your desk and they said I was crying. It's ridiculous. I wasn't crying—"

"But you shouldn't be ashamed—"

"I'm sorry. I shouldn't talk about these things. I don't know what came over me. But I wasn't crying. I explained that to this person, so it's all right now."

XVI

Now that Luther's wife seems to have walked out permanently, there are no major changes in Luther's daily routine.

He spends the evening watching TV, "talking back to the box" when he gets angry at what he is watching. His daughters do not call him. He says about children, "My experience has always been that kids are cannibals and killers." When a child comes into the office, Stephen's face brightens and he goes over to it. Luther calls out sarcastically across the office, "Pet her, Stephen. Go ahead and pet the little killer." He recalls saying good-bye to his uncle on a train and getting caught when the train lurched away—"with three stinking kids waiting in my car for me knowing nothing."

He grows reflective about his life, thinking back to when he was single and running a pottery shop in Santa Monica with his uncle. It was his wife who insisted that they move back East.

"I was a good Jewish husband. I only did things she liked. I never went hiking because my wife Lil didn't like it. I was wrong . . . it demolishes you.

"Judy, my youngest daughter, leaves the curtains wide open at night. She likes to be shocked awake by the dawn. The way I was raised, you lower the curtains. When you piss, you piss on the rim. You don't hit the water and make noise.

"We make the small decisions, Bruce. The big decisions are made for us. We drift in a half-lotus position, in complete unawareness. I used to have this little imp telling me how to think, how to dress, how to behave properly. He's still talking to me all the time. Now I tell the little imp to just fuck off."

XVII

"I know I'm not supposed to say this around here, but it's the Jews who have destroyed this country."

"The Jews?"

"Hear me out. I was . . . slightly gifted as a young man. I published some poems." Luther swallows a handful of raisins and offers the box to me.

"The Jews, with their brazen arrogance, ran Hollywood. Harry Cohn, Louis B. Mayer. Every week I went to the movies and they filled us with all those romantic notions, those impossible illusions of heroism and success. They didn't prepare us for life—they left us completely unprepared for life as it really is. I blame the Jews for destroying my creativity. And don't think I'm the only one, Bruce. The Jews around here don't admit these things."

XVIII

Luther was agitated all day yesterday, bristling at all of us. Today I learn why. He asked his wife to get a kosher chicken for him. She did, and cooked it for him. He invited her over to eat it with him. They ate the chicken together. Afterwards, Luther turned on the television set and settled down to watch all of his favorite Channel 13 programs. About ten o'clock his wife said she thought she might as well leave.

Luther mulls this over today. "I realize now she must have expected that we would talk . . . about something important."

XIX

Luther is haunted by his conviction that he should have been a writer.

"But you published poems when you were twenty. What happened then?"

Luther thinks a moment.

"My wife was . . . counterproductive. She loved everything I wrote. Then I saw that when she had the babies, she gave them just as effusive attention as she did my writing . . ." He shakes his head.

The last time he took a creative writing class, his teacher had encouraged him. This meant a great deal to him, and he had begun writing seriously. Then he had his fourth heart attack, and had stopped writing.

Now Luther is taking a new writing class at the local library. He is trying to regain what he feels he has lost.

"A woman read a sex poem about her husband's cock, using the metaphor of a whale. Jesus Christ. Then a girl read some poems. A businessman, a member of the class, called out after she read: 'Terrific! *Terrific!* I wish more people could hear that! Let's hire a bigger hall!' "

XX

Luther is the chief fire warden of our floor. There is a fire drill on Thursday and Stephen, who is home ill, does not attend. "Don't forget to mark Stephen absent," he tells Bea.

"But he's sick, Luther," she says.

"You're argumentative! Mark him down. Come on, Bea! I also have a memo for you on fire exits. The situation is egregious."

XXI

After twenty-three years, Stephen and Luther have a complicated relationship. Stephen's father was a renowned Hebrew scholar, whose only shortcoming was the inability to criticize people.

Stephen likes everything Jewish; also Tony Bennett, Ray Charles, Leadbelly, Simenon, Robert Louis Stevenson on Edinburgh, Margaret Drabble, Flann O'Brien, Edgar Rice Burroughs, Joyce Cary, R. Prawer Jhabvala, Augustus John, Ruggiero Ricci, Jim Reeves, Betty Carter, Tanya Tucker, Janet Baker, Iris Murdoch, Howard Cosell, Anita O'Day, Peter Pears, Benjamin Britten, Maria Callas, Sinatra, John Jacob Niles, Ruby Dee, Peter Sellers, Peter Allen, V. S. Pritchett, Laurie Lee, Frederick Manfred, James Hanley, Erika Jong, and Helen Humes. He is a compulsive talker and a careful listener. If he does not read an entire book every day, he feels he is losing ground. He is interested in butterflies, ants, and cats. He has raised 120 kittens. He loves London, Scotland, Jerusalem; food; boxing; photography; baseball; literature above all. The author of twenty books, he understands Luther well. He does not agree with his wife Susan, who says, "There's a summer fool and a winter fool. The summer fool doesn't dress up and hide what he is. With the winter fool it takes longer to get past the beard, the moustache . . . Luther is a winter fool."

Stephen brings little treats for Luther every day: an article, a book of interest to Luther. Luther worries him, and it pains him to see Luther retreat more and more into his mysticism books. Luther is quick to say to me, "Stephen has a hell of a lot more blemishes and hang-ups than you know—take his absolute inability to say hello and good-bye . . . he disappears, like a thief in the night . . ." Stephen, on the other hand, is always looking for Luther's good points. "Luther tells a story well, he's intelligent . . ." He pauses and thinks.

At points of tension, Luther says to Stephen, "Hold me up. I'm crumbling." Luther comes in to work an hour after Stephen and leaves work an hour before Stephen does. While he is in the office, he does a fraction of what Stephen does.

Stephen reads every newspaper, every magazine, every literary journal—he bounces around Brentano's every lunch hour. He is highly regarded for his scholarship, buoyancy, and good nature at JFI. But by carving out a creative life of his own, working nights and weekends, he has paid a terrible price. In his mid-fifties, he is deathly sick. Even walking in the New York air— he who loves life beyond anyone I have ever known—leaves him gasping for breath.

Stephen and Luther both read the *Times*—Luther during the day and Stephen at breakfast. Stephen calls out the key stories over the glass to Luther and asks his opinion. Luther welcomes the chance to air his views.

Stephen calls out the important names on the obituary page.

"Don't be a killjoy, Stephen," says Luther.

Luther and I both look up from what we are doing. Stephen is talking to a woman fund-raiser. He is jabbing at the *Times* with a finger, turning the pages rapidly and shouting, "He's Jewish! He's Jewish! He's Jewish! She's Jewish! She's Jewish! He's Jewish! He's Jewish! She's Jewish! He's Jewish!"

The woman is nodding her head.

Luther can't accept Stephen's excellent relationship with his strong wife, Susan.

"The guy is terrified of his wife," Luther says, smiling. "You know, Bruce, I have a gimlet perception of these things. It's fascinating to watch the mechanism that's at work. People simply don't recognize themselves. It's a biochemical process."

Luther sits in Stephen's cubicle talking to him. Through the glass he had heard Stephen summarize an article by Daniel Moynihan. "JUSTIFY THAT FOR ME, STEPHEN!" he had shouted through the glass, jumping up and running into the cubicle. "YOU'RE NOT GOING TO GET AWAY WITH THAT FLIMFLAM WITH ME."

Luther sits on the edge of his chair, his thin, taut body squinched up, his sneakers clenched, questioning Stephen in a fury. "Moynihan is a fool! They stopped Kennedy—why can't they stop him?"

Stephen patiently explains, summarizes the article. "YOU'RE WAFFLING—"

Luther has bought a six-pound pillow. It arrives in the office and he shows it to all of us.

Stephen looks at it and says, "I have a twelve-pound pillow— as big as him." Stephen points at the tallest and heftiest man in the office.

Luther zips across the office, shouting at people at random, furiously: "Do you believe him? Do you believe that? He always has to top me! If I've read one book, he's read ten!"

Stephen, with his patience and understanding, usually wins. But there is one area where Luther has the upper hand.

Stephen has a penchant for reason, calm, and order. He is put off by scatological talk, raunchy sex, deviate behavior.

Luther begins. "Did you see *The Last Detail*, Stephen?"

"I saw it. I have no interest in that—"

Luther pounces. This is his best moment. "Are you listening, Bruce? What do you mean, Stephen, *it doesn't interest you?*"

"Sailor talk, salty language, brothels—it doesn't interest me."

"Just because it doesn't happen to interest *you*—does that mean it's not good?"

"No, I'm just saying there are many other things that interest me more—"

"We don't *care* if it interests you or not, friend; it interests other people. Did it ever occur to you that what you are really saying is that it *threatens* you?"

"Possibly; I think not—"

"BUT HOW CAN YOU SAY IT DOESN'T INTEREST YOU? It's a fact, a reality." Luther's eyes keep darting to me for approval. "You're a college man, Bruce. I hope you're listening."

XXII

On New Year's Eve, Luther prepares to go home alone.

"Ever thine . . . forever thine . . . that keeps running through my mind . . . where do I remember that from?" Luther muses. "Oh yes, this winter day reminded me . . . a picture on the piano of herself that my mother inscribed to my father . . . it was in winter she gave it to him . . . 'Ever thine' . . . we laughed at the Victorian sentimentality."

He talks at random. He recalls being eighteen . . . a friendship with another fellow. On New Year's Eve they would go from table to table, talking to people. "What courage I had then!"

He says to me, "You haven't hit this season yet . . . I look at the books on my shelves and it makes me sick. I should throw them out. I built the library for my family . . . but they don't read. Not one of them is a natural reader. My first greatest pleasure was to read . . . I should unload. How can I take off to Pago Pago if I feel like it?"

Luther tucks his scarf in his coat, and takes his umbrella. At my desk on his way out, he suddenly begins reciting:

When I was one-and-twenty
I heard a wise man say,

'Give crowns and pounds and guineas
But not your heart away;
Give pearls away and rubies
But keep your fancy free.'
But I was one-and-twenty,
No use to talk to me . . .

He trails off and does not finish. "Good night, Bruce," he says.
"Have a happy."

Part Three   I

Ben Knapp, a fund-raiser, dies suddenly, at the bottom of the
stairs of the subway station at Times Square. "Imagine, dainty
Ben—so clean and proper, to go like that!" Luther comments.

Pressure at the office is building. It is a busy month. Stephen
is running back and forth. By noon his face is chalk white; then
it turns beet red. He is gasping for breath. "He is going to have
another heart attack," I tell my wife.

Luther is more crotchety every day. The three of us visit a
bookstore. All the books are marked one dollar. Luther, on the
watch for a bargain, finds a dirty copy that is not marked. He
takes the book to the clerk. "How much is this?" The clerk
looks it over and says, "It's not marked, but all the books are one
dollar."

"That's not what I'm asking you!" Luther shouts. "How
much is this book?"

There is a Chinese fellow in line behind him. He tries to explain to Luther that all the books are the same price. Luther
turns and shouts at him: "I'm not talking to you!"

Standing in line at the bank, Luther's eye is caught by the
sight of a pretty girl. As he waits for his money, he follows the
girl with his eyes. As he leaves the bank, he sees that the clerk,
"a young flibberty-gibbett," has given him one hundred dollars
less than his check. Luther complains to the head of the bank.
At the end of the day his loss is verified, and he receives his
money.

He has written Molly Bethune several times, and after a long silence he receives a letter from her. Shattered, Luther hands me the letter. Addressing Luther as "Sweet Sir," she says that she cannot write him anymore: "I can only answer the first-time people . . . Here's a weird deal: you can write me—and I promise to read your letters—and more than once . . ."

He asks me what I think of the letter. I hem and haw—he interrupts me to say, "Let's be frank. I just didn't have enough to engage her . . . I don't have enough brain for her to pick . . ."

Luther's oldest daughter visits him at the office for the first time in months. All of his daughters live in Manhattan, but he rarely sees them. "How are your sisters?" he asks her.

It is almost time for Stephen's vacation. I hope he will make it. Suddenly his mother-in-law dies. The person who takes it the hardest is Stephen's millionaire brother-in-law, Harry.

Harry weeps and talks on the phone to Stephen for hours. The tears run down Stephen's cheeks. Stephen, who was heartsick for years after the death of his own beloved father, identifies with Harry's feelings about the loss of his mother. Stephen's wife, Susan, tries to remain strong for Stephen's sake, but Harry is inconsolable. He calls Stephen at the office during the day; he comes over to Stephen's house at midnight and weeps. Harry needs a minyan (ten people) for the nightly service of prayer at the synagogue in memory of his mother. When the minyan lacks one, he calls Stephen to drop everything and come across town to the synagogue. Stephen comes.

"Listen," Luther says, "the man allows himself to be taken advantage of. That's the way he is."

"He's sympathetic—" I begin.

"He's a marshmallow," says Luther.

Two weeks pass. Stephen's vacation finally arrives. Stephen is happy on the last day of work; just before he leaves he sings a song that he has heard sung by John Jacob Niles—"Matty Groves," a Tudor folk song. I ask him about it and he tells me all the lyrics, their derivation, and the history of the record.

He begins to sing it again as he scoots out the door.

II

Stephen has a heart attack that night.

We wait for the news. Within two days we know that Stephen will survive. Luther calls him and wants to know when he will be back at the office, whether he will be out longer than the two-week vacation. He does not receive a firm answer to his question. Luther keeps asking Stephen to speak louder over the phone.

Within a week I visit Stephen on a Sunday at the hospital. He is plugged into several machines; a jumping light records his heartbeats. A tube is stuck up his nose and held to his cheeks with adhesive tape.

Stephen is propped up, trying to make me feel at ease, trying to do all the talking and to comfort me, but his voice is a whisper. He has already read today's *Times Book Review* section ahead of me. He summarizes Irving Howe's review of a new book by Lucy Dawidowicz: *The War Against the Jews 1933–1945*, giving me the high points of the review. Then he analyzes Howe's opinions.

Stephen's son, David Ben-Gurion Greenberg, comes in. He is dressed in a dungaree outfit. His hair and beard are in meticulous disarray. David Ben-Gurion is as guarded as Stephen is open, and maybe, I think, he has good reason to be. Stephen's face glows at the sight of his son; it says, this is everything in the world I need.

Stephen says in a whisper, gently, "You look like a hobo."

David Ben-Gurion winces. "Why are you giving me grief about my appearance?"

"What?" Stephen says, amazed.

David Ben-Gurion squirms at having to repeat it, but he does.

Stephen's wife, who has been hovering over him, walks us out. "He worries about Luther—that Luther's whole life is his job, and that without Stephen, Luther would have to retire—he worries about you, Bruce, but you have a life outside JFI—he worries about Bea and Jill—"

I tell her yes, he must quit, the job is killing him. I see him and I know. I tell Luther the next morning that I have seen Stephen. I say, "He was reading—"

"Never mind all that. All I want to know is when he'll be back at his desk."

III

The secretaries want to collect money for a gift for Stephen. Luther forbids them.

"Forbids?" I say to Jill. "How can he forbid you?"

"Luther says that it's too early to get a gift and he won't allow it. He really just doesn't want to have to give a dollar—"

"Well, I insist that you do collect for Stephen."

The collection goes on. Luther is on the defensive. "It so happens that the last time Stephen was in the hospital, I asked him if he wanted a present. He said no."

But the collection of money goes on. Luther watches ruefully.

Abe Stern, a staff member, comes over to us and expresses shock at Stephen's illness. After he leaves, Luther comments, "He's shocked? What do I care if he's shocked? These immature fifty-year-olds looking for self-congratulations!"

IV

It is uncertain when, and if, Stephen will be able to return to work. After four weeks, Luther is climbing the wall, and so am I. He has to come in early in the morning and leave late. He has to report to the director and do most of Stephen's chores. He is very tense and snaps at all of us. Without Stephen's blanket of goodwill to keep things smooth, I find myself more and more impatient with Luther's irascibility. If my eyes turn while he is talking, he shouts, "BRUCE! BRUCE! You're not looking at me!" He is visibly hurt that I do not watch the TV programs he is so fond of—Stephen always made the effort of watching them so that Luther could discuss them with him. He begins to talk about a program and checks himself and trails off, muttering, "Oh, you don't watch TV . . ."

I do not accept Luther's games the way Stephen does.

Luther says that he saw a TV show about cripples.

"How was it?" I ask.

"How was what?" Luther snaps with a straight face. "What are you talking about?"

Later, trying to keep things going for his sake, I make a comment. "Some people feel squeamish about those programs."

"Who does? The people on the program? You, Bruce? People watching the program? Get to the point!"

I finally burst out: "Who do you think, Luther? You know damn well who I'm talking about."

Luther retreats, but he is boiling. The secretaries watch and listen.

v

Each day gets worse. Near the end of one afternoon, I see Luther sitting at Stephen's desk wearing a black skullcap. His head and shoulders are swaying and ducking forward in a parody of Jewish orthodox prayer—"dovenning." He has a crowd around him laughing. "Maybe this way I'll get a little respect!" he shouts.

VI

Murray Farber has popping, frightened eyes, a freckled face, a look of perpetual pain. He is one of us—a former member of our staff—now working for the national office of JFI on the floor above us. Ever since I came to JFI, we go through the same routine once a week.

He comes over to me and says: "You know Hy Bookspan?"

"Yes—"

"What a hostile guy! His wife too. Such hostile vibrations. Ah, the hell with him."

"He never seemed that way to—"

"I don't know the man!" shouts Murray, throwing up his

hands, stuttering, waving me off, backing up, shaking his head in denial. "I don't know him at all." Then he puts his hands in his pockets, approaches me again, and says, "You know Esther Kravitz?"

"A little."

"Such a name dropper. No sense of style, class, intelligence—no d-d-d-dignity. Ah, the hell with her."

"Really? I thought—"

"I don't know her!" shouts Murray. "I saw her in a crowd! Yeah, don't know her at all!"

He is filled with disgust at his present job and associates. He has said to me of Luther: "Poor guy. And so pretentious." Murray is a veteran of the radical movement and Jewish causes. He is also a former newspaperman, writer, and radio commentator for WEVD. "Sure, I reviewed books and did interviews on WEVD. So did Melvin and other people around here. So what? It all adds up to nothing."

When we are walking on the street, Murray suddenly stops me, grabs my arm and shouts, his finger pointing, "There goes Abie the Ape! There he goes. Look over there, Bruce." Later he tells me that Abie is an old anarchist and that he hasn't seen him in fifteen years. "Ah, what's the point . . ." he trails off.

VII

The news comes to us on one of the yellow pieces of paper that daily announce deaths of JFI staff members and their families. Murray Farber's father has died. The funeral is scheduled for that day.

"I'm not going," Luther announces. "We do these things—these so-called good deeds—just to make others think well of us and to make ourselves feel good. Therefore, they aren't really worth doing. Especially in Murray's case, since his opinion of me wouldn't change anyway. I know he doesn't like me."

As the day goes on, only one person on the JFI staff, a secretary, plans to go to the funeral. Usually a dozen or more people will go. But Murray doesn't carry clout at JFI.

The tension between Luther and me keeps building. I write a press release that doesn't follow our usual format. I don't use any of Luther's phrases, which invariably describe our guests of honor as "pillars of strength," "towers of light," "true champions of Israel," and "sources of inspiration to many." Luther grabs my release off the desk and screams, "You could get fired for a release like this! The date and address must be in the first line! I never saw anything like this in my life!"

"Luther, there's no need to get upset—"

"YOU MAKE ME FEEL FREAKISH . . . WHEN I'M THE ONE WHO'S BEEN FIGHTING FOR INDIVIDUALITY ALL MY LIFE . . ."

Later he says, "There are certain things we must do, certain patterns we must follow . . . this is not a creative writing class, Bruce."

Luther hears Bea talking about the restaurant on the corner changing ownership and asks: "Who runs it now?"

"The waitress is the same," Bea answers.

"That has nothing to do with the ethnic cuisine!" Luther screams.

I feel myself bristling. Luther is talking about the national JFI convention that is coming up.

"Where is it being held?" I ask, knowing as I say it I have made a mistake.

"YOU DON'T KNOW? YOU'VE BEEN HERE ALL THIS TIME AND YOU DON'T KNOW?"

"Miami?" I say, but it's too late.

"I MEAN DO YOU KNOW THAT YOU'RE WORKING HERE, BRUCE? I THINK IT'S ABOUT TIME THAT YOU WOKE UP TO YOUR RESPON-SIBILITIES. I KNOW YOU DON'T LIKE TO HEAR THESE THINGS, BRUCE, THEY IRRITATE YOU, BUT YOU'RE A MEMBER OF A TEAM. YOU MAY NOT LIKE IT, AND I MAY NOT LIKE IT, BUT THAT'S WHAT WE'RE BEING PAID FOR, THAT'S WHAT IT'S ALL ABOUT—"

"And I think, Luther, that you are a pain in the ass."

There is silence. The secretaries have stopped their work. Lu-

ther nods his head, "Okay." He does not look at me for the rest
of the day.

VIII

"All right, I'll go to the funeral," Luther announces.

Three of us sit in the car with Luther. We travel through the
Bronx, through Luther's old neighborhood. He sees landmarks
he remembers—even a "Glick House," which he jokes "was
named for me."

We do not talk to each other.

Four funerals are being held in four chapels at the funeral
home. The smoothie at the door makes sure we go into the right
room.

There is Murray, and, near him, his wife. He says to me, "Who
was it—which playwright—who said 'I lived my whole life in
fear of death, but when it came, I wasn't prepared for it.' "

The rabbi greets Luther and asks him only one question—if
Luther knew Ben Elias. Elias, a well-known figure at JFI, had
committed suicide fifteen years before. He had been discovered
stealing over $100,000 in JFI funds.

Before Luther can answer, the rabbi holds up his hands.
"Don't tell me anything. I liked the man."

I sit beside Murray's wife, who is much taller and more solid-
looking than Murray. She carries a little white paper bag. As the
service is announced, she opens the paper bag and takes out little rocks and stones—"from the Jordan, the old city of Jerusalem." They are for Murray's father.

IX

When we are back in the office, Luther continues to avert his
eyes from me.

Just before he leaves, he says to Jill and Bea, not to me:

"My father was in the oxygen tent in the hospital. One night
I said, 'So long, Pop—see you in the morning.'

"My father waved by moving the fingers of his hand.

"I just got in the car and drove home.

"When I got home, my mother said, 'It's over.' "

X

The next day Luther does not look at me. When I come near the office, he tries to go the other way.

By the end of the day, I take a chair and sit down next to his desk.

"Look, Luther, what I said—I meant it—for the moment. I felt you were being a pain in the ass. But I wouldn't want you to think I meant that I felt that way about you—about our relationship, the things we've talked about. I wanted you to know I didn't mean that."

He shook his head. "I didn't think you were that kind of guy."

Our eyes met.

XI

Things have returned to normal.

Stephen is back at work. He now walks with a cane.

Luther is relieved. Before Stephen returned, he was thinking about what he would do if Stephen could not come back.

He told me of the mysterious way the bums in Bryant Park were attracted to him and of his fear that he would wind up like them. He frequently described his encounters with them.

On his lunch hour a big black man came up to him, bouncing a grapefruit in his hand. "Mister," he said to Luther, "this is all I got in the world; could you help me out?" Luther reached into his own pocket, took out an orange, and bounced it in his hand. "This is all I've got in the world," said Luther. "Could you help me out?" The black man laughed, patted Luther on the back, said "Touché," and walked away.

Another day a black man on a bench with a liquor bottle in a paper bag called out to Luther. Luther went over to him. "May I make so bold . . . you have a face that tells me you're someone with a deep understanding." The man talked to Luther about the white man's arrogance and the submergence of the black man. Luther agreed completely with him and gave him a lecture of his own, saying, "You've stopped a talker, you realize . . ." When Luther finished, the black man, pointing to his bottle, said, "I hope you'll forgive this liquid refreshment . . ." Luther took a little paper bag out of his dungaree bag, took his liquor miniature out of it, tilted it back, and said: "I hope you'll forgive mine . . ."

Luther commented about the black man's choosing him to talk with: "I can understand it. I myself wouldn't stop to talk with one of those dressed-up, flashy guys with their business talk, their clever phrases, their rush to nowhere."

Luther continues to be puzzled by me and tries to figure me out. He tends to idolize all "creative people."

"How do you feel about Jane Fonda?" he asks.

High on liquor and boredom with this job, I reply, "I'd like to slit her throat."

He looks at me. "I thought artists were kind, gentle souls. I thought they had an 'is-ness,' a joie de vivre."

"They're not, Luther. I keep telling you."

"Yes, I see that," he says solemnly, shaking his head.

Now that Stephen is here, Luther settles back. "Really," he says, "if you can maintain a kind of panoramic overview, it's all so amusing."

He talks often now about the women he knew before he got married and about his shyness. "I never went near another woman when I was married. Except once. In our car pool, I had seen the other guys, when they were sitting beside a young girl in the car. When she slept, they would put their arm around her. Well, one day, see, I was sitting next to this pretty girl. She fell asleep. After thinking about it for maybe ten minutes, I finally let my hand kind of drop on her shoulder—and then I even let my hand cuddle her breast. I don't know what came over me. Finally she stretched, like she was waking up, and moved away. I worried myself sick about it, about her telling my daughters, or my wife, or both. Just one time.

"When I was twenty or twenty-one, I published maybe six

poems in the newspaper. I got a letter in a perfumed envelope. From a writer. Her name was Magna Wand. Well, we exchanged a few letters and then we arranged to meet in a hotel lobby. She would wear a broad-brimmed hat and I would wear a white flower in my lapel. First I saw an eighty-five-year-old woman and I thought I better get out of there. Going through the revolving door to leave, I got stuck; there, on the other side, also stuck, she was. She was about thirty-five. We walked around the city. Finally we went up to her room. She had a big bottle of red wine. I got out of there as fast as I could. Maybe the wine didn't mean anything, but I thought it did.

"And in a similar way I got together with Lil. You know I knew Lil from way back. She was always the prettiest girl in school and I had a crush on her since I was fifteen. Well, another girl wrote me about my poems in the newspaper. This one lived in New York, but wrote and said she was coming to Toronto. She asked me to rent a room for her." He paused. "We rendezvoused. Well, she had hair on her chest. I have always been one quick to find an excuse not to fuck a woman. I got out of there and that's how I called Lil for a date and began courting her. I remember telling her, 'Do you know, Lil, I've been wasting my time with a girl with hair on her chest when I could have been with you?' "

XII

Luther came in on a Friday morning with a sunny face. "I planted a social seed today . . . with this woman, Yolanda, who teaches a yoga class. I mentioned bird-watching to her . . . and her eyes lit up!"

On Monday morning, he was still excited, but for a different reason. "I went to Yolanda's house yesterday morning. I came into the kitchen. Yolanda wasn't there and the door was open. There was a woman leaning against the edge of the table in pajamas and kimono . . . she had a luminescence of skin . . . a glow . . . and a tight little smile. It was Yolanda's mother. We went outside and sat on a couch of leaves in a grove. Then some stinking little kids started throwing stones at us, and we had to get up. What knowledge this woman has . . . she lives on a hilltop . . . and I went there later in the day to spend more time with her. She has a bad back. She too believes in yoga, yet she said it was caused by the will of God!" Luther smiled and shook his head in admiration.

XIII

He seems to have adjusted to his new life. He does not really form any serious relationships with women. As he has often said about sex: "That's out of my league." He grows increasingly forgetful and absentminded. He continues to watch TV, and write letters of protest—to Barbara Walters: "She has a speech defect that I find offensive in a woman who's a phony"; and to *Time* magazine for their bicentennial issue: "Dear Sirs: I just wasted a dollar. May I proffer the observation that nothing could be more offensive than turning the first page and finding an ad for Marlboro country—not even especially written for this occasion." After dictating the letter to Bea, Luther offered to sell the magazine to her for fifty cents.

The starlings continue to seek protection under the eaves of Luther's house.

Luther has new stories to tell as relatives and friends briefly cross his life. Aunt Ida and Uncle Igor invite him over for an occasional evening in Manhattan.

"My mother wasn't on a straight line, I know, but Ida takes the cake," he tells us. "Aunt Ida visited the bank last week. She sat down at the bank manager's desk, leaned on her cane and said, 'I have $25,000 to deposit in your bank. You may think this odd—but this neighborhood has changed so much in recent years, the kind of people who are handling money. You don't *know* what the person who handled the money just before you was doing with himself. Sir, I want clean new bills.' " She writes letters of complaint to the presidents of companies and the responses, Luther says, come back "with crests on the letterheads." She complains to the president of a tea company that the tea is dyed because it darkens immediately, and to a bank president about the procedure of giving away "cheap merchandise" to lure customers. "Of course," Luther says laughing, "the bank president writes back that he understands Ida's concern—'but we were the last to succumb—and you wouldn't want us not to be able to compete freely?' "

XIV

Luther returns from lunch one day and says, "I saw a man with peace of mind today. I'm in the park. I see a man seated in the corner of a tree in dogshit. I say to myself: 'There's a man with peace of mind.' He's lying on a blanket in the heat. The blanket is held down by a rotten onion and a necklace. He's wearing two hats. He's the most disreputable-looking man I've ever seen.

"I go up to him and say, 'I want to speak to you.'

" 'Can you talk?' he says.

"This immediately got my dander up. I said, 'I want to speak to you because you look to me like a man who has found peace of mind.'

"He was silent for a minute. Then he said, 'And you look to me like a man who's full of shit.'

"He paused again. 'I'm sick. My family hates me, I owe hundreds of dollars, and I don't know how to talk to people.

" I have no peace of mind.' "

XV

Luther is still reading his texts on Eastern religion as well as *The Outsider* by Colin Wilson and Huston Smith's *The Religions of Man*. He goes to the yoga gatherings, although the younger members "look at me like Methuselah."

He sees Lil occasionally. She asks him: "How can you be so insecure and have such an enormous ego at the same time?"

He recalls his wedding day. He went into the boss's office on a Thursday and asked for the next day off. He said he was shaking. The boss said that in view of the wedding, Luther would be permitted to leave at 4 P.M. on Friday.

"Were you that afraid?" I ask him.

"I was full of fear."

He continues to save his money. At a JFI affair at the Plaza, at the conclusion, on his way out, he reaches over to the hood of the piano, lifts it up, and takes his coat out.

He thinks and rethinks his life. "You know," he says, "I don't just wash my face; I *attack* it. My first heart attack occurred when I was washing; I scrunch up my face and smack it. One day my wife, Lil, looked at me and said: 'Just what in the world are you doing to yourself?' I've thought this over and analyzed it. It relates to my childhood—I'm acting out the role of myself as a child who hated to be washed by my parents, and the role of my parents who are vigorously washing me."

But more than anything else, Luther thinks about Lil.

Stephen tells me that what hurts Luther most is that Lil doesn't even have a boy friend. "At least that would be a plausible reason for leaving him," Stephen explains. "But to leave him to live in a furnished room all by herself—that to her even such a life is better than living with Luther—that hurts him most of all."

Luther tells me one day with a look that is full of pain that his wife, who knew he was dating Yolanda, told him that Yolanda was a "man-junkie." He asked her if that was a phrase of the "sisterhood," and his wife said it was. "The implication," he says to me, "is that, one, Yolanda is just hung up on men, so that it could be any man she was dating, not just me, and two, that men are a nasty addiction." I agree with his analysis.

XVI

In a few days, he says, "Something happened last night that tells me it's *fini* with my wife . . . My youngest daughter had called and asked if anything was new. I said no, and hung up. I looked around, and there was . . . I collect bottles. Green ones, turquoise, I put them in little displays . . . and I have begun to collect blue ones. I had put a little collection of blue bottles in my bedroom, including a blue vase, a small one that my wife liked. It had been in her bedroom, and I took it and put it in mine with the others. It had an association, this vase, for us, a memory of an evening, nothing sentimental, but nevertheless it meant something. I know it did, because she never sold it, although she sold many things from the house in her shop. The house is piled with junk and she would just take something and sell it. But not this. But apparently yesterday, during the day when I wasn't home, she came in and took it.

"It means either of two things, and they both mean the end. One, that she just wanted to take it to the shop and sell it for materialistic reasons, even though she saw that I had placed it in my collection. The fact that she didn't feel anything about it, or consider my feelings in the matter. Or, two, that the vase does have meaning to her. She's fond of it, and wants to have it beside her. In which case she's really decided it's over between us, and wants to have things near her that she likes. That she's really moving out for good."

XVII

Luther wants to find out above all why he did not become a writer.

He remembers the six poems he published when he was twenty, and the circle of young friends who regarded him as a "poet-philosopher" who would make his mark in the world.

He recalls the pottery shop he ran with his uncle in California, and that he was happy then.

He draws a blank about what happened then to make him stop writing.

At twenty-one Luther courted and married Lil. "I didn't want to marry her," Luther says, "but I loved her—I always loved her from the first day I laid eyes on her—and she wouldn't agree to anything but marriage. And she had to have kids.

"And it was Lil who didn't like California and the pottery shop. 'It wasn't a realistic way to make a living,' she thought.

Yes, she made me give that up and go back East with her to New York. She insisted I take the job with JFI. She said she was sure I could do it.

"She had that faith in me."

9

The Lost Pigeon
of East Broadway

I

My wife and I are standing over Mrs. Annie Blocker in her kitchen. We have placed a pot upside down on the table. On top of the pot we put a contraption that my wife has invented. We had bought Mrs. Blocker a magnifying glass for her eighty-fourth birthday so that she could keep reading *The Daily Forward*. She has been reading it since 1913. ("Reading the *Forward* is my pleasure," she had told us. "First I open to the front page to look at the troubles, then I turn to the Bintel Brief.") But she was unable to hold the magnifying glass upright with her arthritic fingers. My wife put together a stand to hold up the magnifying glass.

Mrs. Blocker sits at the table blinking. "I can't see a thing, dolling," she says. She holds the *Forward* in her hands.

"Your glasses!" we shout into her ear, relieved at finding another solution. "You forgot to put on your own glasses!"

I find her glasses in her bedroom, and Mrs. Blocker puts them on. Now we are ready. We show her how to place the newspaper next to the glass, and we wait. She tries at different angles.

"No goot," she says finally. "Sorry, dollings." She looks at us.
"The cataracts. I feel like flies are flying out of my eyes.

"To read was my pleasure.

"I am a dead pigeon."

II

On her birthday, she said to us: "I lay in bed and I figure—*I'm*
eighty-four? Me?"

Her back is broken. She has a broken hip, cataracts, arthritis,
hardening of the arteries, a weak heart.

She has a metal walker to lean on when she moves about the
apartment, and five canes parked in corners around the apartment.

A bone in her right foot has become so swollen that it bulges
out. The doctor made a hole in her shoe so that the bulge, which
appears to be permanent, has room.

III

She lives in a project a block from the old *Daily Forward* building, now owned by a Chinese religious order. She is near the
Garden Cafeteria, the Rabinowitz Book Store, and the abandoned yeshivas and synagogues. Her kosher butcher charges
her five dollars for a tiny pullet, delivered to her by an old man
"with a little beardele," whom she cannot send away empty-
handed. She gives him fifty cents. When she protests to the
butcher about his prices over the phone, he replies like the
phone company: "All right, Mrs. Blocker, go to the competition."

Can a Jewish man be a crook? Annie Blocker thinks about it,
and the answer is yes. She remembers the king of the nursing
homes, Rabbi Louis Ribman. She makes a slashing motion
with her finger against her throat to express her opinion of what
his fate should be.

IV

We first met her in the late autumn of 1974. We had signed up as volunteers with a Jewish agency to visit an elderly person once a week. I had asked what complaints she had expressed about her previous volunteer, and was told Mrs. Blocker had said she kept looking at the clock on the wall.

We arrived at one o'clock, and did not look at the clock once. She went through a litany of complaints, and waited for us to leave. She went through the litany again. We stayed. She laughed. "Crazy people," she said. "Oh boy."

She pointed across the way at the apartment building and the lighted windows. "A rabbi, a young man, lives in that apartment. I see him with his children and wife, lighting the Chanukah candles, and playing with the dreidels with the children. I see the dreidels spinning. He moves over to the blinds to shut them, and I think he sees me with my walker, though I try to hide. I see him stop, and instead of closing the blinds, he raises them higher so I can see and makes a movement with his arms to me. And I do this."

Mrs. Blocker pressed her hand to her lips and blew a kiss.

V

There is an eeriness to these streets. The Jews abandoned these neighborhoods years ago, and still there are Jews here. When I was a boy, my father took me down to these neighborhoods to eat pickles and hot corned beef, and to visit an old woman (a relative) who sat in the doorway of a tenement wearing a babushka on her head. She had yellowed piles of Yiddish newspapers and a clock with one hand. I saw only old people down here then—who are these new old Jews? The Chinese and the blacks and Puerto Ricans have moved in, but the Jews have not moved out. Ten thousand are left.

What am I doing here, and what is my connection to this old woman who is so fragile she looks as if she could break at a touch, with a voice that carries a wallop?

I sit opposite her thinking, and I hear her voice saying wistfully: "If only I had a wheelchair . . . I could get around." She had returned from the hospital in one, but had called them to come and pick it up. "I had to return it. It wouldn't be honest."

My wife and I glance at each other. We make a note to try to get Mrs. Blocker a wheelchair. That is something we can do. Then she will be able to get around.

VI

A walker is an embarrassing thing. It is embarrassing to Mrs. Blocker. When she looks out at the other windows, she closes the blinds. "People see me with the walker and feel sorry for me. The only thing that I hate is pity."

She has five canes. "I got a lot of canes—I got everything. My son gave me a black cane to make me look beautiful."

I find the walker and the canes embarrassing too. I am ashamed of myself, but I do, at first, feel that way. I have seen old people in the street inching along, leaning on the walkers, and I have looked away. It is a strange badge of humiliation, a means of transportation that goes nowhere, that allows the old to move a few inches.

At first we sit gingerly in the living room, staring at each other. Mrs. Blocker smiles constantly. (In the kitchen, the black case worker from Home Care, Mrs. Sally Crawford, whispers to me: "I told her she looks pretty when she smiles. And she does, yet she would never smile . . . and now she's smiling *all* the time!")

My wife and I are not professional social workers. We don't know why we are here, but we are, or what we are doing, but we do it. The complaints stop. There is silence. And then we hear Mrs. Blocker talking to us.

"I have a will. Tell me if I don't. My husband felt sick. He suddenly said, 'Annie, I want to talk with you.' We went into the living room and he sat on the chair where you're sitting, opposite me. 'I'm sick, Annie. I won't always be here. It's true. I want you to promise me you won't give up the apartment when I'm gone and that you won't live with the kids; you won't go into a home; you'll stay here.'

"Three hours later he was dead. That was his will to me. And I won't leave. We had a good life. I won't leave the bed I slept in with my husband for fifty years. Why should I leave? I have a stone—double—for my husband and me. And a grave. All I need is a box.

"Every night I call to my husband to take me . . . I tell him I need him . . . why leave me here? I talk to him all night."

Mrs. Blocker takes her cane and walks to the window. "At night I prowl from room to room. I can't sleep. I look out at the parking lot and I count the cars. Last night I got 102 cars. I counted them—today only fifty!"

VII

We get the wheelchair for Mrs. Blocker. Now we can take her down into the street. Suddenly she refuses to go. She does not want to be seen by her old friends on the block in a wheelchair.

The second Sunday we persuade her. Bundled up in the wheelchair, she seems pleased. "Just like a prince!" she says.

But she becomes uneasy as we enter the park where the neighbors sit. As we roll by them, she keeps her nose high in the air. A few women call out to her, but she doesn't respond.

One of them waves and shouts, "How are you, Mrs. Blocker?"

Mrs. Blocker looks at her and says haughtily, "What's the matter, just because I'm in a wheelchair there should be something wrong with me?"

She looks up at me. "Come on. Get rolling."

Each Sunday one of the women talks to her briefly, but they are sick themselves and wrapped up in their problems. They talk briefly about their grandchildren and they pass on, even though Mrs. Blocker always invites them to visit her.

One Sunday there is actually a knock at the door. Becky, a lady we met in the park. I get her a chair before she can back out the door.

They are shouting away at each other. "Let me talk!" Mrs. Blocker shouts. "I'm older than you!"

"Listen to me," Becky says. "My granddaughter brought me a book about people in their seventies and eighties. Know what I mean? They say in the book that in their marriages they still have sex, and if it's not good, nothing else is good."

"Sure," Mrs. Blocker says, nodding, poised forward, very happy with the company.

"I remember a woman our age in Brownsville," Becky continues. "She married a nice man, a tailor. I talked to her one day on the stoop. How's by you, I say. She's not happy. She says, 'I want a *man*!' This is after three weeks. 'Nothing,' she says."

"Sure!" Mrs. Blocker says. "Like Hebrew National corned beef—something!"

VIII

Becky never comes again, and Mrs. Blocker forgets her. She forgets people, and confuses them. Her life is a whirl of pain. "I forget so much. Yesterday to me is . . . history!"

IX

"When I could still walk, I had a dream from my husband. 'Annie! I'm wet—I'm drowning. The water is pouring over me.'

"I called my sister. She was still alive. I had no carfare. She had the money and we took the train to New Haven to my husband's grave. You couldn't see the grave. All you saw was water. It had been raining for days. I had them take the water out. Connecticut is known for that—water—it's very bad for graves."

She was born in Vilna. She had twelve brothers and sisters. All are dead. There is a large, formal, round picture behind glass over her bed of her brother, a cantor, killed by a car. He has a tuxedo on, and a watch fob, but his tie knot is an inch below the collar. Her entire family, except the sister and brother who came to America, are dead, not due to natural causes, but to Hitler.

She was named after her father's mother. Her father was a rabbi, and his picture hovers over us as we talk. "I sat on my father's lap when I was a little girl. He called me mamele. I took a comb and combed his little whiskele and moustache."

She met her husband when she was sixteen at a dance hall in Vilna. One day when we are there she comes across the picture. Taken at the dance hall: a beaming Annie and the boy she has just met: Sam Blocker.

Her husband fled the Czar's army and came to America. She joined him in five months. From 1913 to 1964 they lived on the lower East Side in this neighborhood. Sam Blocker was a tailor and had his own shop.

"He had a name, my husband. The elevators here weren't working last week. I was stuck on the floor above. The colored man Alfred—the janitor—carried me down the stairs. He remembered my husband. He told me. He brought pants to my husband in the shop and didn't have enough money. My husband said not to worry about it. And he still remembers. My husband was known for his kindness. He had a name, I'm telling you."

But times change, and she is alone in an apartment where the doorbell never rings. Along with the pain, the thoughts and memories go back and forth in her head all day and most of the night, interrupted by the Home Care workers who tolerate her and by the suffering of her children. She has a dish of pill bottles and each week she tells us to bring her the dish. She shows us each bottle and checks with us as to what the instructions say. The pills relieve the pain less than they did, and she thinks they confuse her sense of time.

Things still happen to her. Life comes to her from the parking lot. "The things I see from my window. Young girls in cars at night. I hear a girl say, 'Please let me go.' Then he says, 'Not till I'm finished.' Then he tosses her out of the car onto the ground."

The fuses blow out. She calls the phone company. "Mister dolling," she says, "my name is Mrs. Blocker. I'm a handicap and I'm alone in the darkness. Please help me."

The man answers: "You don't belong in my unit!" Later he

calls her back: "We found out what kind of a woman you are, Mrs. Blocker . . . we will help you."

A black boy with a red hat comes to her door. She releases the chain. He comes through the door and moves back and forth. There is a knife in his back pocket. He claims he has a package for her, but that he has to go downstairs to get it. "How much?" she asks. "Twenty dollars," he replies. She notices that some money she had on the table is already missing.

"I sat down on the bed. I was trembling.

" 'Lady,' he says, 'why are you trembling? Lady, you're a very nice lady. I was wrong. The package is six dollars.' "

She gives him six more dollars, and he leaves.

X

As the months pass, the walker and the wheelchair become familiar to us, and we discover the things we have in common with Mrs. Blocker.

One of these things is a sense of hope. Mrs. Blocker says of her body: "Everything is broken"; she says often that she is a lost pigeon, and that God is punishing her by not taking her.

But there is always something she wants—the wheelchair, a lamp to read by in the bedroom, the electric fan that I cart across town from May's for her in the summer, new medicine—that lights up her face with new hope. It fades quickly, but I see it and recognize it so well.

Mrs. Blocker says in Yiddish (translating for us), "Men think and God laughs."

XI

She wages daily combat with the black Home Care workers. Mrs. Blocker is fanatically clean. The apartment glows; the dishes shine; her face gleams. Seated at the kitchen table with us, she suddenly bends forward, trying to get up. She just avoids falling back into her chair. She runs her finger *under* the rim of the chair and shows us the dust. "I like clean. Clean is my whole life."

The workers change with the seasons. "My new girl. I don't know what. She lies on the floor with nothing on. Yesterday, she lays down on the floor in my bedroom with just panty hose on"—she cups her hands under her breasts—"everything hanging out . . . no shoes . . . she says to me, 'This is the way we do it in my country.' What country is she talking about? I'm afraid people will come in and see.

"I know she don't like Jews. She don't say it. So the other day I asked her. She said, 'Jew, schmoo, what do I care?' The way she said Jew, I knew. I said, you know I'm a rabbi's daughter? She said, 'Rabbi, schmabbi, what do I care?'

"I tell her to buy me borscht and she brings me back low-caloric. I've lost fifty pounds and she buys me low-calorie borscht." Mrs. Blocker laughs. "What can you do?

"She looks at things in the apartment and says to me: 'Give that to me, you don't need it.' "

In the third month that we know Mrs. Blocker, she begins to talk about her new daily Home Care worker, a woman from Jamaica, Mrs. Gordon. Mrs. Gordon falls on the floor in fits of fury, mumbling, crossing herself again and again, and thrashing with her feet. "Mrs. Gordon says to me her husband has red hair—and white skin just like mine. I said to her, 'Dot's wonderful, dolling.' What could I say?" She laughs.

When Mrs. Gordon's checks come, she stands over Mrs. Blocker demanding her signature, shouting: "Sign it! Sign it!"

The next Sunday that we visit Mrs. Blocker, she is crying. Mrs. Gordon had put her in the shower, turned on the hot water and walked out. Mrs. Blocker screamed for help, and Mrs. Gordon did not come. Mrs. Blocker crawled out of the shower along the floor to the bedroom. "Please help me!" she screamed to Mrs. Gordon. "Please take a towel and wipe me." Her body was red from the hot water. Mrs. Gordon reluctantly dried her.

Mrs. Sally Crawford, the weekend worker, tells us that something is wrong. "Mrs. Blocker must never be left alone in the shower like that. And her skin was almost blistered."

We call Home Care and tell them what has happened. We say that Mrs. Gordon appears to be unbalanced. The Home Care nurse says to us over the phone: "We've had trouble with Mrs. Blocker before; she always complains." We call the Jewish agency we are working with. "We're afraid something terrible will happen," we say.

The Jewish agency contacts Home Care, and Mrs. Gordon is replaced.

The replacement is a young girl named Jenetta Brown. When we arrive on Sunday, we are eager to hear Mrs. Blocker talk about the improvement.

"She's a pretty goil, I'm telling you. She comes in, and sits down on the sofa in her high boots, her hair made up like a doll, with her homework. And she don't do nothing. When I tell her to do the housework, she tells me not to boss her, she says to me: 'I'm a grown lady.'

" 'And I'm an old lady,' I tell her.

"She can't stand my false teeth. 'Leave them in the bathroom!' she screams at me. 'I can't stand to look at them.'

" 'I'll leave them,' I tell her. 'I'll leave them in the toilet.'

" 'You are a young woman,' I told her. 'Maybe you need a man. You can get one for the weekends.'

"She tells me, 'Mrs. Blocker. I'm not a slave.' What is a slave? Tell me, what is a slave? I thought that was in jail, where they put you in chains.

"I told her, 'Have pity on me and pity on you. Go to the doctor and find out what's wrong with your head.' "

The next week she is crying when we arrive. "I asked Jenetta to take me down in the wheelchair. She took me all right. I asked her to wheel me around the block. She says, 'I don't wheel people!' She said she would be back, and she left me in the park. And she didn't come back. I was outside in the cold for two hours. I cry, and finally somebody takes pity on me and takes me inside.

"When she gets back here, I'm sitting and crying with the cold and I ask her to help me undress. She sits in the corner, her legs crossed, smiling, and didn't make a move. She refused to do anything.

"*All niggers are no good,*" she says furiously.

My wife and I look at each other, and we are silent. A speech is dying to get out, but it will have to wait.

The rules with eighty-four-year-old crippled women are different, and I keep my mouth shut. For the moment.

XII

"I think of my son Sammy dying . . . my daughter, crazy and sick . . . my grandson with his crazy wife . . . and it takes a piece of me."

Sammy, in the picture of him, has a handlebar moustache and quizzical eyes with eyebrows that curve upwards. He is smiling.

He is fifty-nine and dying of cancer. His wife drives him to visit his mother. He sits for five minutes, lies down on her bed and his wife says that she will have to take him home. Mrs. Blocker places forty dollars in her hand.

A hospital bed is brought to Sammy's home, and an oxygen tent. Mrs. Blocker calls and wants to speak to him. They hesitate, and finally they wheel the bed near the phone.

"How are you, Samele?"

"Now that I'm talking to you, Mamele, I'm all right." Then he says, "Mamele, if only I could eat your chicken soup, I would get better."

His daughter is finishing college in Boston, and Mrs. Blocker is paying her rent—fifty dollars a month—out of her disability and social security checks and her savings account in which she has $600 remaining.

Her checks come to $184 a month. Her rent is $38. She pays for her food and rent and the rest goes to Sammy, to her granddaughter, and to her grandson. They all come by, and they all leave with money. The grandson calls her on the day her check arrives.

He drives a taxi three days a week, and is married to a German refugee. Mrs. Blocker tells us that he had a steady job working nights in the post office, but on the honeymoon night his wife told him: "Me, sleep alone nights? It's me or the post office." He chose her. She refuses to work, and spends the day playing bingo and the horses. "What a monstrous creature," Mrs. Blocker says.

The grandson comes by during the week to take a shower at her house. "His long hair reaches down to his big stomach."

Her daughter says of the grandson: "My son is dead."

She tries to divide the money fairly among all of them.

The granddaughter visits and tells Mrs. Blocker to save the china cabinet for her when she dies. "That's mine, grandma—don't forget. You don't know what you've got there."

XIII

Of Sammy, she says: "Such a good man! A young man! I visited him. He tried to hold up his hand in the bed for me to kiss him . . . he couldn't lift his hand . . . it fell back.

"I cry too much—I'm going blind."

She has talked the day before to Sammy on the phone, she tells us. Her daughter-in-law held the phone while he talked.

" 'Mamele'—he calls me like when he was a baby—

"He says: 'How are you?'

" 'HA HA HA'—I laugh like that—'I'm fine! I'm swell!' I'm saying, and he says, 'It's so nice to hear you smile.' The tears are falling off my dress while I'm talking but I say, 'I'm cooking, Samele—chopped meat, split pea soup, kugel. Why not come over and eat with me—'

" 'I'm so glad you're all right, Mamele.' "

I don't know what to say to Mrs. Blocker. "You made him feel better," I say.

"That's right. That's right." She shakes her head.

XIV

In the hallway of Mrs. Blocker's apartment there hangs a sign. It says: "God bless this miserable house." It was placed there by Minnie, Mrs. Blocker's daughter. Mrs. Blocker does not read

English. We ask her if she knows what it says. She says, "Sure! God bless this lousy apartment!"

She tells us again that when she told her daughter over the phone that she was very sick, Minnie replied, "Listen, you're lucky to be alive at all. I won't make it to your age."

Her daughter hasn't visited her in six months. When she came, she saw a hat she had given her mother on the head of Je-netta. "You've got a hell of a nerve," she shouted at Mrs. Blocker.

"Then when my daughter found out I had sold a coat she gave me to Jenetta for ten dollars, she burst into tears and screamed at me. She said she would rather take a scissors and cut the coat into little pieces rather than give it to a colored girl. So I talked to Jenetta. I told her how much the coat was worth. She said would I take another five dollars for it. I said okay. Then I had to tell my daughter. You know what she said? My daughter threat-ened not to come to my funeral."

The pictures of Minnie are of a face edged with sour despair. The mascara is thick over the eyes. She is a heavy blonde. I rec-ognize the look on her face, and I stare at it.

The sour, blank look, emptied of all hope and striving, is fa-miliar to me. It is the expression on my own mother's face.

I recognize it immediately, even though I have not seen my mother in twenty years.

It has always been difficult to answer questions about my mother, since she lives a few miles from my house. It is particu-larly difficult when Mrs. Blocker asks me, but I answer her the same way I answer everyone else.

"Where is your mother?" Mrs. Blocker asks me one day.

"My mother? My mother is dead."

XV

After my parents were divorced when I was ten years old, I stayed with my father on weekends.

One Sunday evening after we heard Tallulah Bankhead sign off at the end of "The Big Show" by singing "May the Good Lord

Bless and Keep You," after Winchell and apples and watermel-
on, my father drove me home.

I took the elevator to the top floor, where I lived with my
mother, and instead of ringing the doorbell, I tiptoed to the staircase leading to the roof, and walked silently up the steps. I
looked at the trees in the moonlight, the breeze stilled my
pounding heart. I would not lose my temper. I would understand. I would remember what, my father had explained,
caused my mother to act so mean to me: the death in the last
year of her father and mother "who had done everything for
her"; the fact that she had been forced, if she wanted the divorce, to go to work. The married neighbors seemed to side with
my mother against me: they knew her familiar waddling walk,
the pretty face and small body and wide behind, high heels un-
steadily pecking away at the pavement, her arms loaded down
with bundles of food and antiques. She had a ready smile for
them, and I did not know how to talk to them.

I walked slowly back down the steps from the roof and rang
the bell. She smiled at the door, removed the latch, and let me
in.

"Bruce, don't you have a kiss for your mother?"

I kissed her.

She served me cookies and milk in the kitchen.

After I finished the milk, I walked into her bedroom. She was
seated on the chaise lounge, her legs folded under her, and on
her lap she held a new pink telephone.

She laughed, she flashed her pretty teeth. "How do I look?"

"Beautiful."

She placed the phone on the floor and held her chin in her
hand.

Suddenly she turned to me and said, "Wash your face, Bruce.
You look like a nigger."

I stared at her.

"Come on. Be a good boy."

"*Negro.*"

"You're starting in?"

"No. But I wanted to say what I feel."

"All right, professor, if you put it that way, I said what *I* feel. You look like a nigger, period. End of argument. All right?" She smiled.

"It's not all right. It's insulting to Negroes."

She fingered the phone. "Come on. You just got home. Do me a favor and wash your face. You don't look like a nigger."

I walked into my room and slammed the door.

A tap at the door. A small voice. "Bruce."

I opened it. I thought I knew what was happening. She was still under the sway of the pink telephone. No grudges tonight.

"Bruce?"

"Hmmm?"

"No more fights. Come sit with me in the living room."

In the living room, my mother took the plastic sheets off the couch and folded them neatly. I sat down, and she sat down beside me. She crossed her legs and folded her hands.

"How's the car?"

"What?"

"The car."

"What car?"

My father had sworn me to secrecy about the new car he had bought. He said it would "make mommy feel bad about divorcing me."

"Mrs. Caruso downstairs told me she saw your father driving around in a red Ford."

"I don't know anything about it."

"What did you do over the weekend?"

"Oh, the usual. We went to the Laffmovie and the Automat—"

She laughed. "That cheap bastard. Where does he leave it at night?"

"What?"

"Does he rent parking space?"

"I don't know what you're talking about."

"There's one thing I hate in this world, and that's a sneak. You're just like your father."

"I'm going to bed."

"Go to bed. Sneak. Dirty rotten sneak. You're the spitting image of him. You tell that son of a bitch for me that he can drop dead with his new car."

She slammed her bedroom door.

In my room I listened. Sometimes she came back.

I got undressed and put on my pajamas.

In bed, I tried to think about my father . . . about the film we had seen at the Laffmovie on Forty-second Street that afternoon: Edward G. Robinson and Slapsie Maxie Rosenbloom as two ex-cons who take over a luggage shop next to a bank in order to drill an underground hole to the bank. I thought about the mashed potatoes at the Automat.

My mother opened the door to my bedroom. "What year is the car?"

I put my hands in front of me.

"I hate sneaks." She slammed my door, and slammed the door to her bedroom.

XVI

Every Sunday evening when we are ready to leave, Mrs. Blocker tries to press things on us: coats, hats, shoes, toasters, bags, sweaters. She is so eager that she forgets her walker and her cane. Her booming voice shouts at us: "Don't gyp me!" She shuffles firmly across the room holding a sweater for my wife. "In the first place, she's so cute," she says to me. "She's an angel, I'm telling you. I got twenty sweaters. Please, dolling, take it."

We shake our heads.

"When I die, my daughter will just throw everything in the incinerator. I know her. Please, dolling."

We think up new ways every time to get out of taking anything.

At the door, she says: "Please promise you'll come to my funeral."

"Yes, Mrs. Blocker," we say, kissing her and taking her in our arms together.

XVII

"People around here are not so good. I sit on the bench. They say: 'So-and-so's husband died. So now she's sleeping with her boarder.' 'So?' I say. 'Good luck to her! What is it your business?' And I take my walker and I walk away. There are *two hundred* benches down here. You think I don't know what's going on? The man comes up to the lady and says: 'You get social security. I get social security. How about it? We'll keep each other company.' And if he has a car, my God! With a car you can get anything . . .

"Before my granddaughter got married the second time, you think they just held hands before marriage? He held her in another place! Mrs. Blocker is no dummy . . . well, well, well . . .

"But a woman has to be able to walk. A woman has to be able to lay good. I'm like a stone alone. At least big stones have little stones. Anyway, if I had legs, I would marry. A man needs legs!

"Oh, yi yi! What's going on today. Even the priests. You know, I wondered how they had babies. Then I found out. I was at a bingo night. A young priest was talking to a young girl, a doll. The next time I looked they were in the next room and, boom boom boom!" Mrs. Blocker claps her hands.

"What can you do? Love—love is like a fire." She spreads her hands. "Then 1 2 3—poof!"

XVIII

She says the doorbell and the phone never ring, but over the months, there is a steady parade of social workers, volunteers, young girls who are getting paid for summer visits. (They always say: "What can we do for you?" Mrs. Blocker knows the question. She folds her hands and says: "I don't know, dolling. What can you do for me?") People with good intentions, as well as the Home Care workers who are waiting for their checks, blur in her memory. She forgets the doctors who see her once every three months, but becomes agitated when she hears that the doctor is "afraid" to come to see her without a nurse to accompany him. She perks up her ears at this. "Afraid of *me*?" She beats her hand on the table. She insists on knowing what the doctor is afraid of, and she is upset for a long time over this.

XIX

She points to her legs and arms. "I have a hitching in my skin like a fire. I'm like a peeled onion. My head is drying up. What's the use of all this? I'm licked. They call me up and want me to go to dances, to camps, to picnics. Should I sit in a corner and cry? I'm better here, to cry alone, to laugh alone."

XX

When she answers the phone she asks: "Who is dot?"

And when she calls us at home, before we can say anything, she says: "Dot is Mrs. Blocker!"

XXI

Watching the TV news, she is furious at Nixon and Rockefeller: "What the hell is going on in this country?" She wants to adopt one of the Vietnamese orphans: "Who will feed them? Where will they live? We have seven-and-a-half-million unemployed. I would adopt them, but I have no hands, no feet, no eyes." She watches the news about Happy Rockefeller's operation. "A poor person would be dead. With money you get honey."

It is only when she can do something for us that she forgets her troubles. She insists on paying us for the string to tie the electric fan securely so she won't tip it over. "Only cash—no mortgage!"

She wants to give all her old clothes away, but finds that people are too proud to take any more. "Where are the poor people?" she asks. She sees a woman in the park she has given a sweater to, and the woman doesn't say anything. Mrs. Blocker goes up to her: "Lady, don't you recognize me?"

XXII

How real is her pain to me? A few times I wake up in the night and I feel that my body is wracked with pain in the places Mrs. Blocker has described. If I cannot sleep, sometimes I think of Mrs. Blocker prowling her apartment until 5 A.M. If I am uncomfortable in bed, I think of how she cannot lie down without pain, or sit up without it, or walk, or see; of how her head throbs; of her constipation; of her inability to swallow sometimes, or bend down at all, but I can never put all these things together to get a sense of how she really feels.

But I do know she thinks of us as her friends. I know this not so much because she kisses our hands when we say good-bye, as because she shows us her gnarled hands with their blue veins. She says quietly, in explanation: "Swollen . . . old, you know."

XXIII

Before the news broke about Rabbi Ribman and his network of nursing homes, Mrs. Blocker had heard all about the homes. She was herself briefly in a Riverdale nursing home when she was sick, and her purse had been stolen. She asked to see someone in charge who could help her. No one came. She pleaded with a guard: "Haven't you got someone for the poor people?"

One afternoon she had sat next to a woman in the park with a nameplate on her wrist. "So I said, 'You're from a home?' She cried. 'If you say the food is bad—if you say anything—they take you before the jury and there's a trial.' And she said, 'I saved all my money and worked and gave it all away for this.' "

I read stories about Rabbi Ribman carefully and tell some of them to Mrs. Blocker, who has already been following the story on television. Of the patients beaten by guards, left to sit in urine and feces.

One night I have a dream about Rabbi Ribman. He is the guest of honor at a dinner given by the Jewish organization I work for.

Since he is the guest, the people in the audience address questions to him from the floor, but they are gentle questions, avoiding the issue of the nursing homes. They don't want to say anything too disturbing. But I notice that people are walking out in droves as a way of expressing how they feel toward him. I want to say the following, but I don't know how to phrase it congenially so that I won't lose my job: "Actually, Rabbi, there is really little difference between what you did and what the Nazis did, is there?"

While I struggle with myself, I hear Ribman answering another question from a member of the audience. Ribman is moving his lips, but his words, and his voice, are those of California poet Charles Bukowski. In my dream, I sit in the audience watching Ribman speak Bukowski's words: "My father was a cruel bastard," Rabbi Ribman says. "He made me mow the lawn, back and forth. He would put his head down, to the grass, eye level, and look for one blade of grass. Naturally he would find one out of the thousands. Then he beat me, he beat me anyway, every day. And I sometimes realize that I'm acting like him, that I'm being like him, and I don't like that. It scares me."

XXIV

It is Mrs. Blocker's eighty-fifth birthday. She is especially excited, as my father is coming up to pay her a visit for the first time.

We have carefully explained to her that my father has a girl friend named Rosie. Mrs. Blocker has questioned us carefully about her, although she does not hear all our answers.

"How big is your father's apartment?" she asks.

"One bedroom."

"That's all? So where does he keep her—on the floor? on the table?"

"She doesn't live with him—"

"In the bookcase maybe?"

She tells the caseworker to go home to her husband: "*Skid-*

doo! You know what that means? You go home. Kiss Willie or someone else will."

This is a new caseworker, a black woman named Dorothy Williams. Mrs. Blocker has formed an affectionate relationship with her, and says she "counts the minutes and hours" when she is away.

"Okay," Dorothy says.

"Do it!" shouts Mrs. Blocker. As Dorothy kisses her good-bye, Mrs. Blocker nods to us: "Dot's a woman! My God!"

After Dorothy leaves, Mrs. Blocker prepares for my father's arrival. She puts in her false teeth. "I'm dolling it up for my lover," she says.

My father has recently recovered from an automobile accident. He spent several weeks in the hospital. He still has a stiff neck from it. On the Sunday he comes to see Mrs. Blocker, he has also been to the unveiling of his closest and best friend, Jake.

My father used to enjoy going out in his Cadillac with Rosie. His Cadillac was smashed in the accident, and so he travels today on the subway to see Mrs. Blocker.

Mrs. Blocker is plainly impressed when he enters and gives him a sweeping look. She leans forward in her walker and smiles at him, scrutinizing him. My father takes a seat beside my wife on the couch to the left of Mrs. Blocker, who sits in her chair. He tries to turn his head toward her to be polite despite his stiff neck. They are both hard of hearing and shout at each other.

"You're not a young man yourself," she shouts. "Jack Benny died at thirty-nine. How old was *he*?"

My father smiles and nods politely, and says to me that Mrs. Blocker has a very strong voice.

"But I wouldn't swear to what he did last night," she says about my father.

My father strains to turn to her. "As a matter of fact, I took out a lovely young lady," he says carefully, letting her know they are not in the same league.

"You took out a young lady?" she shouts.

"Yes."

"How young, may I ask?"

"Rosie is fifty-one years old."

"On the right side or on the left side?" Mrs. Blocker says, with her hands shaking one breast at a time.

My father cannot believe what he sees.

The atmosphere is charged. My father no longer tries to turn to Mrs. Blocker, or even to stare ahead. He turns the other way, to my wife: "You act so polite, so interested. You have to do this every week?"

My wife says that we enjoy seeing Mrs. Blocker.

"I hope you don't mind my saying this. She has such a strong voice. She must have money. She's got it made. Maids every day of the week." Now he turns to me. "I don't mean to offend you, but this woman isn't what I expected at all. I thought you were going to see some poor unfortunate creature! I thought you were doing a good deed. What a voice she has!"

Mrs. Blocker cannot hear a word. She keeps her eyes trained on my father and is shouting at him all the time, and he is trying to ignore her completely.

She tries a new tack. "Mister. I got a neighbor, a beautiful lady. Only sixty years old. She wants, if she gets married, a husband mit a car, money, insurance—"

My father laughs and laughs. "*She* wants? I know hundreds of women of forty who would be happy to get a man without a car, without money, and without insurance. And the fact that she lives on the lower East Side doesn't help her either."

My father says all this staring straight ahead.

"Look," Mrs. Blocker says to us, "he can't turn his neck. Age, I'm telling you."

My father raises himself up carefully and turns to her with a sweet smile. "My stiff neck, for your information, happens to be due to an automobile accident I had on New Year's Eve."

Mrs. Blocker is laughing. "I wouldn't swear to what he did last night."

My father rises, tells Mrs. Blocker how happy he is to have met her, takes his hat and says good-bye.

XXV

We are seated with Mrs. Blocker at the kitchen table after my father has left, although she has not eaten any of the birthday cake we have brought her. "I'm a gnosher," she suddenly says, and picks up the cream pitcher and drinks from it and grabs some of the cake and eats it with her fingers.

After a few moments she says, looking at us, "What should I do? Go in a nursing home, a hospital, or stay suffering as I am? Prowling the apartment all night, or my body lying in a pool of sweat? I tell God every night: 'I'm going to sleep. Don't let me stand up.' But he don't listen to me. Maybe my contract isn't up." She looks at us and extends her hands: "My friends what I got."

My wife gets up to go to the bathroom. Mrs. Blocker says to me: "Watch her like you watch your eyes. An angel!"

We lead her into the living room where our presents are on the table: cans of salmon and gefilte fish, and a picture book of Israel. She hesitates, uncertain: "I don't know the rules."

She sits on the sofa, and we are on each side of her. We open the presents for her. She leafs through the Israel book, and we read the captions to her. I think of her arthritic hands and say, "I hope you'll be able to hold the book . . ."

Misunderstanding or not, she answers, pressing the book against her breast, "I'll hold it to my heart, under my pillow at night, that's how I will hold it.

"You're my son, Brucele."

XXVI

We have been visiting Mrs. Blocker for two years when Sammy, her son, dies of cancer.

The doctor has now diagnosed the wart on Mrs. Blocker's face as cancer. She is taken to the hospital every morning in an ambulance for radiation therapy.

We have not seen her for two months, although we have talked over the phone.

Mrs. Blocker is not standing in the kitchen. She is lying, moaning, without her teeth, on her bed, her head on a single pillow. She raises her head to talk to us. We place a second pillow under her head. "That stupid couldn't do it," she says, pointing. We look up into the eyes of Wilma, a plump black woman in her forties who chews gum steadily. She replaced Dorothy eight months ago.

"I tried, Mrs. Blocker—"

"Go away!" Mrs. Blocker shouts fiercely, waving Wilma away. "You can't do nothing."

Wilma leaves the room. "She can't cook, she can't clean. She's a sick woman herself. I can't stand it anymore. You remember Dorothy: she was so clean you could, excuse me, kiss her ass. I can't take it, I'm telling you. She doesn't tell me when to take my pills—"

"I ast you, Mrs. Blocker," Wilma shouts from the living room, "and you refuse to take them."

"I tell her to write it down so she can remember—"

Wilma stands in the doorway. "I ast you, and you refused!"

"What?" Mrs. Blocker looks with disgust at Wilma. "Go away."

"I ast you to take the pills, and you refused!"

"I didn't feel like it—"

"But I can't help it if you refuse, Mrs. Blocker—"

"You know how much she's earning here? Ten thousand dollars a year! Do you know what I could do with that?"

"But you don't earn it! I work for it."

"Huh?"

"I work for my money."

"You do? What do you do for me? You can't even give me my pills—"

"You won't take them—"

"She won't take me across the street in my wheelchair."

"I can't lift the wheelchair up the curb, Mr. Bruce. Dorothy was a strong woman. I'm not that strong."

"I know you're not strong," Mrs. Blocker raises her head again. "Double fare she gets. Crook! Fourteen dollars a week!"

Wilma stands in the hallway, sits on a chair, hovers over Mrs. Blocker. Whatever she does or says is wrong to Mrs. Blocker. Finally she retreats into the kitchen. She has the air of the unwanted. Her untucked shirt hangs over her slacks.

We move Mrs. Blocker into the kitchen. She sits in a corner. Wilma moves into the living room.

"You know what she eats for lunch? Two slices of bread, with a slice of cheese in the middle!"

"That's all I can afford," Wilma shouts, now from the bedroom.

"She don't eat nothing. She's a sick woman! She didn't tell me. She has a swollen hand! She hides it behind her back. And she can't do nothing. She lied—she told me she had been a nurse before. You know what she did? She served the trays of food and took the trays away! A liar—I could have her locked up."

Wilma comes into the kitchen smiling and snapping her chewing gum. She makes coffee for us.

"Mrs. Blocker is not herself today. I know that. I understand. I know you can't help treating me this way. But I've got broad shoulders. I can take it. Why don't you like me? I like *you*. I really do. But you want too much sympathy, Mrs. Blocker. I can't give it. I'm not that kind of person."

"Stupid, stupid." Mrs. Blocker waves her away.

Mrs. Blocker talks for the next two hours about Wilma and nothing else.

"I buy a chocolate layer cake. Don't worry, I leave Wilma alone in the kitchen and in ten minutes four pieces are gone."

"You offered it to me. You offered it to me."

"People are supposed to ask."

Wilma works for Mrs. Blocker from eight in the morning until eight at night, seven days a week.

"I beg her, Wilma, do me a favor: come a little earlier. Come at seven o'clock so I can take my pills—"

"I have to feed my daughter breakfast!"

"Eleven years old her daughter is. She can feed herself."

"But she would never see her daughter then," Susan says.

"What?"

"She would never see her daughter at all!" we shout.

"I know. She's supporting also her older daughter who has a baby. A woman all by herself. But I need a girl who can cook for me."

"I don't do that!"

"She don't know how to make even cereal."

"No I don't."

"What do you serve your daughter?" Mrs. Blocker says.

"Other things. I don't know about cereal. But I can learn, Mrs. Blocker."

Mrs. Blocker winces and whispers to us that she would never let Wilma's hands touch her food.

Wilma again walks out of the room.

"You know how much money she's making? *Ten thousand dollars*—"

A bloodcurdling laugh from the bedroom, deep and masculine. It is Wilma. We have never heard it before.

Mrs. Blocker shrugs. "Dot's what it is. All day long now: *heh heh heh!*"

The rattlesnake laugh reaches us again.

"I have to get rid of her. You're my friends. Help me. I know all about her. She was married, she had a good, educated husband—"

"If he was so good, why did I divorce him?" Wilma screams, and runs into the kitchen.

"He wasn't a dummy, but an educated."

"I am asting you a question: why did I divorce him, if he was so fucking good? Huh? Answer me that," and laughs and laughs, cracking her gum.

Mrs. Blocker looks at us, shaking her head. "Laugh rather than cry."

She pauses for a moment, and continues: "And she gets twenty-five dollars from her husband for her daughter."

"Yes I do, and sometimes even more than that, Mrs. Blocker; so what?"

"What do you do with it, tell me?"

"What do I do with the money? I pay my mortgage, and I buy food, and clothes—"

"She don't eat—"

"That's my business. I'm fat and I'm getting fatter—look!" Wilma lifts her shirt to show us her stomach, and hits it. We hear the thud.

Wilma reheats the coffee and stands at the sink.

"Who are you?" Mrs. Blocker suddenly says.

"Who *am* I? I don't know. I am a black girl, madam. I am a black, forty-four-year-old woman, love, that's who I am."

"You won't live to see me die," Mrs. Blocker shouts.

"I don't wish that on you. I don't wish that on you, Mrs. Blocker. I hope I live as long as you do."

"Hitler!"

Wilma's laugh shoots through us.

"She laughs," Mrs. Blocker says.

"What do you expect her to do?" Susan asks. "You call her Hitler."

"You are very crazy, Mrs. Blocker," Wilma says. "The truth is you are prejudiced. The truth is you will never be happy as long as a black girl is here, Mrs. Blocker. What you really want is a nice white Jewish girl, but you can't get one. Nobody wants to work for you because you are a very crazy lady. So you're stuck with me. And I know you can't help the way you're acting. You'll be better later. I have got broad shoulders, Mrs. Blocker. I can take it."

Wilma is now laughing and snapping her fingers hard and doing a little dance by the stove. She goes to the bathroom.

"She's a sick woman," Mrs. Blocker screams. "She has a swollen hand! She hides it behind her back! I ask her, where is your other hand?"

A door slams. Wilma comes running in, her palms outstretched, showing us her hands and laughing and laughing and winking at us. "My hands are not swollen! You are crazy, Mrs. Blocker."

"Liar! And both your legs are swollen!"

Wilma jumps, spreads her legs, lifts up her pants to show us her legs. "There's nothing wrong with my legs, as you can see!"

Mrs. Blocker looks. "No shoes! Is that a decent way to dress?"

"THEY ARE SLIPPERS."

Wilma hits herself on the behind, snaps her fingers and wrists, claps her hands and laughs hysterically. She is now dancing around Mrs. Blocker and jumping up and down. We don't know what to do.

She is shaking her hips at Mrs. Blocker. She is beckoning to her with her arms, demanding: "Come on, Mrs. Blocker, dance with me! Get up and dance with me!" She is thrusting her arms at Mrs. Blocker; cooing: "Aww, come on, Mrs. Blocker, you can do it. I know you can." Mrs. Blocker is holding onto her canes and shrinking back into her chair.

"Leave me alone!"

Wilma is saying sweetly, "I just want you to dance! Nothing to be afraid of! I'm here to help you!"

"You are Hitler!" Mrs. Blocker screams.

Wilma laughs and looks to us.

"My son is dead and I don't want to live," Mrs. Blocker cries.

"You want to jump out the window?"

"Yes!"

"Jump! I won't stop you, madam."

Wilma storms out of the room.

Tears in her eyes, Mrs. Blocker whispers: "You are my only friends. I beg you. Help me. That is all I can say."

We shake hands with Wilma, kiss Mrs. Blocker, and walk out, drained and shaken, onto East Broadway.

We spend the weekend writing a report to the agency explaining the situation. We say that Wilma and Mrs. Blocker are victims victimizing each other, that the relationship has become unbearable, and ask that Wilma be given another job. They call us later in the week and tell us that they have visited Mrs. Blocker and Wilma. They found nothing wrong. They have asked Mrs. Blocker point-blank about Wilma. "Let it be," she said. We in-

sist on what we have seen. The director of the agency suggests
that perhaps Mrs. Blocker wants it this way.

We call her. She talks about her illnesses and her complaints.

"But what about Wilma?"

"Let it be."

We do not see Mrs. Blocker very often anymore. She pretends
she does not remember us when we phone her.

"Do you people live in the city?" she asks.

"Mrs. Blocker—it's us!"

"I'm sorry, dollings; maybe if you were to come up on Sunday
to see me I might recognize you."

XXVII

Sometimes I visit my old neighborhood in Brooklyn. I take the
elevated subway, and walk down the stairs to the street. The little wooden cubicle that was a newsstand is gone. When I was a
boy I worked there for free, just to be part of it. All the stores at
the corner are still there: the candy store, the shoe repair shop,
the beauty salon, the tailor. The language that is spoken around
me is new, is Spanish. There is surprisingly little, though, that
is new in the neighborhood. The ice cream parlor is gone. But
the streets are not gutted or dirty. There is no danger, but unfa-
miliarity. And I know very well how my mother must feel
about those Spanish voices and faces—she who could not even
muster up love for her own, who imagined enemies everywhere, who saw contempt in a smile and slapped me sharply
across the face when I was happy, asking "What are you grinning at?"

I approach the apartment house where she lives, where I lived
for so long. It is, as I remembered, a rather nice house. There are
two small stoops, one on either side of the entrance. One was
the apartment where my grandparents lived and where I was
taken care of. I look at the stairs leading to the stoop where I
played, and I look at the door.

The entrance to the house has rock gardens on both sides, and on the right side, a small pond where goldfish used to swim.

I walk around the neighborhood. Amid the concrete, there is, as there always was, across the street a huge old house with land around it: Dr. Lynch's, where my father carried me in his arms for a tonsil operation.

Each street that I approach has an aroma, a feeling to it, the same one it had when I walked it every day to school. Some streets are darker; others are defined by their houses. The green house with the large enclosed porch is still filled with pieces of wood that still look, as they did when I was a boy, as if they were about to be cleared away. There are brown houses with windowpanes lined in green. I cannot find the old house with the well in the garden.

As I walk down the street to P.S. 17 where I walked every day with my schoolbooks, I remember, even before they come into view, the brick apartment house with the brick courtyard across the street from the school, the brick the same autumnal color of brown and gold.

The schoolyard is gone. Most of it is occupied by two barracks-like greenish, round buildings: an annex of some kind. I hear a ball bounce—I look inside the gate. Between the buildings a small area has been left and boys are bouncing a basketball into the one remaining hoop.

I walk back to my mother's house through different streets, and again each one seems to evoke the same feelings it once did. Tense, I go through the backyard into the basement, afraid I may run into her. I take the elevator to the roof, walk up the stairs and open the door, and feel the familiar soft tar surface and see the clotheslines and the steepled, open, doorless little house with triangular windows, the wind blowing through it. I look down at the street, at the trees, at the people. Hiding behind a ledge, I look down at the windows of my mother's apartment. I do not see her shadow.

I liked the neighborhood as a boy, and I like it now, even though there is more concrete. It really wasn't a bad place to grow up in, if there had been other things.

I walk back down the stairs, take the elevator to the basement, and walk to the subway.

There is nothing else I want to see.

10

THE PRINCESS

I

At lunch the other day, my father was musing about why he never really entered the rat race. He recalled another salesman in his insurance office: a fellow who wore a red beret. This fellow, my father said, would choose the Chrysler Building or one of the other tallest buildings in Manhattan and take the elevator to the roof. Then he would walk down the staircase, enter every office on the way down and try to sell insurance. My father remembers this fellow saying to him, "You've never really been an insurance salesman until you've gone to the top of one of those buildings, the very top, and walked down, floor by floor."

II

My father and I met for lunch twice a week in the Governor Cafeteria after I returned from five years in Vancouver in 1973. We talked about his childhood, about my mother, about his male and female friends on the singles scene. We didn't talk much about my life, since it was not going well and my father would stay up nights worrying. After publishing a book, I had decided to enroll in a writing workshop in the West Village to get moving again in New York. I joined the workshop at a happy moment—the instructor was both celebrating his birthday and getting his BA from the New School, and the students were baking him a cake. I came in with ten pages of my story—about winning the friendship of Frank Sinatra (opposites attract, etc.) and was told to put it away for now, roll up my sleeves, and join my colleagues in the kitchen.

My father talked about a fellow in his office, Rupert Pike, a shriveled man with a freckled skinny face, glasses, and a jutting Adam's apple. Suddenly smiling, he said, "When I went to the office this morning, Rupert was sleeping on the floor. He doesn't have money for a place to stay since he broke up with his wife. His wife would get drunk and beat him up every night. He used to have bandages on his head, Bruce. She's an alcoholic. He told me that when she threw him out of the house he would go back early in the morning and knock on the door. 'Evvie, darling? Evvie,' he would say. She would scream at him, 'Get the hell out of here, you son of a bitch.' This went on for years, and he still was crazy about her."

My father laughed. "Explain this to me, Bruce, if you can. This fellow—Rupert—is the most happy-go-lucky fellow in the world. He tells me these things, and he laughs and laughs. He has no money at all. He asks me for a dollar for food, and I found out what he does. He goes downstairs and has a martini! And do you know why he has no money? He has a new girl friend, and he bought her a piano. She lives in a rooming house. Today he said, 'She has an income: one hundred dollars.' 'A week?' I said. 'A month,' he said. 'She's on welfare. I feel so sorry for her . . . I'd like to marry her.'

"Then he said she goes haywire every once in a while. She has a bad face . . . broken down . . . and he'd like to fix it for her. She has black teeth. He said he wants so badly to cap her teeth for her.

"Then Rupert tapped me on the arm and said with a wink:

'She allowed me a kiss on the cheek last night . . .' I'm a bad boy, Bruce, I shouldn't say anything, but I asked him how he could kiss a girl with black teeth. He just smiled at me. He mails her a love letter and a dollar every day. He told me what his secret ambition was: to play piano in a whorehouse!

"I asked him, 'What does she give you?' Rupert replied, smiling, 'Oh, women don't give you anything!' Then he hitched his jacket up and said 'Look!' He proudly showed me the patches on both knees of his pants.

"His other girl friend—the eighty-three-year-old one with one eye—saw him with the girl with the black teeth. The next time he saw her, he told me, she punched him in the stomach so hard she knocked his breath out. He tells me this with a smile, Bruce, and a giggle!

"The other night he went into a bar and just began playing the piano. He told me that after a while the bartender put a mug on the piano. At the end of the evening he looked up and there was three dollars in it."

My father paused. "His wife would get drunk every night and beat him, and he still loved her. Isn't that amazing?"

"My mother slapped and hit me," I said.

My father stopped smiling. "There's no comparison."

III

After a while, my father said, "When I was a boy, Bruce, every time I saw a girl I liked, I died a thousand deaths. I always had a dark complexion. I like clean girls. Like mommy. Clean white skin. She was as cute as a button when I met her.

"Tsk, tsk, tsk. I was afraid of everything, Bruce. I was afraid of my father, I was scared to let him know I was in the house. I was ashamed of my clothes with girls. And I didn't know how to dance. If I liked the girl, I would be so confused I would forget the step.

"That's why when your mother liked me, I was in seventh heaven. I had nothing. So many fears, and I had to be Jewish too. They weren't hiring Jews so fast in those days. I met mommy when I was already thirty-two. She was only twenty-one. She was so small and pretty, and not like the other girls. She wasn't fast, cheap. She never used foul language. She was shy with people. She would hold onto my hand. I felt like a million bucks. She told me I was the handsomest man in the world." He laughed. "And boy, was I ugly! She had to be in love with me to think I was handsome.

"I look around me today, Bruce, and I still think, after all these years, mommy is the prettiest girl. And she loved you, Bruce—"

"She called me 'it'—"

"She wasn't cheap like other women—"

"She called me a moron and an idiot—"

"She even got upset when I used to make up the adventures of Moishe Pippick for you when you were a little boy! Do you know what *pippick* means, Bruce?"

"Belly button."

"Mommy didn't like me to use that word—she said it was dirty." My father laughed softly.

IV

My father watched the Friday ads in the *New York Post* for singles dances and shaped his weekend around them. Being handsome and a fine dresser, he was frequently invited by mail, but otherwise he went to a dance advertised in the *Post* and paid $3.50. He usually went with his friend, Louie, a dentist.

He did not need to go to them—many women sought him out—but he preferred the freedom, ever since his affair with Lillian. During the period my father was seeing Lillian, he lost twelve pounds and looked gaunt. He could not eat. "Men sit on her staircase on their lunch hours," he had told me, "eating their lunch out of paper bags and waiting for her. She has eighteen bikinis."

Now he stayed free. He didn't even like the idea of the bookshelves crammed with my old books at his apartment: "I feel like I'm married—I can't move!" he said.

"This Chinese girl in the brokerage office keeps bothering me, Bruce. She's not too attractive and I think she's marked lousy—"

"What do you mean?"

"She's a girl who doesn't get invited to these dances, so she has to look at the ads in the *Post* and pay to get in.

"She asked me for my phone number and she keeps calling me. 'I want you to hold me in your arms...' she says. 'I'm going to quit my job. I can't stand this anymore, seeing you every day. I'm ashamed of myself.' Then one afternoon I went to the office and I said hello to her. 'Get lost,' she says. I figure, well, maybe she doesn't know the English that well. 'Get lost?' I say to her. I laughed. 'You've been chasing me!'

"I wanted to make her feel better, so I took a photograph to the office, of myself and this beautiful blonde at a swimming pool. I wanted to show it to her to explain why I couldn't possibly be interested in her. She refused to look at it.

"When I go into the office, she grabs my hand. And she keeps calling me. Then yesterday she grabbed me behind the coatrack and said 'Please kiss me. Please.' What an iron grip she has."

My father cut his piece of cake in half, wrapped the second half in a napkin and put it in his pocket. He saved it for dessert later in the evening at home. He was embarrassed about it. "I'm afraid that if I die, they'll find me with a piece of cake in my pocket," he said, laughing.

"We went up to the Concord for the weekend, Louie and me. There was a get-together party, and for some reason, I don't know why, Louie really got mad at a guy there named Sid. He said, 'I just hate that guy!' There was a fellow standing with us, Larry, who I give rides to, and he said to Louie: 'You hate him? I hate him too. You see that girl he's with? I'm going to do you a favor. I'm going to fuck her for you.' "

"Why would that be a favor to Louie?" I asked.

"You ask me questions I can't answer, Bruce. That's what he said. Anyway, last night I got a phone call. It was from Larry. He said, 'Don't tell Louie. But I fucked that chick for him.' "

I shook my head. "Why shouldn't you tell Louie? I thought Larry was doing him a favor—"

"I agree with you, Bruce. But the moral I get from this is . . . everybody uses people. Larry uses me for rides to dances, and then lies to me."

"How does he lie to you?"

"He must be lying, or he wouldn't mind if I told Louie!"

V

Later in the year, my father told me more about Larry. During the rides that my father gave to him, Larry talked angrily about Bill Harris, who went to the same dances and socials. Occasionally my father would also give Bill Harris a ride up to the Concord or Grossinger's. Shortly after Larry had exploded for the third or fourth time about Bill, my father was riding in his car with Bill when he suddenly perked up his ears. Bill Harris was saying, "Larry's a user. I'm going to destroy him."

The next time he was going up to the Concord, my father took Larry along in the car. Within five minutes Larry was going into fits of rage about Bill Harris. Larry suddenly asked my father if he would introduce him to my father's friend Otto Blickstein, a lawyer. When they got back to Manhattan, my father took Larry to the Governor Cafeteria, to meet Otto Blickstein. Otto sat alone at a table, brooding. He was married to a younger woman, in her fifties. Otto had told my father he entered into his second marriage with the philosophy that ninety-seven percent of all marriages were unhappy, and so you had to work that much harder to make the marriage work, and do all the things that you really didn't want to be doing. This made your marriage happy and enlarged you as a person, he said.

Larry shook Otto's hand earnestly and said, "Counselor, I need your advice. I need a weapon." Otto asked why. "Counselor, my life is in danger from this big bruising hulk of a man who is threatening me at dances. He jabs me with his elbow. He takes my Jell-O."

Curious, my father interjected, "Who is that?"

Larry replied, "Bill Harris."

Otto explained to Larry that he needed proof, such as an actual physical attack. Larry said to Otto that Bill was needling and bugging him at singles dances, and that he was frightened.

At the next singles dance, my father took Bill Harris aside. He told him to lay off Larry and not bother him. Bill said to my father, "Larry? I'm scared of that guy. I'm not kidding. I'm afraid he's going to stick a knife in me."

Then there was the unnamed man at a dance who baffled my father, and made him fume. My father was with a girl named Sylvia who had a trick knee. The unidentified man came over to my father's table and asked Sylvia to dance. He kept Sylvia with him the rest of the evening. The next morning, my father, angry, saw him and said that he had some nerve the night before, taking Sylvia away like that.

"What? I wasn't interested in her, pal. There was this other guy with a girl I liked. I thought this other guy might like Sylvia and I could get a shot at the other chick." The man glared at my father. "What are you so huffy about? It had nothing to do with you," he said, and walked away.

VI

These are some of the stories my father told me on those afternoons at the Governor, watching my face to see if he had made me smile—much like the first time he agreed to eat a hamburger. It was at the Bun 'n' Burger last year. He laughed with gladness at my reaction.

"What's so funny?" I had said.

"There's nothing wrong with that," he had said. "I like your enthusiasm."

Food had been a source of friction between us for years: his fear of my chili-eating, my hamburgers, my consumption of spice.

"You're a man, Bruce," he said. "You're thirty-three years old. You've made me so proud of you. If you would only ease up on the pepper and salt, I'd be the happiest man in the world."

Our talks always moved back to his childhood, my childhood, and my mother. When I walked down the street to meet

him at the Governor, he still hid behind a storefront or a telephone pole and suddenly appeared, grinning, realizing it was
the same thing he had done when I was a child.

"That puppet!" he suddenly said one evening. "When you
were in the eighth grade, I looked for a puppet for you for
months. Bruce, when you went away to boarding school, you
came home on weekends carrying a shirt on a hanger. What was
the shirt with the hanger for? Do you remember, Bruce?"

I showed him my passport picture. "You look like a grown
man there!"

He paused. "When I was a kid, Bruce, my father gave me a
penny every Tuesday. You remember him, Bruce. Everyone said
he had such a good sense of humor, but I never saw it. All I remember is that on cold winter nights he made me hold candles
for him in the basement"—as he spoke, my father's hand went
up in the air as if he were holding the candle, and then it came
down again—"and if I said I was cold, he beat me with a poker.
He gave me nothing. Nothing. I'm amazed I function as well
as I do. I never had any decent clothes. I couldn't retain anything in school. I kept thinking about my problems. Singing! I
couldn't keep a tune. Woodwork—I'd die a thousand deaths.
My father wouldn't let me do anything. I wanted to play the sax-
ophone, and he said no. I pleaded with him. He said, 'Let the
rabbi decide.' The rabbi came to the house. I think my father
gave him a couple of dollars. The rabbi said no, that it would be
bad for my lungs.

"I worked as a waiter for the summer and gave him my salary.
He said unless I gave him the tips as well, he wouldn't let me go
to high school! I didn't, and I didn't get to go.

"Then when I met Jake, with his Stutz Bearcat—Jake's
friendship gave me the confidence to go out looking for a job.
When we met, it was like two girls. Jake is so sick now, Bruce.

"My father's English wasn't good. I heard him say on the
phone about himself to his tenants that he was coming over to
collect the rent and that they should look for the man with the
bird. He meant beard. I remember listening and thinking, 'What
can he mean, the man with the bird?' "

VII

The workshop had finally gotten around to considering my Sinatra story. Waiting for their reactions, I could not raise my head. They all knew I was a published writer and had taught creative writing.

The instructor, one year older than I, was bemused. "Not too bad, really."

They were all amazed at the innocence of the idea of a serious young writer traveling to Hollywood and getting in to see Sinatra at his mansion.

Having dreamt the scene over and over before I wrote it, I did not see what was so funny. I perspired, my hands trembled, I almost fell backwards with my chair.

Alfie, a fellow my age who lived with his roommate and mother in Bayside, said, peering at me over his glasses, "I think the persona should come on out of the closet; that would clear up the *déjà vu.*"

"How do you know he's *in* the closet?" I piped.

A significant pause from Alfie. "Oh, *come on.*"

The instructor said, "Of course, these things do sometimes happen in life. The star looking upon the young man as fresh sex, taking him under his wing, a pleasant diversion. I'd like to see if he seduces him—"

"Oh, never, never!" called out Alfie.

"That's not what I intended," I said, but they did not hear me.

Not wanting to go home yet, I tagged along when they adjourned for a coffee klatch at the Blimpie Base. I had raised their spirits. They chirped around me. Alfie took pity and sat next to me, pressing his leg against mine. "I've heard worse. Much worse," he said. He paused. "And better, too." Alfie placed his cigarette in its holder and blew.

VIII

My father and I talked easily now about things that once had ignited my embarrassment. He reminded me of how I had cried at Al Jolson's death, and I chimed in with the date: October 24, 1950. He talked about taking me to the Palace every week when they revived vaudeville in 1948, and about how much I had wanted to be a singer and a comic.

"You were so outgoing, so lively in those days, Bruce. What happened?"

I did not answer him.

"You corresponded with so many of those stars, you called them up on the phone. Dorothy Loudon is a big star now, Bruce. Remember when she was a newcomer on 'The Big Time' radio program with Georgie Price? You wrote her a fan letter and she sent you a picture inscribed 'to my first fan.' Then you called her on the phone. I don't think I ever told you this. Eight years later she was appearing at a night club. She was walking down the aisle and I said from my table, 'I'm Bruce Orav's father.' She screamed. She sat down at my table and we had a drink."

Then he said, "There are things I can tell you now, Bruce . . . after mommy and I were separated, we decided to try again after a while. But I rented a room at the Paris Hotel for six dollars a week just to get away to when I was upset . . . and in case things didn't go right . . . A friend of mine, Hal Saperstein, offered to share the cost of the room. He would use it on certain days and I would use it on others. Then I came in one day and he was there—with a woman! I was so mad I didn't speak to him for months. I assumed he wanted the room for the same reason I did: I never dreamed he wanted to play around. I never cheated on mommy."

IX

My father came to visit me, my wife, and my stepson Danny on a Saturday. It was his birthday. He would not eat and he always felt he was imposing when he visited people's homes, so it was a victory to get him into the apartment.

He was upset about his best friend, Jake, who was very sick and lying in the hospital, near death.

We mentioned the news story about Mama Cass choking on a ham sandwich and dying in a London hotel room.

"I thought the story was anti-Semitic," my father said.

"But she did die that way," I said.

"It's still anti-Semitic."

"You know," he said, "you're half my age now, Bruce. We've come a long way together. I've told you about Rupert Pike. Well, sometimes at the office I'll use his stapler, to staple some papers. Yesterday he suddenly said he was going to do me a favor. He said he had bought his stapler for five dollars, but would sell it to me for three. I said I didn't need one. Boy did he get angry!

"He just needed the three dollars, and I guess in his mind he had it all worked out beforehand. I said why are you so angry, and he said he needed the money to get by. So I just gave him two dollars."

"Did you take the stapler?"

"Oh no. I just let him have the money."

The cat came into the room and my father looked at it. "Does she really recognize you when you come home?" he asked.

We said she did.

"I had mice in my apartment. I came to like them, though. I bought a little mousetrap, and some cheese, and set traps for them. When I came home, if a mouse wasn't there, I'd miss him. Like fishing. It's creative—you should understand, Bruce, it's like writing."

We all went on the Staten Island Ferry, and sat outside, looking at Manhattan and the water and feeling the spray on our faces. My father held Danny's hand, and I sat listening.

"Did you ever realize, Danny, how amazing it is: we all have a nose, two eyes, and ears, and yet everyone looks different. Look at all those faces." They gazed at the people passing by them as they came onto the ferry. "How can that be? Of course, it has to be that way, otherwise it would be so confusing, trying to tell each other apart. It just goes to show, though, there must be someone up there . . . And voices! We all have different voices. It's so amazing. Look at those faces . . ."

X

I had lunch with my father Rosh Hashanah eve at the Governor. Jake had died a month before. My father was preparing to go to services sponsored by a singles group in Great Neck. He was miffed; the ad had said the services would be held in a synagogue. Now "spillover" was causing the services to be moved to a church.

"I was thinking of Jake today, Bruce. He's been gone a month now, may he rest in peace. I never told you this before, Bruce, but I can tell you now. After separating from mommy, I hadn't slept with a girl in six years. Jake was worried about me. He said you had to exercise it or you would never be able to use it again. So he got two prostitutes when his wife was away. We went to his house in Forest Hills. He went running up the stairs, this fat little guy, closing all the window shades in the house so the neighbors couldn't see. Although they saw us arrive anyway. And he said he was doing it for me! But he brought along one for himself anyway. You remember him, Bruce . . . this fat little guy on his short legs running up the stairs. Afterwards he asked my girl if I had done all right . . . "

"Dad, do you ever see Rupert Pike anymore?"

My father's face lit. "Yes. Today, as a matter of fact. He asked me for a dollar for an ice cream soda. He knows that if I think he's going to have a martini I won't give it to him. He has a new girl friend he picked up on the Bowery. He says she's a princess. She told him she has $700,000 but Welfare is keeping it for her because she's unstable. I asked him if she'd ever been institutionalized. He said, 'Mmmm . . . I think so,' and smiled. What a fellow.

"You know, Bruce, you've said some terrible things about mommy to me. Do you think she treated me badly?"

"Yes. Yes, I do."

"Why don't I see it? I think about it and think about it and can't agree with you. How could I expect better treatment? I saw how she treated her own father—like a dog. So I certainly couldn't expect her to treat me better than her own father!

"There were a couple of times I was afraid she was going to poison me."

"Seriously?"

"It was ridiculous . . . I was afraid the two of them, your mother and grandmother, would poison me because I wouldn't give mommy a divorce. But she wouldn't have had the nerve.

"Your grandfather was afraid . . . maybe this is why . . . he was afraid they would poison him a couple of times when they gave him a glass of water. And he hardly even had any life insurance! It was silly.

"When I dated your mother, we would come home to her house and she would put on an apron and go into the kitchen. An apron! She'd come out with some food as if she cooked it. But her mother did all the cooking. She'd never cooked in her life. I found out later. She put a chicken in a pot and burned the whole thing. She didn't even know it needed water to boil. She laughed about it—she had a sense of humor. We laughed together. I can't complain. Those first years we were married, living in her parents' house . . . the two of us in that master bedroom, having a ball, while her mother cooked for us. She was . . . a princess.

"I saw your mother again, about five years ago. I hadn't seen her for many years. I was at the Laurels Country Club for the weekend. She came walking through the door. I was talking to a girl, Rhonda, who had asked me to drive her home at the end of the weekend and I had agreed. That's what these women are like at these places. When you meet them, the first thing they try to get is a free ride home on Sunday nights. But when I saw your mother, I said you'll have to excuse me—that's my ex-wife—and if she needs a ride home I will want to take her. I went up to Mommy. And you know the first thing she said to me? 'You're not going to drive her home?' 'Who?' I said. And she pointed to Rhonda. 'I can't stand her,' Mommy said. After all this time.

"And we danced together, and talked, and I spent time with her. At the end of the weekend on Sunday, she said, 'Please drive me home.' I said of course I would, but that I had promised I would drive Rhonda as well and a promise is a promise. I would take them both home. 'But I hate that one,' she said. I said I had to. Finally she agreed. Then she said—listen to this, Bruce—'Is she going to sit in the front seat beside you?' " My father laughed. "I teased her and said yes. Then I said: 'Of course not. You're my ex-wife. You'll sit in the front seat beside me.' Then she said, 'Who will you take home first?' 'I'll take her home first.'

"So I drove them home, Rhonda first. Your mother invited me up for a drink. So I went upstairs, and I saw the apartment—your little room—after so many years. You can't understand this, Bruce, but I saw the bed you slept in. She said, 'You're not going to call that girl, are you?' I said, 'Of course not.' We had a drink, and talked, and then I got up to go.

"At the door I chucked her on the cheek—like this." My father tapped his cheek with his knuckle. "I know I could have kissed her . . . that she would just melt . . . with loneliness.

"I didn't . . . She has no one, Bruce. If you don't give, you don't receive . . .

"And you know the last thing she said to me? 'I'll bet you're going to call her.' "

My father shook his head.

11

8:30 TO 10:00 P.M.

I learn tonight that, although my seventy-five-year-old father has been claiming increasing deafness for years, he can hear perfectly well. At least, that appears to be the case when he listens to his girl friend Rosie talk. He does not cup his ear, shout, or ignore her words, as he does mine.

My wife, Susan, and I are on a double date with my father and Rosie. It is the night before New Year's Eve. We want to look her over and encourage my father's first real relationship since the divorce—thirty years ago. He agreed to the evening, although he will not tell us Rosie's last name.

Rosie is a beautiful woman, after a long parade of women in their fifties and sixties with peroxide blonde hair, with their minks and jewelry, glistening from every pore. She is dark and smoky. She looks perhaps fifty—a remarkable fifty. My father has always preferred blondes and "clean, white skin." He still recalls with pain his mother calling him "nigger," because of his complexion.

My father calls Rosie—unlike me—by her right name. He has been calling me Louie, the name of his best friend, lately.

Rosie's name is her greatest asset, for it is the name of my mother. "Imagine, after all these years!" my father said when we drove to pick Rosie up tonight.

But she has a fatal shortcoming: a spinal injury that has caused her to lose the use of her foot. She walks with a cane, and has been getting steadily worse. My father says he only sees her now out of pity.

Earlier in the evening, we drove to Rosie's apartment house and found her waiting at the curb at eight-thirty. A neighbor was chatting with her as we arrived. It was difficult to move her into the car; she was almost unable to walk. Once she was settled and introductions were made, my father laughed heartily and said:

"Well, you didn't waste any time."

"Samuel, he is a neighbor—a married man."

"That's all right, you have a right to be friendly with whomever you want. You're a free agent." My father continued to laugh and went on in this way until we reached the restaurant.

My father usually talks to people about his flashy Cadillac (purchased for $2,000), his trips to the Concord, cruises. Then he will deny, with a coy laugh, that he has any money. He does not want to be believed.

But now my father is talking about a subject he is ashamed of: the loss of his office. As an inactive insurance salesman, he had been placed in the bullpen years ago, a nest of desks clustered together in one room and shared by the old-timers. "It's finally happened, what I've dreaded all these years," he says. "The manager called me in. They're taking my desk away. But he was very nice: I asked him if I could keep my mail drop, and he said I could. And the company is shipping my file cabinet to my apartment and paying the cost themselves. Some of the other managers would act as if I was a blind spot in their eye."

A young man with a butter tray greets Rosie and tells her that he is graduating from high school in the spring. They discuss his future.

My father rolls his eyes and says through his teeth, "My God,

I can't turn around for a minute." He says this with his rakish laugh, showing his uninvolvement.

"Samuel, he is a boy. Why can't you trust me?" She places her hand over his. He starts to speak but doesn't. He quiets down.

"My ex-husband has been adopted by a family in Hong Kong," Rosie says to us. "He went there to import kosher Chinese food. Something happened to him in his fifties. He grew afraid, and he became a manic-depressive. Then he started playing around. I'm not sorry about our marriage. There were good years. I wanted to be an actress when I was growing up. I was a member of the chorus in synagogue musicals, then I graduated to speaking roles."

"You didn't tell them you wore tights," my father says.

"I was just getting to that, Samuel. I wore tights—black leotards." Rosie holds out her cigarette for my father to light. He does.

"A legal adoption?" I ask, getting back to her husband.

"Legally, Bruce. They went through the courts. He's a charming man, my ex-husband, when he wants to be, and an erudite man. I learned from him. He had intellectuals over to the house. I listened. But I was never intellectual—"

My father opens his mouth wide in astonishment.

"I've never heard you talk so much."

"Well, Samuel, you generally talk more. I'll shut up—" She continues. "When I was a child, my mother beat me with a cat-o'-nine-tails. And she would get up on a chair to beat my brother—"

"I'm a naughty boy, I shouldn't say anything," my father says.

"That's all right, Samuel. I'm finished." She peeks at him, amused. She smiles and dimples appear on both cheeks.

"I'm mean, aren't I?"

"I find you very kind and thoughtful, Samuel."

My father looks at her and is silent.

Susan says to my father: "Rosie looks very much like Mary Tyler Moore."

"Yes, she does," my father replies immediately. He gazes at Rosie.

My father and I are in the street. Rosie wants to smoke, and so, by mutual agreement, after their biweekly dinner, he goes for a walk. Susan has stayed with Rosie.

"I like her very much," I say.

"Look, I give the devil his due. She's a lovely woman."

"You ought to marry her."

He stops in the street. "You're funny, Louie. I don't even like her. I only talk to her because I know it gives her pleasure, and I feel sorry for her because of her clubfoot."

"You do like her."

"And she's wonderful company—I resent that too," he says.

I laugh.

"I do. I had a car accident because of her. And I like change—excitement. This is a routine, Louie. That's why I make it every other week. And I don't even want that. First I would see her at seven. Then seven-thirty. Then eight. Now eight-thirty. I'm not seeing her New Year's Eve. I'll see her New Year's Day instead. I don't want any responsibility, Louie. Her children treat her badly and I get upset."

"She's a real companion."

He stops in the street and tugs at my arm. He enumerates with each finger all the things in life he enjoys: "I go to these singles dances. I'm the most popular man there. They send me invitations—I don't even have to pay the three-fifty admission. Poor Rosie's been marked lousy with her foot. They don't even send her invitations. You should see me do the hustle. I make jokes to young girls in elevators. I'll say to a girl: 'Is there a modeling school in this building?' At first she'll frown. Then she smiles when she gets it. I wake up when I please. I have my roast chicken from the kosher butcher and yogurt. I read my paper. Louie thinks I'm crazy to be seeing her. He says to me: 'Why are you wasting your time?' "

"You're afraid," I say.

"Of what?"

"Of getting hurt again. Of being betrayed—like my mother betrayed you."

"Louie, I like excitement. She doesn't excite me. I haven't

had sex with her since her foot operation four years ago. I brought her into the hospital walking straight and tall, and she came out with a cane—and she's had the cane ever since, poor thing."

"But she's beautiful."

"She used to be more beautiful. You should have seen her then, standing so straight. It was a pleasure to be seen with her."

He stops in the street again.

"Bruce, I see you and Susan and I'll admit it's very nice to see what you have together. That I admit. But I'm too old and set."

"I think you love her."

He laughs and laughs. "Let's go back to the restaurant. Love her? I don't even like her! If it wasn't for the bum leg I wouldn't even see her anymore! Love her? I wish she'd get better so she could date other men. But she's getting worse, she's so bent over and stooped."

Susan and Rosie are waiting for us. Rosie's limp is worse—she can hardly move the leg.

In the car, my father says, "Maybe your neighbor will be waiting for you at the curb!" He drives her to her house and helps her out into the street. We say good-bye at ten.

We drive off.

When I speak, my father says, "Speak louder, Louie. You know I'm deaf."

12

THE ARREST

I

I was in trouble. My wife was in the hospital and I was stuck with my fifteen-year-old stepson, Danny, at home. A lump had suddenly appeared in Susan's neck. It was very painful. It got bigger. A dental problem, the doctor said. The oral surgeon agreed and made an incision in my wife's neck. The lump got bigger. She lay wide awake in bed through the nights, the pain cutting through her, touching the lump. I would awaken every few hours and know she was up, staring into the dark. A neck surgeon looked at it and placed my wife in the hospital within two hours.

We had been married only four years. Danny was in the shadows. I had nothing in common with him, I thought. I had met Susan when I was a graduate student in Vancouver.

Now in Manhattan I was alone with the kid and two cats and Susan dangerously sick in the hospital and a full-time job. A little freedom might have its rewards, I had thought—more time to work on my writing—but I ran between the job, the hospital, and the apartment, where I cooked or handed Danny money for food, fed the cats, shopped, and drank. I ate after leaving Susan at the hospital at eleven at night, long after my appetite was gone.

Just a month before Susan was hospitalized, we had been on our way to a loft theater in Hell's Kitchen. We passed Polyclinic Hospital, where I was born. I told Susan of this, and she said, "Shalom" (the only Jewish word she knew). I kissed her that moment, and held her.

At 11 P.M. I left the hospital, a gnawing hunger in me, but as usual put off eating until later, after Danny was deposited in bed, after I'd had a drink and fed the cats. A little oblivion.

I had a drink and thought about food. Three Chinese restaurants on the block—which one was less lonely to eat in alone? I thought about it, weighing the differences, the pluses and minuses, and had a second drink, a third. A nuisance, getting into the elevator, to the restaurant, and so forth. I wondered why Danny wasn't home.

I sat down at the typewriter. I decided I would write a letter to Charles Bukowski, who was finally making it since the freaks decided he was okay, that he liked to kick ass, beat up chicks and hassle landladies.

I felt I had a mission. Bukowski had written nastily of Sinatra. "I have long waited to tell you this, Buk," I wrote, "but you are wrong about Frank. I've had a few drinks and now I'll finally tell you. Frank and you have a lot in common. You're both bastards, and you both have talent. So listen to his voice, Buk, get to know one another, and let there be peace between you at last. Doobie doobie doo."

The phone rang. I took it into the bedroom, kicked aside the clothes and shoes and cartons of bones from TV dinners and lay down on the bed.

"This is Officer O'Malley of the twenty-third precinct. Is this the father of Daniel Van Der Dyke?"

"No it is not."

"Who is this?"

"This is Bruce Orav."

"Is not the aforementioned Daniel Van Der Dyke your son?"

"I have no son."

"He says you're his father."

"Look, officer, my wife is in the hospital. I have just left her there. She is very ill. Danny is her son. I am very disturbed. I have had no dinner. I am exhausted."

"I am very sorry to hear that, sir. But your son has been arrested on a serious charge. He has been painting graffiti on subway cars."

"Of course he has. My wife encourages him to do that. She thinks it's a healthy outlet."

"You will have to come down and pick up your son."

I paused, bit the telephone chord, and pounded the bed with my fist.

"Look. Officer. I have just left my wife in the hospital."

"I understand, Mr. Van Der Dyke. But if you don't come to pick up your boy, at dawn he will have to be remanded to reform school. I will give you traveling instructions by subway to Queens."

"How far is it?"

"It's very far, sir. On the tip."

I told him to wait a moment, that I would get a pen and paper. I found a paper bag on the floor and ripped a piece off of it.

"Look, I can't come. It would take me hours to get there. I'd be there at 3 A.M. Send him to reform school. We'll get him back later."

"It is my duty to warn you, Mr. Van Der Dyke, that if you are not here by 3 A.M., and I am not trying to threaten or warn you, that you are the person cognizant and responsible. I am terribly afraid it would not look nice to the judge, and this is not a warning, if you were to shirk your responsibility as the responsible parent. What time may we expect you, sir?"

I had slid to the floor. They had me. They at last had me. They would crucify me.

"What time, sir?"

"I don't know. 3 A.M."

"I would hope by 3 A.M., Sir. 4 A.M. would be too late. We will wait for you until 3 A.M."

They gave me involved instructions, left and right turns at corners when I got off the subway. I scribbled furiously, cursing, all over the rest of the brown paper bag.

I jammed the paper into my pocket and threw the phone against the wall.

"How did this happen to me?" I screamed. "How the fuck did I get into this mess?"

I ran around the room hitting the walls. "And I can't even tell his mother about it. He figured it out perfectly."

II

I had a final drink, stumbled out into the street, and ran into the Kentucky Fried Chicken store. I had to have something to eat. I actually felt less nervous tonight than usual with the street people around me—after all, if they touched me now, I would kill them.

I paid for the chicken, took the box, and went down into the subway station. I looked down the tracks; nothing coming. I was almost alone; just one other person. I noticed I was talking to myself. I ate the chicken and tossed the bones out onto the tracks. "This is not happening to me," I said.

The train finally came. I had made a decision. I got off at Times Square and wandered down the street among the hookers and muggers, looking for a phone. A hooker in platform shoes and a blonde wig grabbed at my balls. I reeled away.

There was a phone by the pinball machine in the arcade. I called my father in Brooklyn and woke him up. I told him what had happened and screamed at him, "I can't take this, I can't take this, I can't take this anymore."

"Listen to me, darling," my father said. "Bruce, listen to me. Everything is going to be all right. I will be there. Where are you? I want you to wait for me. We'll go together to the police station."

"I'm not signing anything!" I screamed.

"You don't have to sign. I'll sign."

We agreed to meet at Nathan's on Times Square. It would take my father an hour—to dress, walk to the subway, and travel there. I walked around the Square and had another drink. Everywhere the landmarks were gone: Toffernetti's had been where Nathan's now stood, with its giant strawberry shortcake in the window and its organist; gone were the Paramount and the Automat off Eighth Avenue and the Laffmovie where my father had taken me every Sunday. In their place was violent porn, blank, sullen eyes, and red hats. A bodiless beggar: a head, shoulders, arms, hands holding pencils, scooted himself along the ground on a wooden platform with wheels. Immaculately dressed Moslems had set up a little table and were selling pamphlets; their hand-lettered sign said, "Whites, nothing you can do now."

As I stood in front of Nathan's, there was my father coming toward me, nattily dressed, handsome, smiling, blowing kisses, walking his jerky walk, making his way in the neon lights among the killers: "Excuse me kindly, thank you, excuse me," to my side. He hugged and kisssed me and said: "Just like old times, Bruce. Haven't I always been there when you needed me? Just answer this question: Haven't I? And you're a man now, Bruce, you're thirty-eight years old."

"I don't want to sign anything. I don't want any trouble. He's not my son."

My father guided me into Nathan's. "I want you to eat something first, bubby—"

"I just ate—"

"How about a roast beef sandwich, a knish, a frankfurter? You have to watch your cholesterol. The roast beef on a bun looks good. You used to love that at McGuinness's."

I said I didn't want to eat, and my father got angry. "Don't upset me, Bruce." He plunked down the sandwich on the table and I began to eat it. "Tell me the truth. Isn't it delicious?" he said. "Anyway, at least I'm getting a chance to see you tonight, Bruce."

I put my hat down on the table.

"Take that hat off the table!"

"What?"

My father bopped it off. I picked it up off the floor. "What should I do with it then?"

"Put it on the chair, naturally!"

My father shook his head at me. "You do that just to be mean, don't you?"

"Do what?"

"Put your hat on the table. Just to mock me."

"I don't know what you're talking about."

After a pause, my father said, "I learned a lesson I never forgot a long time ago. Maybe I never told you this, Bruce. Stop me if I'm boring you. I had a business appointment with a very important, successful executive. He ushered me into his office like a gentleman, and we began to talk.

"I placed my hat on his desk in front of me. As we were talking, his son quietly walked over, without saying a word, picked up my hat, and placed it in the closet. I was so humiliated! It taught me a lesson I have never forgotten. When I was out on the street later, I remembered that I had forgotten my hat in the closet. Of course I couldn't go back. The amazing thing is, I went back to that office for another appointment three months later. On my way out, I got my coat from the closet and looked up: there was my hat! No one had touched it."

"Did you take it?" I asked my father.

"Of course! I grabbed it."

After I finished eating, my father took my hand and we walked across Times Square to the subway. "We've been through a lot together, Bruce. You know I wouldn't let you down."

"I'm not going to sign anything."

"I'll sign. I'll assume all responsibility—"

"But they'll want to know who I am—" I screamed at my father.

"They won't want to know anything. Let me take care of it. They won't even see you. You'll wait outside the police station while I go in and get Danny. Now I want you to stop being so upset, Bruce. What would you do without me?"

We weaved in and out among the crowds.

"I DON'T WANT ANYTHING BUT I RESPECT YOU PEOPLE TREMEN-DOUSLY." A black beggar had touched my father on the shoulder and my father stepped back in shock. "Come on, Bruce," he shouted, and took my hand again. We hurried off, my father's head bobbing up and down in fear. We went down into the subway.

It was 2 A.M.

III

At the subway stop in Queens, we walked down the steps into the street. The subway station had a coal stove and a winding pipe going up to the ceiling. We walked in the pleasant night air. It was an old-fashioned, Irish-Italian neighborhood. After several blocks we spotted the police station in the distance, blazing in the dark night. My father went inside the station. I stood outside among the lolling cops. I saw through the window two young cops boxing with each other. I felt conspicuous, and decided to follow my father inside.

Two cops approached us—the boxers. They were still jabbing at each other. They had beards and jeans. They were supportive, hip types. They said they were in charge of the case. "I'm Chaim and this is Pedro."

"Are you the father?" they said to my father, and told me my "brother" was inside. My father signed the papers.

The two cops were very hip; they kept boxing and wrestling with each other. They fell to the floor and wrestled. My father and I waited.

Chaim got up first and said, "Look, this is all bullshit. But we got to enter it. Your son got caught painting graffiti on a subway in the trainyard." He moved closer. "Generally kids committing crimes like this—and I'm not assuming anything—are from broken homes with emotionally disturbing factors. The kids are trying to get attention—love—"

Then we saw Danny standing there, not particularly upset, but solicitous, concerned.

"How could you do this to your mother?" my father asked.

Danny thought about it and shrugged. "I don't know." I knew
Danny found it an irrelevant question. He hadn't done it to his
mother. He had done it to me.

I could not bear to look at him.

The trial date was set.

IV

The three of us walked to the subway. Danny led us, since my
father and I had already forgotten the way.

"Aren't you ashamed?" my father kept asking Danny, holding my hand as we walked on the lamplit street.

"Sure," Danny said. "Yeah."

We waited at the station platform for the train. Danny kept
trying to reassure us: that the train would come soon, that he
knew the way back to Manhattan. My father and I held hands.

Danny, getting no response, stood farther away from us. From
a distance, he said to my father, "I hope you feel okay. I really
feel bad about this."

At Times Square, Danny and I took the uptown train and my
father took the train back to Brooklyn. I watched my father
walking off. He was suddenly walking very slowly.

Sitting side by side on the train, Danny and I did not speak.

V

Susan was operated on later that week. Looking up at me just
before the operation, she had said, "Whatever happens, I will be
happy, because I know you love me."

I wept and walked the streets.

The operation took seven hours. Susan recovered completely.

The doctor appeared and probed the open hole in her neck.
Jesus. This is life. I am watching life.

I watched, clenching my teeth.

What might my own son have been like? Would he have looked like me?

Only once have I seen a child who reminded me of myself.

A little boy of four or five on the Greyhound bus with his parents. The mother was an obese Oriental. The father was a chunky, handsome, blonde man with a comb in his back pocket. The father made the child sit in his own seat adjacent to him across the aisle. The child looked like a cross between the two parents. I was seated behind them.

The child tried to climb on his mother's lap.

The mother screamed, *"I could kill that kid!"* She lurched away, pushing him off.

She hissed, "Don't let him come near me. I've seen shit. Don't tell me about shit, man, I've had it with shit."

The child tried again to climb on her lap. She pushed him away.

The father put the boy back in his seat and gave him a bun to eat and a comic book: *Archie Junior*.

The child gnawed at the bun, and kept peering at the mother. He had a sunny look that darkened when he looked over at her.

The father reached over and stroked his son. "I hate that kid," the mother said.

The mother quieted down when the bus started to move. She purred and kissed the father on the lips, running her hand through his hair.

The boy kept trying to join them. The father gently put him back in the seat, mediating between them. The boy looked at the other children on the bus. I watched him as he looked at them, then at their parents, observing their relationships. The boy watched hungrily. When the other children laughed, a laugh began to form on his face. He would begin to read his comic book, look around, look at me, and turn his head to stare at the other children again.

When I looked up later, the boy was silently vomiting. His mother stared. His father took a paper bag and handed it to the child. When he finished, the child glanced at his mother guiltily.

The father took the boy in his arms and carried him to the bathroom in the back of the bus.

The hours went by. I could not bear to watch the child, and could not pull my eyes away from him.

The mother did not speak to the child once. When she finally fell asleep, the boy climbed into his father's arms and the father held him, cradling his head. The child slept, remaining in the same position, without moving, for the rest of the trip.

VI

I waited two weeks to tell Susan about the arrest. I seethed, waiting to tell her. I led up to it, and she could see how upset I was. "Something's wrong," she said. She asked me to lie down on her bed in the hospital room.

"There isn't room for the two of us," I said.

"I'll sit on the chair," she said.

"No," I said.

"It's okay, honey, I feel much better," she said.

I lay down on the bed.

"I have a headache," I said.

"I'll get you a cold cloth."

She laid a cold towel over my forehead, and sat down in the chair by the bed, waiting for me to speak.

Looking up at her, I began. Slowly and dramatically, punctuating my account with little outbursts of outrage, I told her about the arrest.

13

A Sense of
Responsibility

I

I was forty years old and I was about to quit my job. I would have to tell my father.

I had decided during a lunch hour break. I realized I did not care as much as I once did for the suffering of other people. It sprung to my mind—beggars were beggars; the elderly were just old; criminals were constituted that way; children were cunning; all blacks were anti-Semitic. Did I mean this? The day before I had watched my wife, Susan, pick up a twenty-dollar bill from the ground and go running after a woman with a baby tied crooked on her back who she thought had dropped it. Was Susan certain? I was surprised at her spontaneous action, and I was surprised at my own reaction to what my wife had done. Would I have given the woman the money? I wondered. Is this the way it went, sneaking up on you? "Slip sliding away," sang Paul Simon. Libriums all day long, then alcohol. I had watched a colleague in the office, a man in his sixties, each day turn the newspaper first to the TV page, then the obituary page to watch for the deaths of friends.

I had returned to my cubicle, exhausted from the hour.
I had decided then to give notice.

II

"I want you to know, Bruce, that no matter what, my every
thought was my love for you, day and night." I read the rest of
the death note my father had left on the desk. There was the
usual information about the will, the stocks and bonds. My
father was in the bathroom shaving. I had traveled out to his
apartment in Brooklyn to tell him about my decision.

When he came out of the bathroom, my father snapped up the
note, folded it, and put it away in the desk. "I hope you didn't
read this, Bruce. You probably did, didn't you?"

"No."

"Well, it doesn't matter. You need to know these things in
case something happens."

My father was seventy-four and healthy. For many years
there had been a ritual: roundabout instructions about what to
do if he died. He had given me a key to a safe deposit box—and
taken it back. Whenever he brought up the subject, I was embarrassed. "There'll be plenty of money for you, Bruce," he said
as he closed the desk drawer. Was I supposed to smile? Shake my
father's hand in gratitude? Show despair? Wasn't this supposed
to be good news? I tried to keep my expression noncommittal—
my father watched carefully. Then he told me about a file cabinet at his office where there was spare cash—two or three
hundred dollars. "I used to keep thousands there—when I was
doing a lot of business. But don't worry—there'll be plenty for
you." Then came a hasty roundup of more instructions, which
I would need to write down to remember. But could I actually
sit down and write out the information then and there? My
father was still scrutinizing me. Suddenly he said, "Don't look
so interested, Bruce. I'm not leaving you so fast."

I did not tell my father my decision that evening.

III

My father had lived in a one-bedroom apartment since the divorce, in 1947, and had always had a Cadillac to greet the world with, and dapper shirts and ties—all purchased at a fraction of their cost. "The only thing that counts in this world is money," he had repeated ever since I was a child. "Love, friendship—nothing lasts."

Money, and a smile. I had recently watched television with my father. We had seen a commercial about a denture cream that allowed the woman on the screen to "have her smile back." "Isn't that wonderful?" my father's voice came from behind me in the darkness.

I remembered driving alone with my father when I was a boy, the two of us singing "When You're Smiling," my father hitting the wheel as we sang. My father had talked constantly about the importance of smiling. A smile made people like you, and it didn't cost anything. He sang to me at bedtime—"Smile, Darn Ya, Smile," "There Are Smiles That Make You Happy," "Let a Smile Be Your Umbrella," and "Powder Your Face with Sunshine."

IV

The following week, my father called me at my office at *Animals* and asked me to come out to Brooklyn. "Can you give me a little time?" he asked. "Not a chance, huh? No luck, huh? Are you so hopped up on your writing you can't give your father a break?"

"I'll be over at eight," I said. "I have something I want to tell you."

I sat across from my father in the living room and felt an old feeling—that once again nothing would be said.

"Bruce, you aren't listening to me. I have to give you my safe deposit key one of these days. We never really talk, Bruce. I feel you're so far away. What's your favorite TV show?"

"I don't watch TV."

"I was just watching a show about the rise of the Nazis. Tsk, tsk, tsk. It was expensive: parades, rallies, uniforms. Where did they get so much money, Bruce?"

I didn't answer.

My father got up to put cheese in the mousetrap.

"What do you do with your extra time?"

"I write."

"I know that. I meant besides—"

"Then why do you ask me such a question?"

"I know you're a writer. I'm very proud of you. I think your writing is terrific. You're busy as a cockroach."

I began to think about the money: why couldn't I have some of it now? Just how much was there? Even that letter of instruction was odd—the most concrete thing in it was the initial to look under in the file cabinet. Without the safe deposit key, how would I get in? Could my father read these thoughts of mine? How did they creep into my head? If something real was said between us, these thoughts would go away—but in the boredom, there they were.

A real thing to say might be: Do you think of me as a cockroach? But my father would deny the matter any importance. He often said to me, "You're the one who saw the psychiatrists; you have the understanding—so you should be the one to forgive." (Yet my father, ten years ago, had seen a psychiatrist too—the one he suspected of tearing checks out of envelopes while he lay on the couch talking.)

My father snapped his leather easy chair backwards and stretched out. Now he came to the books he was reading—usually biographies of Hitler, Nixon, FDR, Churchill, Goering, or Joe McCarthy, or the story of the tortured life of a famous writer. "I'm reading about Dostoevski's life," he said. "What a terrible existence! And his wife was a pretty young girl. What did she want him for? All great writers, all great artists, live such miserable lives. Are you a great artist?"

I didn't answer.

"How are you feeling, Bruce? How's your sinusitis?"

"I hate my job at *Animals*."

My father sighed, clamped his jaw shut, and then said, "Well, that I can't help. Everyone hates their job. I always hated mine. In Bridgeport, I used to sit in the bathroom for hours, afraid to come out. What makes you think your job should be any different? What I went through, nobody will ever know . . .

"I want to tell you the latest about Louie, Bruce. He's so fat, Bruce. You know how he's been taking the tickets at these singles dances we go to. He volunteered. It's five dollars a week, but that isn't the reason he does it. He likes the authority it gives him—taking the ticket, greeting the girls. A dentist, and so insecure. And he gets free drinks. With a few drinks in him, he loosens up. Stop me if I'm boring you with this. Louie got a phone call from the hostess of the party. She told him they would have to stop giving him free liquor. It was really their way of getting rid of him. After all, he doesn't even take the tickets right. He gets flustered and lets people go through. Louie told me about this, and boy was he upset! He sent them a telegram offering his resignation! But then the days passed and he started thinking about it and decided he'd been rash. He called up, rescinding his resignation—sad, isn't it?"

"Dad, I'm quitting my job."

"You think it's sad?"

"I'm quitting my job."

There was a pause.

"Uh huh. Going on welfare? Food stamps?"

"I'm going to devote full time to my writing."

"You don't have an honest bone left in your body, do you?

"After all *Animals* has done for you. Medical benefits, pension, a month vacation—"

"I want—"

"You want, you want. We all want. I want. Everybody wants."

"I want to work at my writing."

"So keep your job and write when you can, like you've been doing."

"I can't do that anymore, I can't keep up that pace. It's one or the other."

"Bruce, I can't tell you what to do. You have a good job, security, you're functioning better than I ever dreamed you could, and you want to throw it away. What will you do all day long—you'll go crazy."

"I'll be writing."

"You'll have too much time on your hands, like me. You have no hobbies, like me. You can't even dance, while I at least have learned to do the hustle. You just don't want to work—"

"I do want to work."

"You know what I mean. You want to do what's pleasant, what you like. That's easy. Everybody likes to do what's easy. I would myself, but I don't let myself. That's always been your problem. Buying all those books. You'll never get to read them. You like to write. That's easy for you. The challenge is to do what's unpleasant, what you hate. While I've denied myself my entire life. I could be having a ball—buying books, going to the theater and movies like you and Susan do. I could travel all over the world. Instead I've been saving it all for you."

"Oh, for Christ sake. You haven't worked in thirty-five years!"

"What are you talking about?"

"Didn't you retire at forty?"

My father laughed. "Are you crazy?"

"Well, what the hell do you call it? Sleeping until noon, moseying by bus into Manhattan to look at the stock exchange, dropping by to kibitz with the boys in the office, where you told me you took your afternoon snooze on the couch, then picking up your roast chicken and your yogurt and taking the subway home. Wasn't that your goddamn routine? It still is!"

"I'm seventy-four years old! I'm an old man!"

"But you've been doing it as long as I've known you! And I want the time to work, for Christ sake."

"I worked like a dog, and for you! When I lived with your mother, I worked day and night, going into all those strange offices and houses. I cringed every time, knowing they didn't want me. I was just a stranger to them, trying to sell them something they didn't want. I died a thousand deaths, I was so shy. And this is the thanks I get. Coming home at 3 P.M. to pick you up from school when you were a little boy and take you home—"

"You wanted my company."

"Who else did I have? You were my life, you were the only person I had, and you were so sweet then, you loved me."

I stood up. "I'm going home."

"You loved me when you were a little boy. You used to say, 'Daddy, I love you more than anything in the world.' I have your postcards and letters from camp. Here, I'll show them to you, since you've forgotten everything." My father rummaged through the desk and took out a stack of letters and postcards and held them out toward me.

"Take them!" I took a postcard and saw all the X's at the bottom of the card under my name.

"You loved me then."

"I love you now."

I took my father into my arms.

V

I met my father for lunch in front of the *Animals* building at noon on the Wednesday after I had told him of my decision. As I walked toward him, I saw that he held money in his hands, glinting in the sun. He tried to jam it into my pocket. I moved away. "Take it! Take it!" my father shouted. "The dollar-fifty for lunch at the Automat last week; I forgot to compensate you for it. You know I never let you pay for our lunch."

My father again tried to shove the dollar and two quarters at me. "*Take it! Take it! Take it!*" A small audience of staff members of the magazine gathered to watch. The old man's face was flushed with anger.

I walked off. "Come on, goddamn it," I said.

My father hurried beside me, holding the money, aiming it at my pocket.

We walked to the Fifty-seventh Street Horn and Hardart. It was one of the last remaining Automats. As a boy, I had loved them. My father and I had eaten almost all our meals at them.

Now they were empty and abandoned, the flies hovering over the food. A tiny woman, her face frail as a skull, her eyes hollow, sat all day at the middle table, her booted foot marking time. I tried not to look at her. The wall behind where we sat boomed and shuddered as we talked; the employees in the kitchen were clattering dishes. One of them kept screaming, "Rack and ruin!"

After a moment, my father said, "Bruce, I read a very interesting story the other day by Somerset Maugham. It was about a young man who was very dedicated to art. He wants to be an artist, you know? A pianist. Despite his father's opposition, he quits his job and goes to live in an artist's garret, practically starving to death. For years he practices on the piano. Guess what happens?"

"I don't expect a happy ending," I said.

"How did you know, Bruce? Have you read the story? At the end, the young man realizes, after years of practice, that he has stubby fingers! He will never be a great pianist. And he shoots himself."

My father smiled peacefully and settled back.

Now my father took an envelope out of his jacket pocket and dangled it in front of me. I knew what it was. "The premium on the life insurance policy is due again, Bruce. Three hundred and fifty-four dollars."

My father waited for my response.

I gritted my teeth, and said, "Lot of money."

"It *is* a lot of money. And I'm not doing any business anymore. I'm not sure I can keep it up much longer. Should I give it up?"

"Dad, we go through this every six months."

"Well, I'm serious. You're not showing any sense of responsibility."

"Give it up."

"Well, I may."

"Give it up. Don't give it up. Have it your way."

"You resent my bringing this up," he said.

"Right."

"Why?"

"I don't know how to tell you."

"Try."

"It shouldn't . . . be spoken about."

"How would you know I was paying it?"

"My God, I know by now."

"It's not easy for me to raise this sum of money. Nothing's coming in anymore. I'd like a little appreciation."

"You'd have it if you didn't ask for it."

"I don't understand," my father said. "I just want a little pleasure from it, but you won't give an inch. You deny me the least satisfaction."

We walked down Fifty-seventh Street together.

"I really do appreciate it, you know," I told my father, who looked at me in pained puzzlement, kissed me, and walked off shaking his head.

VI

I imagined what would happen when the members of the staff of *Animals* heard the news of my resignation. At first they would be terrified for me. I seemed sweet to them, I guessed. They would hang around my cubicle, expecting to hear of extenuating reasons—mental crack-up, fatal disease. Then, as they realized what I had been concealing from them, and that I did not have an excuse, they would come to dislike or hate me. Small talk would cease. The personnel office would work overtime to end my medical coverage as quickly as possible.

I was terrified, walking off a cliff, my dollar value over, my father's generosity in danger.

VII

On the last day at *Animals* the staff gave me a farewell party.

After the last good-byes, I said good night to the Irish guards at the door, who shook my hand.

Well, I thought, I had certainly been wrong about the staff's resentment—and my thoughts of the guards being ordered to accidentally shoot me seemed absurd.

These thoughts had hovered on the fringe of my mind—additional reasons for not quitting: the guards . . . my father contriving to have me arrested in his anger at my freedom . . . my father and mother getting together, boiling, conferring on how to nab me.

Now that I had quit, I saw I had no reason to be afraid. My father was on his best behavior, elaborately polite, fearful of permanently alienating me. Only in the off moments did unpleasant conversations occur. One morning I woke my father up in Brooklyn by ringing the doorbell. My father muttered at the door as he let me in: "I thought there was a chance you'd have a best-seller sometime. That's dead, huh?"

I sat down without answering. "Let me tell you the dream I was just having, Bruce. It was about a crippled dancer."

14

Jolson Sings Again

I

"Jolson was never any damn good as a singer," said Billy Eckstine recently. Well, fuck you, Mr. B.

Well, maybe so. Ersatz, yes. I was—am—one of the millions of little Jewish boys who dreamt of him: our rabbi, Moses, Judaism. On one knee in the living room grimacing: "Rosie, you are my posie"—Jewish boy athletics. Running, jumping, flying through the air. October 24, 1950: Jolson dead. The *New York Post* is still in my scrapbook, yellowing pieces of the blintze wisdom of Max Lerner ("Campus Morals Today: Twenty Part Special") and Barry Gray and James Wechsler.

Now my Protestant stepson Danny is into other shit: the Stones, Led Zeppelin, the Who, the Doors, Jimi Hendrix.

Danny—seventeen—is waiting for a sign, a stairway, a flash, road, star, and he is sure it will come—as I stood at seventeen behind the apartment house, in the courtyard, with Esther, beneath the stars, in the moonlight, on concrete, near grass in a backyard closed off to us by a wire fence. Esther is holding a cat (for that is the snapshot); she is wearing a white, men's shirt tied in front, her soft midriff is bare; she wears jeans cut off hillbilly style. She is wearing thick fifties lipstick, and smiling. I can taste her.

I am sure that Danny would have loved her very much.

A ghetto love, by a peeling radiator next to a fire escape; an upright piano.

In Seattle, far from me, where he is safe—Danny called from his father's house and across the wires shouted, "I am reading Sartre's *Anti-Semite and Jew*."

II

Images of Danny:

1. Trying to hold in his laughter: a sputter, then a cackle, hand over mouth. Looking at me to share it.

2. Enduring my stare of hatred: cornered, his eyes trying to look straight ahead, darting about. His head rigid. Cool and frozen.

3. Danny high tonight. Lit up, he shines like a polished apple. Susan is delighted with his good mood, not thinking about the Heinekens he has drunk through the late afternoon, or what he has smoked.

He says an amazing thing to me in his slurred voice, beaming: "*I want to be like you: wine, women, and song.*"

III

My father, the other day, peeling an apple, finishes his childhood litany and adds something new:

"One day my father came home loaded down with presents. This must have been in 1908. I was so excited I jumped up and down. He was so infuriated he smacked me—hard."

He pauses and looks at me. "I was a good boy. Why was he so mean?"

IV

Thirty-nine. Feeling tired and old. Rapping with the reaper. So *that's* what it's all about. The warts fall off my father's face: I love him again.

V

Ghettoization. 1975. Manhattan. Bedroom, kitchen, Danny's room in the back. Every time he stepped over the line, I banged the wall.

1977. Lefrock Block. Taboo areas in the tiny apartment: the living room because it adjoined the bedroom, the kitchen because he banged around so much, the bathroom because I took hours in there.

In the Israel Day parade, Danny and I marched hand in hand.

VI

Spring, 1978. Danny is expelled from school. I go to school to plead for him with the director. He will not relent, but will allow Danny to take his final exams. If he passes, he will get credit for the term.

VII

Summer, 1978. With our last breath, we move from Lefrock Block back to a tiny flat in Manhattan. Danny's room is in the back. I know he feels he will be isolated in the apartment. I feel his thoughts and accusations.

On the night after the move, we go out to celebrate. Danny is cool and sullen. I am high.

"What is *he* so miserable about?" I ask Susan at the table.

"Look, leave me alone," Danny says.

"We make this great move, and *he's* miserable—he's wrecking it."

I feel my face wrenched out of shape with fury.

"He's not."

"Oh, I see. Both of you. Well maybe I should just leave, so the two of you can enjoy your dinner—"

"Oh, Bruce—"

"Oh Bruce what? What? What am I saying? *Isn't* he wrecking it? No, I'm wrecking it. Is that it?"

"I wish you'd leave me alone," Danny says. "I don't want to fight you."

"*Shit*. That's what it all comes to." I bound out of the restaurant.

I install a door in the Manhattan flat between the living room and the long hallway leading to Danny's room. When it is built, I feel big about it. I summon Danny and say pleasantly and expansively: "I installed a door there, but I want you to know that when it's open you can come in. When it's shut, please knock. It's not meant to shut you out, just give us some breathing space."

I look up. Danny is standing in the forbidden area staring at me. I hadn't heard him come in. I am seated reading beside the open window, and know that he wants to push me out. I keep reading. Danny walks out of the forbidden area, back to his room where he lies on his bed on his back.

If I were Danny, I would want to push me out the window.

VIII

The final summer that Danny lived with us. 1978: We suffer in the intense heat in the new miniscule apartment. Danny lies around in his room after the expulsion. When he comes out of the room, wearing only his undershorts, he has a stricken, pained look. His face is blazing red from the sun—his body red and peeling like an onion. He looks as if the top layer of his skin has been stripped away.

He exercises with his barbells, drinks, reads *High Times*, and goes downstairs to buy joints.

One day a butcher knife lies beside the bed.

Knives are stuck in the wall of his room; another knife juts out of the desk. On the wall: Laurel and Hardy, Groucho, W. C. Fields, rock groups.

1972. Vancouver. Danny drops a lit match in a barrel of gasoline. His eyebrows are singed from the explosion.

IX

Father's Day, 1978. I hand my father his annual tie. "Thank you," he says, smiling, to my wife, Susan. He holds it, strokes it, and says again, nodding his head to her, "Thank you."

"Bruce got it for you," she says.

"It's very nice. Thank you so much," he says, looking directly at Susan.

Danny looks at me sympathetically and dizzily shakes his head again and again, silently laughing at my father.

My father's reasoning, such as it is, goes like this: I have quit my job to write. Susan is the breadwinner. Even if I bought the tie, it is her money.

X

Summer, 1978. I am drunk. Danny, drunk, is making himself comfortable in the forbidden area. He is stretched out on the big chair in the living room, his feet up.

"You haven't done the dishes for days," I say.

"I'll do 'em."

"When?"

"I'll do 'em."

"*When*, God damn it?"

"Look, I said I'll do 'em. I don't want to hassle with you."

"You lie around all day drunk and stoned, you do nothing, you think nothing, while your mother sweats her ass off—"

He puts his hands up: "I don't want to—"

"*Now.* You'll do them *now.*"

"I said I would do them."

"*Now. Now.*" I stare at him wildly and stomp into the kitchen. I pound my fist against the wall. Then I take my briefcase and leave.

I take the subway to my writing studio in Times Square. I walk up Forty-second Street and watch the sights. The Jewish Feminists have set up a booth on the Holocaust and hold up signs to advertise a rally "IN MEMORY OF THE THREE MILLION." Their newspaper has a picture of Joseph Papp on the front page nursing a leg: the headline proclaims with approval that Papp has shot himself in the right foot in self-criticism for making a chauvinistic remark.

When I arrive at the building, I take the elevator to the twenty-sixth floor and then walk up a narrow, winding, orange staircase to the top. My studio is in the tower. It has twenty-two little windows. It isn't very safe. Big chunks of plaster keep shooting down from the ceiling and narrowly miss me. One night the chunk was five feet wide. I had to close off some areas entirely, and I keep moving my desk, a card table. I drink two cups of black coffee and begin writing about my childhood and my father. Tonight I wrote about the day he came home in the middle of the day to the boarding house and found me dressed up in a suit and tie. He exploded at me, claiming he wanted me to be out playing with the boys. This scene has stayed with me over the years and this time I'm going to get it right. I do.

By 3 A.M. I wind it up. I have a shot of bourbon to steady my nerves for what is to come: the trip home. First I take the same route down to the first floor. I have to ring the bell for a long time to wake up the guard, a black man named Harper. He has the front door key. He needs to talk. He is very lonely, in the building by himself. Tonight he talks about his family. I learn that his son was shot in the head and killed on the first day of his first job, before "he'd had a chance to scuffle up the ladder." I am exhausted, but I listen carefully to Harper. I am stunned by what he tells me, and I have decided I can use him as a character in my novel. And I like him. And he holds the keys. I don't know what to do: to just walk out seems now like the most insensitive thing I could do. So I put my briefcase down and we talk for almost an hour. Finally he lets me out. "How's your young fella?" Harper asks. I start at this. Then I say, "Fine, fine." We shake hands in the doorway. It is a very dangerous neighborhood, so he stands there watching me run down the block, making sure nobody gets me. But when I am out of his sight, I jump into a doorway and write down in my notebook everything of interest that Harper has said.

Then I begin the most difficult part of the night: getting safely into the subway. I have to get down the Forty-second Street block past the muggers, the pimps and hookers and the killers. I am vulnerable, with my beret, my books and notebooks and briefcase, walking in the neon lights past the porn shops. But I have certain advantages too: I look weird, I'm drunk from the shot of bourbon, and I deliberately talk to myself and act paranoid. I fit in a little better that way—even though the things I am saying aloud are really perfectly rational: stuff about making progress in my writing and avoiding summarization and cerebral content.

As I get closer to the subway entrance, it is really dangerous, so I run again instead of walk. The biggest challenge is when I reach the subway entrance. That's where they wait with their knives and guns. But I've worked out a strategy that works pretty well. I run up to the entrance and then, to everybody's surprise, I throw myself down the steps, landing at the bottom, where the token booth and the cops are. This is painful, but it works. Of course, I pad my knees with foam rubber. I am never mugged. Then, when I get on the subway, I look so ragged and wild, nobody messes with me.

XI

Some horrors are ridiculous: little thirty-year-old Jewish boy horrors. In 1968 I traveled to the frontier: to Vancouver to get a masters in creative writing. Alone and poor again at twenty-eight: no girls, no car or friends: dinner—peanut butter crackers, a sausage stick. If the head rabbi of Vancouver had known about me, I would have been a prime subject: a guest at people's homes on Friday nights, dentists and lawyers offering me philosophy. At bar mitzvahs they would have stuffed my pockets with kishke for a rainy night.

It rained in Vancouver endlessly, day, night, weekend, pouring down on my body and will.

The chairman of the creative writing department suggested I turn the protagonist of my novel into a mouse. He suggested at one point or another with conviction that every writer in the department use a mouse as a protagonist. He always explained his reasons at length and with compassion.

During my first year in Vancouver, I put an ad in the newspaper and a teacher answered it. It said: "Graduate student seeks friendship with serious girl." When she called me, we discussed the import of the word "serious" and agreed it was what made the ad unusual. She came to my apartment, with its bridge table, typewriter, TV set and cot.

Two days later, after I kissed her, she called me to tell me her old "beau" wanted her back. I felt weak in the knees at this news and had to sit down on my cot.

1970. The masters degree, a teaching job, meeting another faculty member: Susan. Marriage, and Danny.

XII

Spring, 1979. *Danny will visit us in July for the summer.*

Susan and I are at the Ensemble Studio Theater in Hell's Kitchen. Here, on a tiny stage, are small miracles. Mistakes cohere into art. Poor and small and confined. Small, hard-backed chairs, no air. The atmosphere is electric and tight. We wait. I read the program. They are forming an acting school.

Wow. This is my chance. What I've been waiting for.

Fuck. I don't want to be an actor anyway. I haven't wanted to be in show business in fifteen years. It's too late, too late, far too late, incredibly late.

Susan is shifting beside me. I know what she will say.

"Bruce, look at this—"

"I saw it. What about it?"

"Maybe Danny could—"

"Could? Could what? He doesn't live with us anymore."

I can't breathe. My head is spinning. "I have to get out of here. I feel faint."

I keel over onto the floor.

XIII

I call Eichner, Danny's psychiatrist when he was here, tell him what has happened, and ask to see him.

I sit in the child psychiatry clinic—the only adult—smug and pleased as punch. I am snagging Danny's shrink. I knew he preferred me all along. I pop two Valiums. I will not be droopy during this first interview.

But I don't like being the only adult here. The other patients are drooling, reading comic books, sucking on candy. Even the other shrinks look like kids—swinging singles in their twenties, from Grossinger's, with tiny moustaches. Entering the waiting room, they stop in their tracks when they spot me and seem to buzz together about it.

Eichner is a string-bean German, thirty-five, legs twisted around each other with delight, pasty complexion, glasses with a dangling pearl string. He takes wild stabs.

I tell him about fainting in the theater. "Danny is coming and I have to move out of that room of his—the only space I have to work when I'm at home—"

"So. You are furious! And for very good reason. His arrival means a suspension of your being."

"Well no—"

"Oh yes! But why do you seem to think he has to stay in your apartment with you and his mother?"

I pause. "What do you mean?"

"So. Aren't there hotels in this vast metropolis?"

"But he's a child. You mean he should stay on his own?"

"Why not? If he can play with knives and drugs, if he can steal, why can't he stay on his own at a hotel?"

"He's only seventeen years old. And what about Susan? She only gets to see him once a year now. And it would make him feel unwanted."

"Why would it do that?"

"The problem is . . . I'm frightened of him."

"Of course. You should be frightened! Herr Daniel had *knives* of many sizes, he was into *drugs*, and his animosity was directed at you. His fist almost shattered the plate glass table top in this office." Eichner stood up and made clawing motions with his hands. "*Knives*! He had *knives*!"

XIV

1953. Showtime at Grossinger's. I worship the MC, Harry Spear, for his style and his showmanship. Tonight before the main act (young singer Harry Belafonte) he allows me and my buddy Mike Lobell to do a comedy skit. I must do this; shadows are falling on my life and a comic has to feel funny.

The lights are on us. I hear my beating heart, but our act is so funny that it breaks us up as we do it. But there is no laughter out front. One thousand people are silent. We walk down the stage steps into the blackness of the aisle to our seats. I hear Harry's apology to the audience. Mike and I were both short and we didn't reach the microphones.

I approach my seat.

One person in the audience is laughing, and it is my father. It is a silent laughter, filled with satisfaction and joy. I do not feel like a funny fellow.

XV

Fall, 1977. Danny is falling apart at school. He makes strong resolves which last for a few days. I map out a space for him to

study in the cramped Lefrock Block apartment. I tell Susan to
check his homework every day. I wrench these steps out of myself, reluctantly. They take my time, and they are ineffectual
anyway. For Danny is a charming bullshitter. Soon he works his
way out of the net: with a damaged look, he tells Susan he
thought we respected and trusted him, yet we wanted to check
up on him daily—as if he were a child. Susan is moved. No more
checking: no more homework. I feel rage. He is back to his old
schedule—staying out until midnight or all night with his
friends. This partly pleases me—the part that wants him to fail.
One night he sleeps on a park bench in Riverside Drive and his
wallet is stolen.

We clamp down again. I supervise Danny's English homework. For a week things go smoothly. He is friendly and communicative. After he leaves the house one morning, I hear a
buzzing in his room. I open the door and trace the sound to his
closet. I open it and a grow light stuns me. I shield my eyes from
the blaze. It is poorly connected by a nest of wires hooked up
haphazardly and seems set to explode. It is shining down upon
a fresh marijuana plant. I unplug it. I pound the wall: sin and pu-
trefaction. I am betrayed.

XVI

Danny's sweeping, hungry glances at my bookshelves climbing to the ceiling. His eyes grow large, intent. He takes books
out with care. "So many books," he says.

I feel a surge of jealousy.

A rare moment when I write at home. He comes upon me at the
typewriter, my fingers flying. He makes a typing motion with
his outstretched fingers, smiling and approving, and says, "Keep
making that beautiful music."

How does he know I am really a writer? When I am home, I am
drunk, or raging, or listening to Sinatra.

XVII

Fall, 1978. "School is bullshit," I tell Danny. "What really matters is zeroing in on what you care about and learning to do it well. Not scattering and dispersing yourself."

He shakes his head, which is bowed.

"I think you want to be in the theater."

He nods his head silently.

"Yes."

"If you could get to work with a small drama company, would you do it?"

"Sure." He looks directly at me. "I'd really like that."

Later in the week I call the Equity Library Theater and ask them if they can use an apprentice: my son.

"Does he have any experience," they ask. "Yes, in lighting."

They say they want to meet him. He races into Manhattan for the interview.

Danny is taken on. He is placed in charge of lighting for *The Crucible*.

He works every afternoon, evening, and weekend. He is very happy.

Susan and I go to see the production. We wait for Danny outside the theater afterwards as snow falls lightly upon us. When he sees us, he throws himself into our arms. We kiss and hug him.

"This is the best thing that's ever happened to me in my life. Thank you," he says to Susan, and "*thank you*," he says to me. We all walk arm in arm up 103rd Street, from Riverside to West End, the old brownstones covered with snow and shimmering with Christmas lights: the old West Side, scene of my early struggles in a Communist lady's boarding house, the prim lady spinning around with her flyswatter to crush cockroaches climbing up the refrigerator. Oh what outrage. One wintry night a telegram appeared under my door: Kay Boyle praising and criticizing a story I had written for her New School class. May Kay Boyle live forever for that gesture, which I needed more than food.

XVIII

Girls. No one failed with them the way I did. How they fell for the cool, the uninvolved, and how they turned away from awkward passion. An upright prick is a walking wound. What do you do with it? The guys who got cunt didn't seem to want it. And it wasn't even cunt I was after: breasts, dimples, wide eyes, long black hair, a warm, live hand, a shoulder to hold, a particular voice, a particular laugh—and they were enough to make me cross to the other side of the street when someone I wanted was approaching, as my father had done before me.

XIX

Winter, 1977. Danny is on his back, in his room, drunk and miserable. He should not be there, for the girl he has confided in us about, the *first* girl he has been able to approach this year, a new girl in his class, whom he asked out before the other boys got to her, striding toward her, introducing himself, challenging the odds—this girl is waiting for him for their first date. His friend John has gotten him drunk—John, who, I told Danny when he came home, wants him to be a loser like himself.

Danny is lying on his bed, and we tiptoe around the apartment. At ten o'clock I knock on his door.

"Danny," I say, "You know, Nicole doesn't know why you didn't show up. The way you described her, she sounds like the kind of girl who would understand if you called her and explained."

He opens the door. "I've been thinking of that."

"I don't want to tell you what to do. But as it is now, you're just a bastard to her. You've hurt her, you know?"

Danny nods. "Sure."

"But maybe if you tell her all about it, you could just start over again."

Danny strokes his chin. "I'd really like to do that. I didn't want to hurt her."

"Okay, Danny."

I close the door. We listen for creaks and noises. After an hour, there is the dialing of a telephone.

A knock at our door. "I'm seeing her tomorrow night." He comes into our arms.

XX

What surprises me are his deepest affinities: the Columbia area of the upper West Side, the lower East Side, blacks and Jews, Durante, pushcarts, Coney Island, James T. Farrell, Mike Gold, Richard Wright, a threnody of the lost and dispossessed, the old alliances of my youth that I have lost. Plucked from the West Coast, how did he get this way? He is recreating my dreams; he is walking the ghetto streets my father found as a child, reading the books my father, hovering in the Bridgeport library from the cold, once read.

XXI

Summer, 1978. Danny, Susan, Eichner and I in a circle at the clinic.

"His real father wouldn't put up with this shit—" I say.

"He wouldn't deal with it this way," Danny says.

"What would he do?" I ask.

"He would talk it out, and try to understand—"

"Then why don't you go back to him in Seattle?"

"*Because*—" Danny rises and covers his face. Looking away, he lunges blindly for the door.

"Danny!" Eichner calls.

He slams the door and we hear him run down the hallway. Then we hear a crash. Eichner runs out after him.

We pace the room.

After a long wait, Danny returns with Eichner.

We sit in a circle again.

"Bruce feels you want to hurt him physically, Danny."

"I did that minute. I wanted to hit him hard. I mean it."

"He means beyond that. That you generally want to."

Danny looks up. "Oh no," he says.

Later, I say, "I've been awful to Danny, and I don't know why. I understand his rage. Everything he does infuriates me. My criticism of him is worthless. After all, if he was perfect it wouldn't make any difference. I would still resent his presence. And I've caused him to act this way. Every movement of his in the house has enraged me . . ."

"I really admire your honesty in saying all that," comments Danny. "That takes courage."

Eichner tells us later that the way things are, there would be danger. Danny is to go to Seattle to be with his father.

Summer, 1979. I am glad to see Danny when he returns for the summer. He has had a good year: catching up in school in Seattle, playing basketball, hiking and swimming and finding some new girl friends. He has made his own movie in English class. He has gone to AA meetings.

The first day we go jogging together around the Central Park reservoir. He contrasts the "natural highs" of exercise, nature, and friendship with drugs and alcohol.

The second day we go to the Thalia to see two Rossellini films, *Shoe Shine* and *The Bicycle Thief*, and at a bookstore haunt in the old Columbia neighborhood, I purchase Brendan Behan's *Borstal Boy* for him. It is very easy to give Danny things he will enjoy: all I have to do is think of those things that have meant the most to me. And he remembers every single gift I have ever given him—he ticks them off unconsciously whenever he wants to boast to a friend of what "his father" has given him. I would think the reference to "his father" would be confusing for him, but he manages nicely.

He sees his buddy Joey a lot of the time this summer and dates a girl named Shelley. When he finally makes his move with her, she says: "What took you so long?" He calls us excitedly—he has gotten a job. After a day it is over. I ask him what it was: "Giving out handbills for a fortune teller."

We talk when he gets home evenings, quite sober, at two or three if I am up, our legs stretched across tables or chairs. We have a beer. "Remember that housing project we lived in at Le-frock Block?" I say. "No space, no privacy. That fucking bus ride from Manhattan, then the long icy walk up the hill against the slamming winds, and no taxis even willing to go up there. Wait-ing for hours for cabs just to get back to civilization, and some-times they just never came—and your mother and I slipping and falling on the ice. And those dead faces on the express buses. All this to save money so I could write, and the express bus and the cabs cost more than our great West Side apartment. I thought that was it, that I'd really had it—that we'd die there." Danny is silent. "Those paper-thin walls, hearing people screwing in the next apartment, those all-night parties upstairs with Latin mu-sic, the thieves next door coming home from their thieveries and staying up all night counting their money, playing jazz and plotting and saying: *'Shit. Fuck. Piss. Motherfucker. Cock-sucker.'* And us unable to make a sound, afraid they'd hear us hearing them. But one night, Danny, I heard the little girl in the shower singing to herself, 'Thank Heaven for Little Girls.'

"Your mother and I walked outside among the slivers of glass and the tons of dogshit and somebody called at me: 'Goldberg.' When I looked up a brick fell with a thud just behind us."

XXII

"When mommy and I married," my father recalls, "we had a bedroom in your grandparents' house. Her mother did all the cooking. When I came home after work, mommy would put an apron on and serve the food as if she had cooked it. But her mother did all the cooking. We had a ball though, Bruce. When you were born, you slept in a crib in your grandparents' room."

"Why didn't I sleep in your room?"

"Well . . ." My father smiles apologetically. "You see, mommy wanted *me.*"

XXIII

Summer, 1979. I love Danny. What has happened to me? Why did it take so long?

The rancid jobs by day, traveling to the Times Square studio at night, then Lefrock Block. Trying to keep going. I had thought it was a matter of Danny—with his great need, his tremulous emotions—or me. I would have nothing left, I thought.

The night before Danny will leave to return to Seattle, he is upset. His best friend, Joey, has taken over with the girl, Shelley, he has been dating.

"But it wouldn't have worked anyhow. I kept trying to really talk to her all summer in a human way. She said she didn't know how. And last night we tried for hours and hours. That's really what it's all about, anyway. Like the way you guys are," he says to us. "Like a couple I know in Seattle. They're older than you, but they keep growing and changing. They're into yoga, stuff like that."

After a while he says, "But he could have waited before he made his move."

He is going to return Joey's bicycle to him, and have it out. It is midnight, but we wait. When he gets back, he says things are okay. "We talked it out. I guess Shelley wanted some reassurance that she'd have somebody when I left. But anyway he's still my buddy."

As Danny packs, Susan is lying on the bed, silently crying, her shoulders heaving. I hold her, and kiss her. It is not enough.

I go into Danny's room.

"Danny, your mother is just so miserable that you're leaving. She really needs you."

"Oh, sure."

Danny goes into the bedroom and takes Susan in his arms. I stand at the door. He holds her and pats her tenderly. "That's right, mom, let it out. That's the best thing to do."

Susan weeps and smiles and blinks and shakes her head. "Where did you get such a lovely way with people?"

It is 2 A.M. We are all still in the living room.

Suddenly Danny says, "Something happened that really made me think. I went back to our old neighborhood on the

West Side. I liked that neighborhood, it's alive. So many different kinds of people. But a guy on our old corner killed somebody who gave him bad dope. He killed him. Shelley *saw* it—so did some of the other kids. This was a guy who'd gotten me joints when we lived by Columbia. He'd taken me over to 104th Street and said to the others, 'He's okay.' "

Danny shakes his head.

We kiss each other good night.

XXIV

In the morning, Danny finishes packing. He is about to leave with Susan for the airport.

He sits down beside me at my desk. He is smiling. I try to begin.

"Danny, we had a real dialogue this time—"

"You mean a human relationship."

"That's what I mean."

"You know," he says, "I really understood you better when you talked about Lefrock Block. That place really sucked."

We laugh, and then we are embracing. Danny's face is very warm.

"I love you so much," Danny says. He is weeping.

"I love you very much, Danny."

Then Susan is there, and we are all holding each other and crying, and do not stop.

XXV

Beside the *New York Post* story about Jolson's death is a picture of Jolson and his new wife nursing their baby. The caption title reads: "One Role: Jolson as Daddy," and beneath the picture: "Taking time out from his comeback as an entertainer, Al Jolson looks the part of a perfect papa as he watches his wife, Erie, give month-old Asa his feeding. The Jolsons adopted the baby."

XXVI

My mother hands me a bundle wrapped in cellophane: my baby clothes.

Susan cradling our cat in her arms: "He's just like a baby when he looks at you and recognizes you for the first time."
"When is that?" I ask.
"At about four months."

I am jogging in Central Park behind a father and his two children: a boy and a girl. With his backhand he tosses a football to each of them in turn as they all run. What an effort that must be, I think: fatherhood.

A mother with a baby in a carriage stands at the bottom of the subway steps. I offer to carry the carriage up the steps for her. She accepts, and I do so.

On the bus, a black mother sits, her baby carriage before her. With a lurch of the bus, it begins to roll. I put out my hand and stop it.

XXVII

My fortieth birthday. My mother calls: I hear a child's voice, high and birdlike. She is chewing gum, snap, snap. "Happy birthday. How does it feel to be twenty-eight?"
"I'm forty."
"I tell my friends you're twenty-eight."
"But I'm not."
"Don't you dare tell them," she says sharply. "Are you crazy? Me with a forty-year-old son? Never!"

XXVIII

I was ten years old when Jolson died. I heard the news on the radio when I woke up. I lay in bed. I remember the morning, my father tiptoeing around the apartment, waiting sadly to tell me, my mother banging around as usual.

In 1950 in New York the trolleys were disappearing, and the Third Avenue El; Runyon and Winchell sat at Lindy's; there were stage shows at the Paramount, the Roxy, the Strand, the Capitol, eight acts of vaudeville at the Palace and five acts at the Jefferson on Fourteenth Street. The songpluggers were in the Brill building, still writing the kinds of songs Jolson had sung.

I listen to them now: "Rosie, You Are My Posie," "Give My Regards to Broadway," "Let Me Sing and I'm Happy," "When You Were Sweet Sixteen," "Sonny Boy," and "Back in Your Own Backyard," and despite the schmaltz, they bring a smile and a chill: I am still a Broadway baby.

> Her baptismal name is Rosie
> but she puts the rose to shame
> and every night you can hear me
> call her name—Professor!
> Let me sing about my Rosie . . .

These Jewish and Irish immigrants, infusing America with their joy at being here.

To be a Jolson, strutting across a stage before the footlights: every day I practiced, a magician, flying across the room, down on one knee, or singing on the rooftop, my arms outstretched, stopping in midsong when someone appeared with a cart of clothes to hang on the lines. (They flapped on the lines, the flapping sound and the wind greeting me when I opened the roof door.)

In 1974, I bought a bottle at the corner liquor store on 110th Street and Broadway. The owner noticed that I had a copy of *Variety* and said, "Are you in show business?"

"No. I've been reading it since I was ten years old."

"Then why?"

"I enjoy it. It has a feeling of fun—"

She interrupted, and nodded. "I understand. I understand. It helps you forget your troubles."

XXIX

"Shhh. I'm on the phone with my father in New York—Hello—Hello—Bruce?"

It is Danny, his emotion surging across the wires from Seattle, his thanks for my letter (he answered it immediately in class, but in tearing it out of his notebook tore it in half, and had to recopy it), his voice strong, sober . . . his new girl . . . the part-time theater work he's gotten in Seattle a success.

I think as he talks: here is my chance, my second chance. Hear my voice, vulnerable and soft now, without rehearsal, without preparation, trying, trying. Danny applauds my missed notes, my off-key, irresolute openings—ah, now I'm getting better pitch. He encourages me as I do a little soft shoe, a stumble or two.

I think I am getting through.

XXX

As I was at seventeen with Esther in the moonlight, I see Danny now. Esther: little body bursting with feeling, perched upon the upright piano singing Judy Garland as I played. Esther: beside the milk bottles at the door, on the stoop, the fire escape, comforting her small brothers when they cried. Doing my Jolson imitation for her the first time. Seated beside her, watching Danny Thomas and Danny Kaye on TV. Opening the door when I rang the first time, her eyes wide, signing my petition to protest the beating up of Barry Gray by hoods, asking me over brownies and milk: "Don't you recognize me?" and I suddenly remember the girl sharing my seat in homeroom, pressing her body shyly against mine, my thinking it must be a mistake, but being afraid to glance at her. Her spicy, delicatessen smell, her mouth and breasts, black hair; her passion and Talmudic kindness and fairness.

This was before I stopped singing. And it would be a long while before I would try to sing again.

Design by David Bullen
Typeset in Mergenthaler Trump
Mediæval by Wilsted & Taylor
Printed by Maple-Vail
on acid-free paper